Do Unto Others

KRISTEN HOUGHTON

DO UNTO OTHERS
by Kristen Houghton

© Copyright 2017 by Kristen Houghton. All rights reserved

ISBN-13: 978-0-692-44769-7

Library of Congress Cataloguing-in-Publication Data
Houghton, Kristen
DO UNTO OTHERS: A Cate Harlow Private Investigation crime novel/Kristen Houghton-1st. ed.

1.Cate Harlow (Fictitious character)-Fiction 2. private investigator 3. crime 4. female sleuth 5. cozy mystery 6. detective mystery 7. New York City

Published by *Criminal Element* an imprint of
Skylight-NYC Publishers, LLC
175 Fifth Avenue
New York, NY, 10010
Skylight-NYCPublishers.com
skylight-nyc@outlook.com

Cover by 2Hopper Production & Design Studio
in association with KH Koehler Design

Do Unto Others

A Cate Harlow Private Investigation

Kristen Houghton

Skylight-NYC Publishers, LLC

Books by Kristen Houghton

CRIME AND MYSTERY

CATE HARLOW PRIVATE INVESTIGATION SERIES

For I Have Sinned
Grave Misgivings
Unrepentant: Pray for Us Sinners

FANTASY

THE TEDDY JAMESON CHRONICLES

Welcome to Hell, Teddy Jameson
Leaving Hell with the Angel of Redemption

HISTORICAL ROMANCE

The Anchoress: A Romantic Tale of Terror

ANTHOLOGY

No Woman Diets Alone-There's Always a Man Behind Her
Eating a Doughnut

And Then I'll Be Happy! Stop Sabotaging Your Happiness and
Put Your Own Life First

YOUNG ADULT NOVELLA

Remember, Hetty?

COMING IN 2018

Lilith Angel, a YA fantasy series

For Alan...this crazy adventure continues...

And a special dedication to the brave men and women in blue, New York City's Finest, who truly do serve and protect...

CONTENTS

CHAPTER 1

"**W**ILL'S BEEN SHOT. LISTEN TO ME, CATHERINE. Look at me, honey. Do you understand what I'm saying? Will's been *shot*."

Will's been shot. With those three words, the evening that had begun with so much promise, suddenly turned into a living nightmare.

August in New York City is a pleasant time. I'm back from New Orleans, and nicely settled into the hectic routine at *Catherine Harlow Private Investigations*. It's been a month since my return from the land of jazz, incredibly great food, and mystery. The little girl, Mireille, the one I helped rescue along with the other girls destined for the sex trade in New Orleans, is doing well. She is living peacefully with my friend Melissa's mother and has sent me a few pictures of animals and birds that she has taken with her 'toy,' her beloved cell phone. She's happy and I'm happy for her. After what she's seen and knows, she deserves a normal life.

As much as I loved the magical feel of NOLA, it feels *so* good to be back in my own home and walking the familiar territory of my own city. As for cases at *Catherine Harlow, Private Investigations*, there's only one pressing one on my agenda. A missing woman case that has hit a bit of an investigative snag. But that's happened before with these cases, so I'm not concerned. Nor am I willing to give over tonight to thinking about it. I spent a lot of time on it today and tonight is mine.

Soaking in a warm tub after a hectic day, I smile to myself and take a deep breath of the jasmine-scented bath salts. I lay comfortably relaxed in the large tub and allow myself no distractions. To achieve an uninterrupted hour of relaxation, I turned off both my landline and cell phones. The only sounds I hear are those of warm water gently filling the tub and good music from my Bose.

Thirty minutes later finds me humming *California Gurls*, by Katy Perry, while pulling on cream-colored pants and a soft, cobalt blue top. It's still summer and people are eager to make the most of the summer nights. That's the reason I'm getting dressed to meet my friends for a nice late dinner out. 'Livin' the life while it can still be enjoyed;' that's my new mantra. Visiting one too many cemeteries after midnight in New Orleans has taught me that. Life is for the living, and it is be lived now.

I'm in the middle of putting on the delicate gold earrings, a gift from Will for my birthday, when I hear my doorbell ring repeatedly and annoyingly. I know it's not Will doing the ringing; he finally has his own key.

After months of debating the issue, I made the decision to give in to his repeated requests for a key to my brownstone. It was a big step for me, allowing easy access to my home to my ex-husband. I made certain stipulations about that access, though, one of which is he can't just let himself in unexpectedly. I at least want a call or text that he's coming over. A girl's got to have some privacy and alone time, after all.

The doorbell chimes ring again and again. "All right, all right, I'm coming," I call out, quickly placing the back on one earring. "Stop with the doorbell already."

Probably some kids selling something for school or a fundraiser. I sigh with annoyance as I hurry to the door. Who else but kids ring a doorbell over and over again to get your attention?

But I'm wrong; it isn't kids doing a staccato doorbell ring at all. Standing on the front stoop of my brownstone are Giles, Myrtle, and Harry. My first thought is: why aren't they at the restaurant? They know Will and I are usually a bit late for one reason or another. No one seems to mind. Why did they come here?

The last time I spoke with Will, he was running late at the precinct and told me he was going back to his place to take a quick shower before coming by later to pick me up.

"Hell of a day, babe, you know I hate writing up these damn reports. Of course, I *had* to spill coffee on one of the damn reports to screw up my day even more." He laughs. "Plus, something unexpected was dropped on me last minute. All work and no play. I need a hot shower and, later tonight, some after-dinner play. I'll be a little late but I'll make it up to you, baby."

That made us both laugh and I was looking forward to a long and very pleasant night, including the *after-dinner play*, with the very hot Detective Will Benigni.

So why are Giles, Myrtle, and Harry standing here and not waiting at the restaurant? Something's not quite right, I can feel it. I can feel it—and I don't like it.

"Hi," I say surprised and, suddenly uneasy. "I thought we were going to meet up at the restaurant. Melissa should be there already. Will's running a little late, something at work. I called him a while ago, but he was probably in the shower or something. He didn't answer his phone."

"Cate?" Giles looks so serious. Harry looks a little scared. Myrtle comes over to me and takes my hand.

"What's going on?" I try to back up a little as if I want to avoid something I feel sure in my gut is going to be bad. A glance at Harry shows me tears in his eyes. Whatever happened to make them come here must be serious; Harry doesn't cry over nothing. Suddenly I have difficulty breathing. All three of them come in and close the door.

"Take a deep breath, Catherine, just breathe slowly," says Myrtle looking pale and more serious than I have ever seen her. "I called Melissa and she's coming over here now."

"She's coming here? What do you mean? No, she's waiting for us at the restaurant. Why does she have to come here? What is it?" I ask, afraid to hear the answer. "Has something happened?"

"Will's been shot. Listen to me, Catherine. Look at me, honey. Do you understand what I'm saying? Will's been *shot*."

"What?! No, no. He was on desk duty all day doing reports and some other unexpected stuff. He wasn't out on the streets. He can't be shot." I step backwards and bump hard into a large floor vase near the door, losing my balance. Giles steps forward and grabs me.

"Cate, look at me, look at me, sweetheart. Will was shot outside his condo building."

"Oh, my God! Will shot! When? He called me just before he was going to leave the precinct. Everything was fine, he was laughing over something that happened at work. When did this happen? Why didn't someone from the precinct get in touch with me; call me or come here?"

Suddenly I put my hands over my eyes as I remember that I had turned off both phones. I forgot to turn them back on. And the music! With the faucet running and the Bose turned up loud, I would not have heard anyone at my door.

Then a question too horrible to voice comes into my mind. But I have to ask it, I have to know. "Giles? Oh, God, Giles! Please tell me he's *alive*!"

Giles looks directly into my eyes, so that my attention is focused only on what he is saying. He nods an affirmative yes. "He's alive and being taken to Lenox Hospital, Cate. Believe me they'll do everything, *everything* they can to save him. You remember my friend, Dr. Felicia Hayden? The internist?"

I nod dazed, thinking only that he's alive, Will's alive. Thank God, he's alive!

"Lenox Hospital is where Felicia has medical privileges and she's there now. I'm going there with you. I wanted to see you first. Listen to me, Cate, Will's going to have the best surgeon I know, Dr. J.T. Charles. Felicia recommended him herself and she told me he has an excellent reputation. Do you hear me? He is the *best*."

Myrtle takes my hand again. "Will's captain and his partner did try to reach you but, when they came to your door, no one answered so they thought you were out. No one knew where you were. All their calls went to your voice mail. When they couldn't get in touch with you, they called your office. It's a real blessing that you and I decided to have all after hour calls forwarded to my cell phone, Catherine," says Myrtle.

"I have to see him before he goes into surgery. I have to go there. I have to go now!"

"Of course, of course," says Harry. "We'll take you there right away."

My bell rings again and Myrtle opens the door to a terrified-looking Melissa. I've never seen her looking anything but self-possessed and calm, even when her beloved aunt, Anjali, was facing murder charges. "My God, Cate!" she says grabbing me in a tight hug.

Gently disengaging myself from Melissa, I ask Giles, "Were there any witnesses? Anyone see this happen?"

"A couple who lives in the same building saw the whole thing and called 911. They're giving statements now."

Myrtle takes charge of us all. "Let's go to the hospital. Let's go!" she says in her firm no-nonsense teacher's voice. "There's a police car and escort to take you to the hospital. Melissa and I will go with Cate. Harry, you drive Cate's car. Giles, you ride with Harry."

I see flashing lights outside my brownstone as two squad cars pull to a screeching halt.

"We've got green lights all the way, honey," says Myrtle as we rush down the stairs to the waiting cars.

CHAPTER 2

WE REACH THE HOSPITAL just as the EMTs are wheeling Will inside the Emergency Room doors. I open the door of the cop car before it even comes to a complete halt and pitch forward onto my knees. Struggling up, I race to get through the sliding doors after the EMTs. Once inside, I see that Will is immediately surrounded by medical personnel. I've got to get to him.

"Let me see him please!"

"We're taking him to surgery, miss," says one woman in the group of nurses and doctors surrounding the stretcher.

"Just one minute, please!"

"Then you'd better come with us," says someone in the group. "He's sustained chest trauma and a head injury. We gotta go now!"

I grab Will's hand as we race through the hall toward the surgical theatres, wincing at the amount of blood on his clothes. His chest is bandaged and there's another one around his head.

"Will? Will, can you hear me? I love you. You're going to be all right, you're going to be okay!"

He opens his eyes groggily. It seems as if he is looking right at me, but then his eyes close again. The pain must be incredible. The loss of blood terrifies me. It's on his shirt and seeping through the bandage on the side of his head. I hear the doctors talking about units of blood needed. We're approaching surgery and I know they won't let me come in with him.

"Will?!" He opens his eyes again at the sound of the desperation in my voice.

"I," he mumbles struggling to speak. "I..., kuh..." I can barely hear him.

It sounds as if he's trying to say the word okay.

"Yes, Will, yes. You *are* going to be okay." I choke back tears, hoping that by telling him he'll be okay, he really will pull through this.

"No, no, I...you...," he licks his lips, looks at me, and tries again. "I, I-shh, kuh, I shh kuh...kree..., you, you..."

Is he saying 'I'm sorry Cate' as if he feels he has to apologize for getting shot? He's trying to say my name. Oh, God!

"Yes, baby, it's me. Cate. I'm right here. Don't apologize for anything, baby."

He slowly shakes his head. "No. You..., I, I-shh, kuh, kree, I shh kuh..."

"Yes, Will, Cate. It's me. I'm here." We're almost at the door to surgery.

"I-shh, kuh, kuh..." He tries to moisten his lips again. "Shuh, kree...kuh."

He thinks I don't understand so I reassure him.

"I know, Will. I know what you're saying. Don't worry!"

The fact that he's attempting to talk, to say my name, is encouraging. He tries hard to focus and suddenly his eyes lock on mine and I see complete coherence there.

"I understand, Will, baby. I know."

"Kna..., know?" The word comes out with effort.

"Yes, I do. I know. Don't worry about anything. I know. It's me, Cate."

He seems to breathe a sigh of relief. I squeeze his hand. Then he closes his eyes and passes out.

"Miss, we have to take him into surgery now! You have to stay here."

I give one last squeeze to his hand and reluctantly let go, watching helplessly as they vanish behind the doors to the surgical unit.

∽⚬∽

"This didn't just happen, Cate."

Joseph Jacoby, Will's precinct captain and good friend, tells me as we sit in the third floor hospital waiting room. He and a bunch of cops have just given blood and he's drinking a small paper cup of that syrupy orange juice they give to blood donors.

Joe looks like the grandfather every kid wishes they had. Still slim and fit, thinning grey-hair, and a gentle look. Looks deceive because I have seen him being tough as nails with hardened criminals.

"This was an outright murder attempt on Will's life. Whoever shot him wanted him dead." He looks at my stricken face. "I'm sorry, Cate. I shouldn't have said that. I'm so used to talking to other cops and we don't sugar-coat anything. Sorry, honey."

"No, no it's better to be blunt, Joe. Will needs protection now. I need to know that."

"Listen honey, no one has any chance of getting to him here. No one will get *near* him. There will be two cops outside his hospital room in eight hour shifts, twenty-four hours a day. Plain-clothes cops in and around the hospital, too. And we're giving nothing to the press. We're hoping the shooter will come out into the open and talk to someone. You know, bragging rights about shooting a cop, the lousy son-of-a-bitch."

I put down the stale-tasting vending-machine coffee and look at my watch. Will's been in surgery for over four hours. I left a message for Will's mother, Francesca, on her cell phone. She's traveling in remote areas of South America looking for primitive art for the Metropolitan Museum of Art where she's a collections curator and I don't know if the message will reach her anytime soon.

I didn't say why I was calling, I just said that I needed to speak with her. I couldn't leave a message telling her that her son has been shot and is now in a dance with life and death. Francesca has always been good to me, even after Will's and my divorce. She didn't blame either of us. I feel horrible for her. It was the hardest message I ever had to leave because I had to make my voice sound normal and all I wanted to do was cry. Thank God Myrtle was right here with me.

I'm sick to my stomach and my voice is edgy and raw with emotion as I question Jacoby. "Who? Who wants him dead? Has anyone checked any of his files to see if there were threats made against him? I know Will would take that seriously and report it, so don't give me any bullshit that he'd turn all macho and just ignore them. What about some son-of-a-bitch who Will had just arrested and somehow got out on bail? Or someone who was sent to prison years ago and has just recently been released? Those been checked yet? That couple who saw the shooting? Were *they* questioned thoroughly, I mean *really* thoroughly? The shooter's description, height, clothes, coloring, the whole fucking scene? Seriously, come on, Joe! Is anyone *doing* anything now?"

I know I sound angry and bitchy, but I'm scared, and I want whoever did this to be caught as soon as possible. Jacoby knows the strain I'm under and he responds kindly.

"We're working overtime on it, Cate. You know that when it's one of our own, no one sleeps until the bastard is caught." He looks at me with complete seriousness and determination. "Have some faith in us, honey. Will's one of us and, believe me, we will get whoever did this. You can make book on that."

I give a half-hearted smile at that comment. Everyone knows that Joe's uncle, the so-called black sheep of a prominent family of New York City cops, was a notorious bookie in his day. He's eighty-six now and still dabbles on the illegal side of betting.

"Yeah, Joe, I know how it works. I know, I do know. Hell, I was a detective's wife, you know that. But there *has* to be something missing, something we're not seeing. I mean, damn it, Will was in the precinct all day, he was doing paper work, all that stuff every police officer totally hates doing, but has to do. What happened between the time he left the precinct and arrived in front of his condo?"

Joe Jacoby looks at me in mild surprise. "Honey, Will wasn't in the precinct *all* day. He got a call and left early. I don't know what it was about. He just said he had to look into an old case. Something about how the legal system can screw the victim instead of the perps, and how restraining orders are worthless."

"What case?" I sit forward. "He said something unexpected was dumped on him but I just assumed it had to do with more paper work. What case are you talking about?"

"It was some domestic abuse thing. All I know is he mentioned it briefly just a couple of months back, too." He sighs deeply and shakes his head. "You know how it is with cops. There're some cases that kinda stay with you. Makes you wonder, every once in a while, just how the vics are doing. That's especially true if the criminal wasn't brought to justice, so no real closure. But that particular case? I don't remember the details, but I'll check his older case files later tonight."

"Thanks, Joe."

"Yeah, this case. It was before he partnered with Javier, but, you never know, Javy might know something about it. Partner talk and all. We all bullshit about old cases. You can ask him now," he says with a nod towards Will's partner who has just come back from the cafeteria bringing us more stale coffee and a paper plate filled with plastic-wrapped cookies.

"Cate, can I do anything for you? Anything?" Javier offers me a cookie, which I decline. For once in my life, my healthy appetite has left me, replaced by a nauseous pain of fear and confusion. I'm wondering why Will let me think he was just leaving the precinct when we talked on the phone. Why not tell me that he was out on the streets checking an old case of domestic abuse? Who called him? Was the case that confidential? I know that we've both had cases we didn't talk about, even with each other. Did this old case have anything to do with the shooting?

Javy sits down next to me and awkwardly pats my shoulder. He repeats what Jacoby said a few minutes ago. "We'll get whoever did this Cate. We will. And, listen Will is going to pull through. You know, my girlfriend is very religious and she's praying to her favorite saint for Will right now. She swears that this saint is the reason I'm still alive."

"Javy, do you know anything about a domestic abuse case that Will worked on before you became partners. Did he ever say anything to you about it today or any other day?"

"A domestic abuse case? I mean we're homicide so we're dealing in a different area here even though we've all had experience with domestic violence and abusers. But, no, he never said anything directly about any one particular case, only, well—"

"What? Well what, Javy?"

"He *did* mention some case from maybe a year ago, I think. That was a few months back. Something about how the vic was safe now that she had moved, and all that stuff. He was happy for her, he said. I think he helped her in some way, but I don't know for sure. But, there was nothing new he mentioned, nothing that was recent. Why do you ask?"

"Jacoby said something about Will leaving the precinct earlier and he thought it had to do with that old case of domestic violence."

As soon as the word violence is out of my mouth it reminds me why I'm here. Thinking about Will getting shot hits me hard and I close my eyes. I am not religious by any means but suddenly I find myself repeating to Whatever Higher Power might be available, "Please, please let him live."

I'm not above making deals so I also make wild, desperate promises to this unknown deity that only someone who is terrified will make. Stupid promises like giving all my money to the homeless, never eating Harry's divine pastries again, becoming a hermit and spending my life in contemplation and charitable works. I concentrate. Isn't there a patron saint of cops or something? Who is it? Does Javy's girlfriend pray to *that* saint?

"So anything you need. I mean it, Cate. I am—Cate? Cate?" Javier is gently touching my arm. "Cate? Did you hear me? I am going to find the person who did this."

I open my eyes. "I know Javy, I heard you. I'm just a little out of it right now."

"Yeah, yeah, I'm sorry Cate. But, you know, anything you need or want." He lets the words drift away.

Dr. Felicia Hayden comes into the waiting room followed by

Giles and an older doctor. I stand up, take a deep breath, and face them making one last mental plea, "Let Will have made it through the surgery. Please!"

Giles comes over to me. "Will's out of surgery, Cate. We've got him being monitored in ICU. This is Dr. J.T. Charles. He has all the details."

I breathe a shaky sigh of relief. He made it through! Oh, God, he made it through! Dr. Charles comes over to me and I see that his eyes look tired but he manages a small smile.

"He's sustained penetrating trauma in the chest area and he's in critical condition. The bullet pierced the right side of the heart which, fortunately, has lower blood pressure, and thus less bleeding, so we were able to do immediate damage control. The bullet has been removed, and we're sending it to the police lab, but he's not out of the woods yet. There's also the trauma to his head."

"Head trauma, yes. I guess he fell after he was shot and hit his head. Is it bad?"

Dr. Charles looks at Giles questioningly. Giles touches my shoulder and explains.

"Cate, Will was struck in the head and *then* he was shot. It looks as if the shooter hit him in the back of the head with the gun first to stun him."

"He's in a medically-induced coma at present," continues Dr. Charles. "This is to reduce any possible swelling in the brain. We're keeping him in the ICU as long as we need to do so. He's in critical condition, but he's a fighter. We're monitoring him very closely. The next twenty-four hours should give us a good indication of his condition and what else may need to be done."

"But the head trauma! Swelling in the brain? How bad is it?"

Dr. Charles comes close and looks at me with compassion. "It's a serious concussion which normally would be treated on its own. But the chest wound he sustained, and the subsequent surgery, put his body in somewhat more danger. As I said, he's a fighter and we're doing everything we can to save him. Right now, he's doing as well as can be expected for a person in critical condition."

"Let me see him." A medically-induced coma! I'm shaking but

I make myself stand straight and unmoving.

"Just for a few minutes. He's still unconscious. I'll have a nurse take you there now."

Felicia, of whom I was once jealous because she was dating Giles, comes over to me, gives me a hug and says, "I'm here late tonight. I'll keep checking on him, don't worry. And I'll keep in close contact with you."

I nod, numb, but grateful for her kindness

As a nurse comes to escort me to see Will, I turn to Joe Jacoby. "Joe, promise me you'll check to see if there's an old case on domestic abuse. See who the perp and the victim were."

Joe nods yes. "You got it, Cate."

I turn to Will's partner. "You asked if there was anything you could do for me, Javy?" He looks up at me. "Find the scum who shot Will and let me know as soon as you find the bastard. Let me—*talk* to that son-of-a-bitch first, got it? That scum's ass is mine."

CHAPTER 3

I REMEMBER THE FIRST time I saw Will. He had walked into the Office of the Public Defender with a young, inexperienced lawyer. They were going over some papers in the client rooms before leaving for the courthouse. These men and women who were public defenders, many of them first or second year lawyers, were eager and had good hearts, but they lacked the savvy of their older, richer counterparts in private practice. They tried really hard to help their clients, but their success was limited.

I was a legal linguistics translator there, a fancy name for someone who could translate Latin terms into coherent English. It was my job to sit in these rooms and explain to their clients exactly what the court papers were saying. When Will came in, I was finishing translating the legalese of a warrant to a woman whose husband had been picked up by two cops on his way to work.

"What does that mean, those words Capi Mitti-something?" she had asked me, showing me the crumpled paper in her hand. "They took my husband while he was at his job and put handcuffs on him. In front of his boss, they did that. For what? This paper? They bring him to jail. Can they do that? He needs his job. He'll get fired, and then what will we do? What do these words mean?"

"*Capias Mittimus,*" I explained kindly to the distraught

woman with the crying infant in her arms, "literally translates as *'We are sending someone to take.'*" In the language of the court that means that the judge gives police the authority to 'take in' a person who has failed to appear when so ordered. Your husband was taken from his place of employment and brought to jail in restraints because he had failed to answer an original summons."

Rocking the crying baby, trying to soothe him, she asked again, "But what does it *mean*?"

"Okay," I said calmly. "This paper means that this is an arrest warrant used to get a person physically into court to respond, to answer, a specific charge. Your husband was driving illegally, he had no driver's license, and there were several summonses out for him."

She shook her head confused. I explained again. "It means that your husband didn't answer the original court summons and so they had to issue a bench warrant, a paper saying that the police can bring him into court. The handcuffs are a necessary requirement. I'm so sorry, but the police have to cuff anyone they bring in."

After I handed her, and the now squalling baby, to one of our public defenders, I sat back and felt the sadness of what she was going through fall over me. I wanted to cry over all the heartbreak and despair I dealt with on an everyday basis. I felt helpless. I was so tired of all the pain. There had to be more to a work life than this.

My best friend, a pretty redhead named Marley Weiner, was at the desk next to me. She nudged me to take a look at the guy who had come into the room while I was busy.

"Lookee, lookee, girlfriend. *That's* the guy I told you about, remember? Will Benigni, the hottie hotshot who, I hear, is the youngest person in the history of the NYPD to make detective. *And—*," she draws out the word importantly, "It's not just that he's really good at being a *detective*. I have heard through several women that he's supposed to be the best at *everything*, you know what I mean, Ice Cream?"

She waggled her eyebrows and ginned wickedly. Ice Cream was her nickname for me because of my deep devotion to the pistachio flavor of the delicious treat.

She got my attention with that last bit of info and I took a long look at this new detective. His head was down and he was in a serious discussion with the lawyer. He was in charge. From his lean and muscled body, and the casual way he leaned over the desk, I figured his height to be about six-one or so. The suit he wore was nicely tailored, a better cut than the usual suits worn by the older male detectives who came into this building. Prep school, I thought. The suit and the relaxed, but take charge demeanor, say this guy went to a prep school. So why did he become a police officer? If he was that interested in the law why not become an attorney? That's interesting.

If he knew he was being scrutinized by the women in the office he paid no attention. But, suddenly he rose up to his full height and turned in my direction, looking first at Marley, and then at me. He gave us a smile and then turned his attention to the young lawyer. Helping the lawyer with two heavy boxes of files, Detective Will Benigni walked with him toward the exit. I sighed. Walking away from me without us ever being introduced.

But at the door, the handsome young detective stopped and turned. There was no mistaking the fact that he was looking directly at me and smiling. I smiled back and gave a half wave of my hand. And then, he did something so simple, yet so tantalizing—he winked at me. It was a very sexy thing to do as far as I was concerned. There was a world of erotic promise in that wink. I could feel my face get hot.

Then he turned and walked out the door of the office, probably unaware what that wink had done to me.

"Oooo, Ice Cream, looks like Detective Hottie likes you!" Marley said with a knowing laugh. She tossed a paper clip necklace she had made at me. "God knows I wouldn't throw *him* out of *my* bed! Go get'em girl! Woof!"

Suddenly I wanted to know more about this hot, young detective.

The afternoon was more than chilly for the end of April. It was only 3:15 and, technically, I was supposed to be in the office until 4:00, but I had had enough sadness for the day. Pleading a headache, I grabbed my things and headed toward the door.

I stepped outside of the building that housed the Office of the Public Defender and shivered. I hate the cold. Pulling my jacket closer around my body, I crossed the street to Timothy's Coffee Emporium, the best coffee shop in New York City, to grab a caramel macchiato.

Inside the coffee shop I went right to the counter and ordered a Timothy's large and a huge macadamia nut chocolate chip cookie to go with it. Truthfully, that was more than likely going to be my dinner since I hadn't gotten around to food shopping.

"Want it heated?" asked the braces-wearing, squeaky-voiced teen named Jeffrey behind the counter.

"Yeah, I do. Let the chocolate melt into the cookie really well, okay?"

"Gotcha. Take a seat. I'll bring it over in a few minutes."

I found a seat near the back of the shop, as far away from the constantly opening door as possible. Sighing, I closed my eyes and thought about my day. All the sad, confused, and angry people. Even though I consider myself to be a pretty upbeat person, this job had a way of bringing me down really hard. Maybe, I thought for the one-hundredth time, maybe I should pursue my dream job. I daydreamed about having my own business and being a private investigator. The problem was my finances were a little light now. I had put a down payment on a brownstone fixer-upper with money I had inherited from my parents. I could easily handle the mortgage, but the fixing up was costing me a fortune.

"Here you go, miss. Caramel macchiato and macadamia nut chocolate chip cookie, properly melted."

The voice was definitely not Jeffrey's. I opened my eyes to see Detective Will Benigni standing in front of me with a tray holding two coffees and two large cookies.

"Mind if I join you? I'm Will Benigni. I recognized you from the Office of the Public Defender." He smiled charmingly at me as he placed the tray on the table.

"Oh, um, sure, sure. Have a seat. I'm Cate—"

"Harlow, Cate Harlow. I know. Daniel, the lawyer I was helping? I asked him your name." He looked at his watch and grinned. "I'm not going out to dinner until eight, so I figured coffee and a cookie will keep me from starving until then."

Going out to dinner. Nice. Probably a date with some gorgeous prosecutor I think, as I push the too-long bangs out of my eyes. He's looking at me with that same sexy smile and I feel shaky.

"So tell me something about yourself, Cate Harlow."

"What would you like to know?" I asked, a little nervous to be talking to this utterly charming and good-looking detective. What could he possibly want to know about *me*?

He holds up the cookie in his hand and nods toward the one on my plate. "Why a *macadamia* nut chocolate chip cookie and not the *walnut* chocolate chip one? Personally, I'm partial to the walnut ones." He winks at me and we both laugh.

My life just got more interesting.

Four days later we had our first dinner date. We were going to an upscale Italian restaurant. He picked me up at my brownstone at 7:30 on the dot for an 8:00 dinner reservation. I had been ready for over an hour.

Standing on my doorstep, he looked hot as hell in dark grey slacks with a black sweater over a light blue shirt, and he smelled fantastic. I looked pretty good myself in a short black pencil skirt, soft white blouse, and three-inch black heels.

After dinner we walked and talked for a couple of hours before going back to his car. Just after midnight, he left me on the stoop of my brownstone after a kissing marathon in his car that was unbelievably hot and left me aching to jump his bones.

And—two weeks later he brought a willing and eager me to his loft apartment where we had incredibly mind-blowing sex over and over again. Passionate, hot, unbelievable sex. He led me every erotic step of the way, teaching me exciting new paths to pleasure.

I followed like a happy puppy until the puppy became a knowledgeable she-wolf and it was my turn to lead *him* on a sexual adventure.

CHAPTER 4

SEEING WILL HOOKED UP to a drip of pain killers and life-giving fluids makes me gasp with fear. The endotracheal tube is in his mouth and held there with surgical tape. His chest is covered in bandages and one is wrapped around his head. Will looks helpless and that's not something I want to see. It hurts me. He always seems indestructible and the one person who can fix anything in life. Oh Will! Please, please fight to stay alive. I squeeze his hand but it's limp, cold, and clammy.

A sob breaks from my throat and the nurse touches my arm. "He's out of it Ms. Harlow, but he's not in any pain. The morphine drip takes care of that very well. Believe me, he's seems to be a strong man. He looks like he takes good care of his body and that's a plus. A person's physical condition is really important in this type of injury. If it's good, if the person is healthy, then that helps a lot in healing."

I just nod, not trusting myself to speak. I take a couple of deep breaths and focus on what the nurse has said about health and healing. Okay, all right.

Giles and the surgeon come to the door of the room. Standing next to them are two of Jacoby's people, good solid, take-no-bullshit cops. Opening the door slightly, Giles beckons to me, letting me know that my time is up. I nod and the surgeon comes in to check on Will.

Before I leave, I bend down by Will's face and whisper, "I love you, baby. Please live, please!" Then I squeeze his hand once more.

Maybe it's my imagination or maybe it's what I want to believe, the power of my own need, but I can swear that I feel the slightest bit of pressure from Will's hand, trying to squeeze mine in return.

⎯◯⎯

Back in the waiting room, Melissa is on her cell phone. When she sees me she asks the person to whom she is speaking to wait a minute. "It's Tante Anjali. I called her to ask her to do a healing spell on Will. Believe me, Cate, they do work."

"Okay, thanks."

The New York City sophisticated Melissa Aubrincourt has tapped into her New Orleans voodoo roots and called on her aunt Anjali, a 'person of great magic,' to help heal Will. Oh, well. Any spells or prayers are more than welcome right now.

"Anjali says she's so sorry this happened. She is lighting her candles and casting a spell now."

Melissa ends her call, drops her cell phone into her Hermés bag and comes over to where I'm standing. She puts her arms around me and hugs tightly, whispering, "I'm here for you, Cate. We all are—Myrtle, Harry, Giles. Lean on us."

Spells, candles, magic, prayers and promises to the saints; what the hell? I'm up for anything that works. I rest my aching head on her shoulder for a minute. Myrtle and Harry are talking quietly with Giles. We're the only ones in the waiting room.

"Where're Jacoby and Javy?" I ask, raising my head and seeing them gone. I direct my question to Myrtle.

"They left to go back to the precinct. The chief wants to get started on finding the person responsible for this."

I nod my head. Good. Get going, Joe and Javy. Uncover any clues to this attempted murder and find the bastard. I look around at my friends.

"I'm staying here tonight," I announce to everyone in the room, daring them with my eyes to even attempt to convince me to go home. I refuse to leave. "Giles, I want to be in Will's room. I need to be there. Can you please see what you can do?"

Giles nods his head. He also knows exactly how important it is for me to be with Will at this dangerous time. "It's really against protocol to allow you to stay there, since it's ICU, but—"

"I don't give a damn about protocol! This is Will, do you understand? This is *Will*!"

"Let me finish, Cate. It *is* against protocol, but I'll make sure that they let you stay. They probably won't let you in there for another hour or so, though, so you'll have to wait here. I'll get Felicia and we'll go talk to J.T."

My phone buzzes and I check the message hoping against hope that Joe Jacoby has found Will's shooter. But it's simply a message from the husband of the missing person.

"I haven't heard from you for a couple of days. Got any news about Wendy? I really need some closure on this."

Wendy. I'm the queen of finding missing persons it seems. A sad, but true, fact. Bread and butter of the private investigation business.

But tonight, nothing, nothing will tear me away from Will. I don't respond. I've got too much on my mind to even think about someone else right now. In a few days I'll check my sources, maybe even bring my tablet or laptop with me to the hospital. Maybe. Not tonight, though, not tonight. Tonight, I need to focus all the positive energy in the universe on Will.

"Cate?" Giles is standing next to me. "You'll be able to go stay with Will in a couple of hours. I arranged for a small lounger to be brought to his room."

"Thanks, Giles." I heave a sigh of relief and tears drip down my face. "I would've stayed in the waiting room if I had to do so. No way was I going home."

He touches my face gently, wiping away the tears. "Just remember that you won't get a lot of sleep. Nurses will be checking on him all night long."

Sleep? I look at him in amazement. How the hell can I sleep until Will's completely out of danger?

CHAPTER 5

D ESPITE MY FEELING THAT I can't sleep while Will is in critical condition, the adrenaline rush that has kept me going for hours, crashes, and that first night, I fall in and out of a dark, troubled sleep. I am aware that the nurses and doctor come in periodically to check on Will, but exhaustion keeps me prone in the lounger. Once, during that night, I heard Giles ask me if I needed anything but I don't remember what I said, if I said anything at all. My sleep is uncomfortable and stressful.

It isn't just my worry for Will that makes me tense and scared. It's the environment. A hospital at night is more frightening than it is during the day time. The eerie darkness outside the windows, the distant sound of ambulance sirens bringing someone to the hospital, and the too quiet hallways create a primal fear inside the human heart. I hate hospitals. To me they're places of death. I've been to too many hospitals that involved death for my clients. My dreams are haunted by cases I've had that have led me to morgues and bodies on slabs.

I come fully awake in the very early morning hours, scared, disoriented, and sleepily wondering where I am. I stand up too quickly and a wave of dizziness hits me. It's been thirty hours since I ate anything. I stare at the floor until the wave passes.

A quick glance around the room reminds me that I'm in a hospital room and I immediately look toward Will. He is in the same position he's been in since right after the operation. No movement, very still. Too still. Fear clutches my heart as it does every time I look at him. I bite my lip as I walk over to his bed.

Gently, very gently, I put my fingers under his nose and am relieved when I feel his shallow breath on them. I lean over him, carefully, and touch his cheek and chin, feeling the rough, unshaven bristles on them. Come on, Will, fight to live. Live, please live, for me, for us!

Behind me I hear the gentle click of the room door handle and a woman's voice whispering my name. "Cate?"

It's Felicia and she walks over to the bed. Gently she touches Will's body checking his vital signs. Then she looks at the chart hanging by the foot of his bed and makes a quick notation on it. She does the same on a pocket tablet she takes out of her lab coat.

"How's he doing?" I ask, my voice edged with fear.

"A notch above status quo, which is a good thing. It means he's not any worse and that's a definite sign that his body is responding to everything that's being done here."

She looks at me and I can see her medically evaluate my own condition. "How are *you* doing?"

"I'm okay. Some good coffee would help right now." I stretch achingly. The lounger is no substitute for a bed.

"Good. And the key word for what you want *is* good. You're getting excellent coffee this morning, not this institutional swill. Your friend Melissa is in the waiting room with what she told me is worth more than gold to you. *Real* coffee from Timothy's Coffee Emporium. She brought me a cup and it was heavenly. Why don't you go out there and get some too?"

Seeing me hesitate she adds, "I'll stay here until you come back. I would let your friend come in here with you but, two in the ICU is definitely not allowed. Go ahead. I'll be here."

Glancing at Will, I take a breath. "Okay. I'll only be a short while. I'll be right back."

Dr. Felicia Hayden nods at me, and I go out the door, saying good morning to the two new cops who have come on duty. On my way to the waiting room, I look at the large clock that seems to hang in all hospital hallways. 4:17 in the morning.

⸺∝⸺

Melissa is standing in the doorway talking to a good-looking doctor in scrubs. He seems utterly fascinated with her. That makes me smile a little. She is a true man magnet. Seeing me approach, she excuses herself from the conversation and comes over to hug me. The doctor walks away looking disappointed that his time with the lovely Melissa has ended.

"I've got coffee, your favorite, hazelnut cream, right? And I brought you a cheese croissant. Come on over here and sit down. Oh, and over there," she points to her small elegant Louis Vuitton overnight bag on the floor next to the chairs, "I brought you some fresh clothes. Are you all right?"

She leads me to the small table which usually holds magazines. I noticed they've been neatly stacked on an empty chair. She's covered the table with pretty paper napkins and has set the coffees and croissants on them.

"I'm okay, just overwhelmed, I guess. But, Melissa, it's just after four in the morning. You really didn't have to bring me this or go and get my clothes. You should be home sleeping."

"No, darling, I shouldn't be. You're here and that's where I want to be. With you. Myrtle and Harry were here until I came back. You're not to worry, darling. We're taking care of everything. Kitties are fed, plants watered, mail brought in."

"What? No." I shake my head vehemently. "No. Harry and Myrtle? They've done more than enough. They don't have to be here all night. I'm fine, really."

Myrtle and Harry are in their sixties for Pete's sake. Don't they need sleep? Myrtle has already told me that, if she has to, she can run the office of *Catherine Harlow Private Investigations* from an improvised command center and laptop in the waiting room.

"Nonsense, Cate. All of us want to be with you and believe me, no one minds. We love you, darling."

"Giles was here too. I know he came into the ICU room more than once last night."

"Yes, he told me he would check on Will." She smiles. "And check on you, too."

Sweet Giles, he must've been here all night. Truthfully, he's a good person. Not many men would worry about his ex-lover and the man she loves. I basically dumped Giles for Will, but the man harbors no anger, no hard feelings towards either one of us. How does someone live like that? I know that I hurt him. How is he able to put that hurt behind him and still care about what happens to me and to Will?

I stumble a little and sit down abruptly.

"Cate? Are you sick?"

"No, I just feel a little bit dizzy. I'm okay."

She touches my hand with concern, then quickly uncaps the lid from the container and hands me the coffee. "Here. Drink this."

I inhale the delicious aroma. The smell alone revives me a little and I take the first sip with pleasure. Then I take the croissant and find that I'm hungrier than I thought I could be. We sit quietly and I see Melissa delicately and discreetly cover a yawn. She is my best friend and there's no other like her. Her 'profession,' and her well-heeled clients don't take away from our friendship. I don't care what she does for a living. Melissa is one of the best, most loyal people I know. She gives with her heart and I love her for that. I cradle the coffee with both hands and rest my head on the back of the fake leather chair.

We sit quietly, both of us involved in our own thoughts. The quiet is interrupted when my phone buzzes, alerting me that I have three new messages. One is from Joe Jacoby asking how I'm doing and telling me that there are no new leads on the shooter. I'll text him back later. The other two texts are from the husband of the missing woman, a man I've yet to meet, who engaged my services over the phone. Boy, he's up early. Too bad I have no news for him. In the three weeks that I've had that case, there is very little to go on.

The story, as told to me by the husband, was so textbook. The woman, who had suffered two miscarriages during their six-year marriage, had simply left one night, over a year ago. Her house was tidy, her husband's laundry done and put away. The couple's car was in the garage. She just left.

The husband wasn't able to provide me with a picture. The strangest thing about this case was that he believes she took all pictures of herself, all albums where she might be seen, with her when she left. Even took her picture out of her husband's wallet, probably when he was sleeping or taking a shower. She had no social media accounts, so that was no help in finding a pic of her, either.

No female matching her description was ever found dead or alive. There was no evidence of foul play. No abduction theory. Her clothes were missing, but the luggage was untouched in the basement. Except for the clothes and the pictures, and the fact that she was nowhere to be found, the house and contents were as they always were; clean and orderly as if they were just waiting for her to walk in the door.

My immediate thought was that this woman left of her own accord. Her getaway wasn't spur-of-the-moment. She had planned it, probably months ahead of time. However, families, especially spouses, find it next-to-impossible to believe that a husband or wife would just walk away and out of their lives.

The husband—Eric Wigand is the name—asked me if his wife could have divorced him without his knowing about it. He said he'd heard that it could be done. I told him she would be able to do that only if *he* was the one who was missing.

"It's called *in absentia*, Mr. Wigand. In most states, a person can legally divorce a missing spouse by an action known as 'service by publication.' You announce that you're looking to find this person via the classifieds of a local print newspaper and state your intention to divorce said person. It takes a couple of months before you're able to get a divorce decree, but it has been done. So, no, unless *she* couldn't find *you*, I'm certain she didn't do that."

He sounded relieved and said that definite closure, no matter what I found, was necessary in order for him to move on with his life. And, in a way, I understood that perfectly. I don't like loose ends either. I like everything neatly tied up and put away.

He told me that he had moved out of the house in Rural Valley where they had lived. "Too many memories," he'd told me. "Too empty without Wendy." Now he was settled in Philadelphia. I guess I have to call him back. But, not yet, not yet. Maybe I can have Myrtle call him.

I finish half my croissant and then tell Melissa that I have to get back to Will's room. As I get up, I pause and put my hand on my chest. Damn, but my heart is pounding like hell. Melissa looks at me with concerned eyes.

"What's wrong, darling?"

"Nothing, it's nothing. Just a caffeine rush making my heart race a little." I take a breath and try to will my heart to slow down.

"Cate, let me ask you a question."

"All right. Ask it while you walk me back to the ICU," I say, putting the lid on the container of coffee and moving forward. I sway a little and steady myself against Melissa. She grabs my hand as we slowly walk down the hall.

"Cate, tell me. Why do airline attendants tell passengers to put their own oxygen masks on first before helping other people?"

"What?" Her question makes no sense in my disoriented mind.

"*Why* do airline attendants tell passengers to put their own oxygen masks on first before they attempt to help *other* people?"

She repeats it slowly and with emphasis, then answers her own question. "They tell you this for one simple reason; you can't help someone if you don't take care of yourself first. If *you're* not all right, how can you help someone else?"

Melissa pauses and asks, "How can you help Will if you're not feeling well yourself?"

"I'm fine, I'm okay, really." The dizziness hits me again and I lean against a wall.

"No, you're definitely not fine."

She plops me down into an empty wheelchair in the hall and, over my protests, pushes me down to the ICU and parks me outside of Will's room. She opens the door and has a whispered conversation with Dr. Felicia Hayden, then wheels me inside the room.

"Cate, what happened?" Felicia comes over to me and squats down looking into my eyes.

"Nothing happened. I just got a little dizzy that's all. My friend Melissa is kind of overreacting."

"Okay, just let me check you out. I'm taking you to an empty room. Will's doing about the same and his vitals are steady," she adds seeing me look toward his bed. "Melissa can stay here while you get checked. All right, Melissa?"

Melissa nods and Felicia says, "Cate? Let's go."

I grudgingly agree and Felicia whisks me off to an empty room three doors down from Will where, she says, she'll give me a quick check-up.

CHAPTER 6

"**Y**OUR RAISED HEART RATE and the dizziness you experience are a combination of the heightened stress of the last twenty-four hours, no restorative sleep, and very little in your stomach. You have had quite a shock. Other than all that, you're fine. I recommend that you go home, take a shower, eat something packed with healthy carbs and protein, then get a couple of hours of solid sleep."

"I had a cheese croissant," I say grudgingly. "Doesn't that count? I mean at least the cheese would be protein, right?"

Dr. Felicia Hayden shakes her head and laughs. "Well, technically, I guess the answer is yes. But I still stand by my diagnosis and recommendations. You really should go home for a hot shower and a couple of hours of sleep."

"I'm not leaving Will. I need to know he's completely out of danger before I leave here even for one hour. And as for showering, I'll do what's called a whore's shower in one of the bathrooms."

I know I've probably shocked her with that comment. As a private investigator, I've spent some interesting times with hookers and am very up on their jargon. But I can't worry about shocking anyone. Right now I'm overwhelmed. I can't be weak or sick. I have to be okay to take care of Will.

Felicia suddenly laughs at my crude remark and sighs. "All right, Cate. Let me see what I can arrange for you here. We'll start by ordering you a good breakfast. There's a place near here that delivers, the nurses use it all the time. They say the food is excellent. First I'll take you back to Will's room and then I'll place the order. And maybe I can arrange for you to shower in the interns' bathroom so you won't have to do a, how did you phrase it? *A whore's shower?*"

We both laugh at the way she says that but as we get to Will's room, I stop the wheelchair by placing my feet on the ground. "I can walk. I want to walk."

Before she can stop me, I get up, lean against the wall to get my bearings and then walk through the door. Felicia laughs again.

"What's the joke?" I stop and turn toward her.

"Giles was right in what he told me about you."

"Giles? What did he say about me?"

"He said, 'Cate will always do exactly what *she* wants to do. Don't even think of trying to stop her.'"

I face her and give her a half smile. "He knows me. He's right about that."

"Well, Cate, that's a damn good thing, isn't it?"

⎯⎯∝⎯⎯

I come back to Will's room to find that Melissa has gotten permission to stay with me. It seems that the surgeon, Dr. J.T. Charles, who is examining Will is inclined to break the rules of protocol for her. He tells Melissa that she can stay with me 'for a short while only.' I am very grateful to have her here with me.

"How is he, Dr. Charles? What's Will's condition?"

Dr. Charles finishes his examination and asks me to join him in a nearby examining room. My heart jumps in my chest. Why can't he tell me in here? Please don't let it be bad news! Melissa comes with me.

"What's wrong?" The words come out of my mouth as soon as the door of the small examining room closes.

The good doctor looks at me mildly surprised. "Wrong? Nothing is wrong, Ms. Harlow. Why?"

"Cate, please call me Cate, doctor. Anyway, you asked me to come in here rather than talk in Will's room. In my experience, a private talk usually means something is wrong."

"I'm sorry if I gave you the wrong impression, Cate, I truly am. The truth is I don't like to talk *about* a patient *in front* of a patient, even if they are not conscious. It puts them in the third person, almost as if they weren't there or had no concept of what we say about them. That isn't fair to them. Believe me, even in a coma, it's been proven that patients can hear what is being said.

"However, the news I have is fairly good. His heart and lungs are steady and strong. He's healing from the surgery but, I'm still concerned with the concussion. If brain scans show no swelling and all goes as I hope, I may be able to begin to bring him out of the coma by the end of next week. That's done by gradually reducing the amount of sedation over a set period of time."

I sigh and hug Melissa tightly and smile at the good doctor.

But Dr. Charles looks at me without smiling and says in a serious tone, "Please remember, that waking up is a gradual process after having been this sedated. It is not instantaneous. You won't see immediate results."

"So, how long after you begin to wean him off the barbiturates, will he regain consciousness?" I take a deep breath. "I mean, is there a specified window of time in these situations?"

"Most medications used for inducing coma can have effects even after they are stopped. However, by and large, the effects are over in a maximum of about twenty-four to forty-eight hours. Understand that it does take time for a patient to fully come to consciousness. And, when he does regain consciousness, the detective will still be very weak. He'll be sleeping a great deal due to the pain medication. Any other questions you might like to ask?"

"Does he still have to stay in ICU? I'd like to know how long he's going to be in there."

"I can't say right now because it all depends on his progress. Heart trauma surgery is a serious procedure. That plus the head injury, well, for now, ICU is exactly where he needs to be."

CHAPTER 7

I SPEND ANOTHER RESTLESS NIGHT sleeping in ICU next to Will's bed. He mumbles words, or sounds that I know are *meant* to be words. When he does that, I hold his hand and tell him that I'm here, me, Cate. Physically, he's not out of the woods and that scares me.

I help the nurse bathe him and, when Melissa comes to the hospital, she and I rub his legs and arms with essential oils to keep the muscles supple and to increase healthy blood flow. On the sage advice of Melissa's Tante Anjali, I also massage Will's temples and scalp with a special oil that darkens his hair and my fingertips.

"Tante Anjali says it will heal the concussion," Melissa informs me. "The dark color acts as a protective barrier against negativity which can slow healing."

But, besides the bathing and massages, and taking turns shaving him oh, so gently, I know I'm not doing Will any good by just sitting anxiously in this room twenty-four hours a day. I need to be out there doing what I do best—investigating what happened and following any leads, no matter how small, to find the shooter. In other words, I need to get my butt up and moving, fast. Will is stable and, though I really don't want to, I have to feel that I can leave him for short periods of time. I make Melissa promise me that she will call me if there's any change at all in Will's condition, at any time.

"*Par le sang de mon cœur, je promets,* "she says solemnly. By the blood of my heart, I promise. I believe her.

A day after the shooting, Will's captain updates me on everything they have. So far Joe Jacoby has no leads other than that the shooter was a muscular male, shorter than Will, and that he was in dark clothes wearing a hat and shades. That's all the couple who witnessed the close-range attack can tell the police.

"Both the woman and man are in shock, Cate, and unable to give any more details than that. Witnessing something like this kinda blinds them to details. All they remember is the shot and the blood, and that the shooter ran down the block and got into a black van or SUV. They weren't positive which type and they couldn't give us a plate number. Nothing more. But I'll keep having a go at them on the chance something clicks in their memories. I've got my team canvassing the area again in case something was missed. Or if there's someone else who may have seen something. The CSU gathered what they could from the scene and that evidence, as little as it is, is over at the forensic labs.

"The bullet removed from Will's chest is also being analyzed. Preliminary data says that it's looks like it's a bullet from ARX ammunition which is consistent with the use of a Ruger Redhawk Revolver. The gun and the ammo go together. That's about it, kid. Call you back when we've got more."

I call Javy to find out if he remembered any details about Will's old case concerning domestic violence. He says he had thought about it all night, couldn't sleep and then some of the details came back to him. Will mentioned the case only once. He and Will had been on a stake-out and, to alleviate the boredom of it, they had talked about old cases.

"Will didn't say a lot about this particular case, just told me that he calls the victim every month to see if she's still okay. As I told you, I think she went into hiding or something. Anyway, I guess the abuser went free because the vic refused to testify against him for fear of her life. Will said no matter what she was told about being protected by law enforcement, she still refused to testify. Because of her refusal, Will said the only option open to her was to go into hiding. He helped her relocate. That's all I remember, Cate. He never told me who she was, or who the perp was. Sorry."

"You look through his files? Hard copy, computer? No names or anything came up? No record of the domestic violence calls or police response?"

"No, nothing there. Nothing on his computer, nothing in the paper files. Which in itself is strange, right? I mean, it's like the records never existed. He ever mention it to you? I mean we're not supposed to talk to civilians or non-department people about the crimes and calls but, well you know, sometimes we do. I know I do."

"Nope, I never heard of this case and, in the past, Will *has* mentioned some cases to me. You're on the mark when you say that it's strange that there are no files on this. Doesn't make sense. Not much to go on there, Javy," I said. "You know, if there's anything else on this old case of Will's, call me. And keep me updated on the search for this damned shooter."

The building housing *Catherine Harlow Private Investigations* suddenly appears in front of me like a longed-for haven. Just walking through the door, a simple everyday routine for me before Will was shot, makes my day seem as if everything is fine and that Will might just call me, as he sometimes does, asking me to meet him for lunch.

But I know there'll be no call from Will, no happy lunch. I know everything isn't fine, and won't be fine, until he's out of the hospital and back to being Will.

Before I mount the stairs to my office I glance outside and take a look around. I feel as if someone is watching me. I know Jacoby wanted to have a plainclothes detective follow me at all times, and he wasn't happy when I turned down his offer. Knowing Joe Jacoby as I do, though, he probably didn't listen to me and has someone following me anyway. Keeping an eye on me 'just in case.'

Myrtle has been doing double duty taking over here, besides being with me at the hospital. She greets me as I walk in and immediately gets up to give me a hug. Then, standing back, she looks at me with an appraising eye, and nods approval.

"You look better, honey."

"I went home to shower and change clothes. I'm still sleeping at the hospital, but I have to admit that going home for an hour did make me feel better. Melissa is staying with him until tonight, then I'll go back."

"Any change, Catherine? Everything was the same when I called this morning."

"No, he's still out. But his vitals are normal so Dr. Charles said that maybe by the end of next week, they'll bring him out of that coma. God!" I say my voice breaking, "Let it be soon. I'm so scared."

Myrtle hugs me again. "All right, honey. It will be all right."

I grab onto Myrtle as if she was a lifesaver thrown to me in a raging ocean. She holds me tightly and leads me to the sofa. "Now come over here. Look! Harry made chocolate-filled cannoli just for you, honey. Sit down and have one."

More food. Why is it that in times of crisis, everyone wants to feed you?

"Thanks, Myrtle. Harry doesn't have to do this. He's done so much already, bringing pastries to the hospital."

"He wants to do this and, anyway, baking keeps him calm. He needs distraction. Have one, honey."

I take one to be polite, but the aroma and the chocolate cannoli cream sticking out from each end do me in and I eat it in two quick bites. I've come to realize that while food doesn't solve problems, it can help make them just a tinier bit more bearable.

I sigh and sip from the bottle of water Myrtle hands me. "What's on my agenda, Myrtle?"

She looks at me and nods, knowing that, in the same way

Harry needs to bake to keep himself distracted, I need to work. Myrtle walks to her desk and comes back with a yellow legal pad, then sits across from me. Even though I gifted her a top-of-the-line tablet for her birthday to make keeping track of cases at the office easier and more modern, I secretly like the fact that she still uses paper and pen to write down information. She likes hard copies.

"A few things, nothing pressing. Several you can do on your laptop—you know, simple security checks for potential new hires at these three companies." She shows me the names of the companies on the pad. "Oh, and you need to write that report on the babysitter the Wolowitz family wants to hire; you checked out her credentials last week. All's good there. Your notes on her are in a file on your laptop.

"The only case that may need your personal attention is that missing spouse one. The woman Wendy who went off the grid more than a year ago? Now I've dealt with this man, her husband, myself, telling him nothing more than that you were bogged down in work and it would be a few days before you could respond to his call. I gave no details about Will or anything, just told him you'd get back to him as soon as possible. You should never let clients know too much about your personal life, keep it professional."

She's right. I agree wholeheartedly. Clients need to see me as someone who can get the job done for them without thinking that I'm being hindered by any personal problems.

"However," Myrtle arches her left eyebrow in consternation, "he's insistent that *you* call him today. He's called three times already this morning. Sorry honey. Are you up to it? Because if you're not, I'm going to call him and recommend that he find another private investigator. He does live in Philadelphia, maybe he can find someone there. Or what about Barry O'Connor, that young man you met at a PI crime conference last year? You said he was smart and I believe that you also said he's in New Jersey. That's not far from Philly."

I wrinkle my nose at her statement. I'm too much of a professional to farm my cases out to someone else. As worried as I am over Will, I know that I've got to deal with the everyday business at *Catherine Harlow Private Investigations*. On top of that, in a practical sense, I need to keep the money coming in for bills and living expenses. Plus, I *have* to keep busy so I don't go crazy.

"No, Myrtle, I'll call this client. And speaking of calls," I lean forward and grab another cannolo "any word from Will's mother, Francesca? She hasn't returned my calls."

"Sorry, honey, absolutely nothing. I keep trying, but all I get is voice mail. We know that she went on an expedition in South America searching for primitive art for the Metropolitan Museum's new exhibition. Depending on where she is will determine if she got your, or my, messages."

"Yeah, I figured that. I just wish she was here, though. I mean he's her child, you know? Her son is in a medically-induced coma after having had his head bashed, been shot in the heart, and gone through major surgery! She needs to be here!"

"I know, honey, I know. I'll keep trying her cell phone. I'll make sure I get through."

Myrtle, my rock. She firmly believes that if anyone can get something done, she can. But this time I think that, unless she hires a plane and flies to where God only knows Francesca might be, contacting someone in the far inner reaches of South America may just be beyond her skills.

With a sigh and the beginnings of a headache, I guzzle the bottle of water and walk over to my desk to call my insistent client.

CHAPTER 8

"**T**HIS IS CATE HARLOW RETURNING your call, Mr. Wigand. I do apologize that it's been a few days. I had a case that had to take priority," I say, in total agreement with what Myrtle said about not letting clients know too much about my personal life. "But I'm available now and I'll be going over all the info I have about your wife. Is there further information you want to give me?"

The gruff voice on the other end sounds genuinely relieved to hear from me and, in the midst of my own fear and turmoil, I feel sorry for his misery. As horrible as the scenario in my own life is right now, at least I know where Will is and that he's getting the best of care. But someone you love just walking out of your life without leaving a clue, and you don't know if they're even alive or what horrible thing may have happened to them, that's got to be really hard.

We talk for about twenty minutes and I ask all the usual, pertinent questions that I've asked him before when he first engaged my services, hoping that maybe he's remembered something new that could help me crack this case.

"Did you get the money I sent you to retain you?"

A money order made out to *Catherine Harlow Private*

Investigations, came in the mail the day after he had contacted me. I found that a little odd. Most of the times I'm paid by check, PayPal, credit card, or, in a very few instances, cash. But Myrtle said that maybe he had bad credit or didn't have a checking account.

"Yes, I did," I tell Eric Wigand. "That covers the first month."

"Good. Just let me know when there are additional expenses."

"I will make sure to do that. Listen Mr. Wigand, is there any possibility that we can meet sometime this week? I can make an arrangement to meet here in my office on, maybe Friday at 4:00 in the afternoon? It's really best if we can meet in person. I'd come to you in Philly but, umm, right now I have to stay in the city."

There's a short pause before he says, "You gotta stay there, huh? I hope it's not family problems. You know, no real problems. Nothing you can't handle."

"I handle problems very well, Mr. Wigand," I say in a professional tone.

"I bet you do. I bet you can handle just about anything. Anyway, I'll try to make it but, like I told you when I first contacted you, my boss is a real bastard when it comes to anyone taking time off for personal reasons. Unless I'm calling from my death bed, he'll, uh, get pissed if I miss work. I've only had this job for three months. I can't lose it. Let me see what I can do and I'll call you."

"Okay, sure, I understand. You can leave a message with my secretary. In the meantime, I'll start checking the info you gave me. Oh, and Mr. Wigand? I really do need a picture of your wife if you can find one. I know you told me that she took all the pictures and albums with her but maybe she missed one."

"Yeah, sure, I'll keep looking for one."

"Maybe her family has one? Even an old one will be fine."

He doesn't answer right away, then says, "Wendy has no family, all dead. All she has is me. Look, I need to know what happened to her, understand? I need to find her." His voice breaks slightly and I feel sorry for him all over again.

"I'll do more than my best to find out, Mr. Wigand. But, seriously, see if you can make the meeting on Friday. I like to meet my clients, helps me get a solid feel for the case."

"I'll try."

The way he says it, I know damn well that he will not come in on Friday or maybe any other day. I've worked cases before where I only met the client after everything was neatly solved. They were minor ones, though, security breaches at a company, identity theft, credit card fraud— none of them involved a missing human being, a real person. I have never worked a missing person's case without meeting a relative or good friend of the one gone missing. This is strange, but he has paid my fees, so I have to get to work.

We say good-bye and hang up and I begin to sort through what facts I have about the case. He sounded genuinely upset and sad. Either that or he's a good actor. Who really knows what goes on in a marriage? What made her leave and take every photo of herself with her? Was she trying to erase any memory of herself and her life with him? Did she destroy the pictures in a fit of anger? Why do people leave each other?

For a variety of reasons, really. Money problems, an affair, who knows? Bored with the same-old, same-old life and looking for something better? Maybe she committed a crime he doesn't know about yet and left to avoid jail time. It's possible he cheated on her. Maybe she's vindictive, wanted to hurt him badly, and figured this was the best way to do it.

Or maybe she found someone, fell in love, and they left together. But, if that were the case here, why not just ask for a divorce? Divorces can be messy and painful. I should know—I went through one. But still, why just vanish into thin air? Something's not right here and now my PI-self kicks in and I want to find this woman, not just for Eric Wigand, but for my own curiosity.

A missing wife who left of her own volition with absolutely no trace. Why?

∞

I look through everything Eric Wigand sent to me via email and print out copies to study. This woman seemed to mingle with absolutely no one. No friends, no contact with any neighbors. She had no children, so no parent-teacher or Mommy-club contact. Wigand mentioned that they'd suffered through her two miscarriages. I had asked him about any medical personnel attending her at those times.

"Can you give me the name of her gynecologist or any doctor she was seeing during that time? It would be good if I could speak with them."

"Her doctor retired. I don't know where she is now."

"Her gynecologist?"

"My wife wasn't seeing a gynecologist, just a general practitioner. As I just said, the woman retired."

Nothing there.

"Any places you and Wendy had frequented in the area? Restaurants, maybe?"

"No. Wendy cooked a lot. We'd go and get a lot of stuff from Farmers' Markets. I like those big tomatoes, the sweet, juicy ones those Amish people grow."

She belonged to no social organization, either in real life or online. She didn't work outside the home. I knew nothing about her, except what Wigand told me. So, where to begin. Even if I don't want to leave the city because of Will, I can still do some investigating long distance.

Eric Wigand told me that he moved to Philadelphia about three months ago to find work. Before that he and his wife Wendy used to live in a place called Rural Valley in Armstrong County, Pennsylvania. A quick search on the Internet tells me that it is one of the most remote places you can live. According to a 2000 census count, there were 922 people, 382 households, and 267 families residing there. No stores nearby, no areas of entertainment, not a hell of a lot of human interaction. Maybe that's why she left. I'd leave too if I had to drive any great distance to get to real civilization. Real civilization to me has restaurants, pizzerias, shopping malls, and medical centers within twenty minutes driving time from my brownstone.

This woman Wendy Wigand lived in Pennsylvania and she had to have had contact with someone besides her husband.

What's her real story? What or who was she running to? Or, maybe, running from?

CHAPTER 9

I MAKE IT BACK TO THE hospital a little after 6:00 pm to spend the night with Will. At least five times during the afternoon I've called for any and all updates on Will's condition. All the info I've gotten is that 'nothing's changed, all is the same, vitals are steady.' The news is as comforting as it is frustrating. Comforting that his condition is not worse, frustrating because he's still in that damned medically-induced coma.

I have to admit that Dr. J.T. Charles and Dr. Felicia Hayden have been very good and patient. I think that maybe Giles spoke to them and asked for their patience in dealing with me. He knows me, and he also knows how persistent and, sometimes pushy I can get, especially when I want immediate information. Giles also know how utterly terrified I am at losing Will now that he and I are back together.

I wonder if I could ever be like Giles. A good, decent person who holds no resentment toward anyone, especially toward me. After all, *I* was the one who left *him* to go back with my ex-husband, even though I have no intention of getting married to Will again. It was pure lust on my part. Will knew exactly what erotic itch to scratch and I willingly let him. How decent was that move?

I think I'm basically a good person. I will use illegal methods to solve a case if I think it's in the best interest of my client, so that's why I say *basically* good. But Giles is not only genuinely good and decent, he's unfailingly kind. I know he was in love with me and still is. I know he wanted to make our relationship permanent. Giles knew that I still had feelings for Will, even after we started dating, yet he patiently waited for me to get over Will and begin a new life with him.

When that didn't happen, when I left him for Will without explanation, he was gracious and kind, if not completely baffled. Now he's being kind again by making it easy for me to be with Will in ICU and making sure his colleagues give me frequent updates on Will's condition.

If I'm truthful with myself, and, even though it hurts sometimes, I always try to be, I can admit that, if the tables were turned, I would have a hard time being as gracious as Giles. I would help him, of course, because I'd be upset for him and I would do everything in my power to ease his pain. But I'd be just the slightest bit bitter seeing him crazy in love with someone for whom he left me. I remember how jealous I was when he started dating again, even though I was back with Will. That's a part of me that I do not like and have a hard time controlling. That damned green-eyed monster who lives secretly inside me will pop out every once in a while.

At my office, I checked data on the internet and found that Dr. Charles may be right. Most medical professionals believe that comatose patients do hear what is being said. Research also shows that talking to the patient in a matter-of-fact manner is not only therapeutic to their healing, but also is a primary factor in helping them access memories. They hear your voice. I told Melissa to talk about anything and everything when she's in Will's room.

I make my way to the nurses' station and ask to speak to either Dr. Charles or Dr. Hayden. Within five minutes Felicia Hayden comes down the hall and gives me the standard update.

"I know you're frustrated and scared, Cate, but believe me when I tell you that the most telling signs about a patient's recovery are his vitals. Will's vital signs are steady and that is good."

With that I have to be content. I'm beginning to hate the word 'vitals.' I thank her and hurry to Will's room where I speak with Melissa for a few minutes, hug her good-bye, and then sit down in a chair next to Will and grab his hand.

After spending an hour with Will, where I tell him about my day in the hopes that hearing my voice really will speed his recovery, I stretch and walk to the waiting room. One thing they don't allow in the ICU is electronic equipment and I need to use my laptop.

Getting started on my missing spouse case, I check various places in Rural Valley where Wendy Wigand may have been or visited. There're not a whole lot of places to check. There is, however, a barber shop that caters to both genders. It's possible that she went for a haircut at some point. There's also a small general store. Two possible leads.

I type questions on the computer about this Wendy Wigand and then type a few more about the husband Eric. He seems to be sincere but I can't get a good read on anybody unless I have a face-to-face. I realize he wants to move on with his life. That's a phrase that people always use when a major crisis hits. After a while, nobody, not even the closest of friends, wants to be around the sadness or pain you're experiencing. It's too depressing. So, they tell you that *'you have to move on with your life.'* Suddenly I feel a chill come over me. Would Myrtle, Harry, and Melissa say that to me if—I shake the horrible thought from my mind. Will is going to be all right!

The waiting room on the ICU floor is empty which is good for me. I work uninterrupted for over an hour, intending to grab a cafeteria cheeseburger for dinner and then head back to Will's room before eight o'clock.

My phone buzzes and I see an incoming call from Captain Joe Jacoby.

"Hi, Joe, what's the update? Any news?" I say this without any preamble. "I hope that you have something for me. You know that the longer the investigation goes on, the better chance there is that the witnesses might forget something crucial or the crime scene might be compromised."

There's a pause and then Joe's tired, and totally pissed-off voice, comes back at me. "Now *you're* telling me how to do *my* job? We got it all covered. Hell, you little punk, *I* helped train *you* when you were going for your PI license! You came to *me* for advice. Remember? Don't tell me what I already know and what I'm already doing."

Oops, went too far with that one. My mouth has a life of its own sometimes. I should know better than to tell a seasoned police captain how to do his job.

"God, I'm sorry, Joe, I really am. I do remember, I do. I'm sorry. I'm just overtired and getting anxious that this guy won't be caught. This is killing me, seeing Will in a coma."

I wait for a few precious moments while he draws a deep breath and cools his well-justified anger at me.

"Yeah, right, gotcha. Apology accepted. Listen Cate, I called you because we may have a small lead on the shooter. It seems that the female witness says she remembers the shooter saying something to Will, right after he shot him. Got a call from her about an hour ago. I had the two cops guarding them bring her and her husband down here. I got them round-the-clock protection. Poor bastards; they're both emotional wrecks having witnessed the shooting and all. Civilians. Seeing something like that at close range, it shakes'em up. Got them sitting in a room down here with a violent crimes counselor right now."

"Can you keep them there until I get there?" I ask jumping up from the waiting room chair and running for the elevator. "Please, Joe? Please keep them there and let me talk to them."

"Ah, Cate, c'mon. Give me a break here. I gotta say no. I don't need you coming in here all gung ho scaring the shit outta the witnesses. We know what we're doing here."

"Joe, I know that. I do know you know exactly what you're doing, and that all of you want to catch the shooter as much as I do. But, I've got a stake in this that none of you have."

"What's that?"

My voice breaks. "I love Will. So, please, just let me talk to them. I love him, Joe and I couldn't live with myself if I didn't personally help gather all info crucial to finding his shooter."

I'm annoyed as hell at myself that I start crying, but maybe the tears help plead my case because, after a pause, Captain Joe Jacoby says very gently, "Okay, kid. How fast can you get here?"

"Fifteen to twenty minutes, tops. Put it out that if I'm speeding, I'm not to be pulled over, okay?"

"Sure, just don't kill anybody or yourself for that matter. I'll hold the witnesses here."

"Thanks, Joe. I owe you."

"Yeah, yeah. Anyway, maybe it *will* help if you talk to the them, especially the woman. You seem to have a way with scared women if I remember correctly from your other cases. Women trust you. She's still shook about what she saw, but she was pretty coherent and positive about what the shooter said."

Getting into the elevator, I lean forward and push the button that says lobby. "What? What did he say?"

"The witness says the shooter struck Will on the head with the gun, and right after he shot him, he said 'Your little bitch lost is as good as dead. You should have stayed out of my business.'"

CHAPTER 10

"**Y**OUR LITTLE BITCH LOST is as good as dead. You should have stayed out of my business."

I repeat this over and over again as I navigate the congested New York City traffic, honking my horn and cutting people off in my rush to get to the precinct. What the hell does that mean? Who is 'your little bitch lost?' One of Will's CIs, a confidential informant, a snitch on the streets who is a source of vital info to law enforcement? It has to be. A hooker, a small-time thief or pot dealer. Someone 'lost' to what we consider normal society.

All cops, especially detectives use confidential informants, who are basically bottom tier in the criminal world. A detective and a CI have a strange relationship that is beneficial to both of them. The detective looks the other way at the CI's small crimes and in return the informant provides crucial info that may help in major crime investigations.

Occasionally, if it's necessary to gain info on violent gang against gang crime, with a real possibility of innocent citizens getting killed in the cross-fire, they'll use a gang leader as a confidential informant. That gang leader then expects the detective to protect his turf against his rivals in exchange for pertinent and detailed information. I know that Will has more than one CI whom he trusts, including gang leaders. As a private investigator, I have a few reliable sources who are on the outskirts of the law, myself.

Was Will working a major case on someone and somehow his confidential informant got made? That's got to be it. I have to get Javy to check all Will's CIs and see if any have disappeared recently. That might be hard to do since, even though partners share a lot of info with each other, they don't always give away the names of their top snitch. It's a personal and sacred bond between an officer of the law and the CI.

Finally pulling into Will's precinct, I park in a space reserved for visitors. I run up the two steps to the front door and then just stop, my hand on the glass. How many times have I gone in this door to see Will? I've come here to pick him up for lunch, to talk about a case of mine, to laugh and joke. Sometimes I'd come in with a head full of steam ready argue over some mundane topic that seemed so utterly important at the time. Now it seems that I can't move, I can't walk inside. My legs feel like lead

"Going in, miss?" Two rookie patrolmen I don't know have come up behind me and one of them holds the door open, looking at me expectantly. I shake my head yes. I can't speak but I walk inside and head slowly for Jacoby's office.

I stop by Will's desk. It's neat, the way he always leaves it. "I don't know how the hell you ever find anything on your desk," Will has said to me more than once when he's been over at *Catherine Harlow Private Investigations*. "Would it kill you to have some order here?"

My eyes tear up remembering this and I take a deep breath to stop myself from bursting into tears. Neat his desk might be, but it looks unused and lonely. I touch the scarred wood and close my eyes. I can see him sitting there talking on the phone, calling out to another detective, eating a hurried snack because he's working late and didn't have time to get dinner. Damn it Will! You have to come back here, you have to!

"Cate! Hi, sweetheart. You need anything?"

Suddenly I am barraged by the concerned voices of detectives and cops. The blue brotherhood and sisterhood gathering around me.

"Hey, Cate! How are you doing?"

"We're gonna get this bastard. Tell Benigni."

"Cate, what's going on? How's Benigni?"

"Harlow, how's Benigni doing? Don't worry, honey. God damn. He's gonna be okay."

"You need anything, Catie, anything at all, you let me and my partner know."

I try to smile and respond to greetings and questions. "Yeah, he's, um, yeah, Will's holding his own. I'm just here to see Jacoby. Thanks, guys, really, thank you for everything."

I move away from the group as politely as I can, assuring them that I'll keep them updated on Will's condition. These people are a united front against crime and most people don't realize how hard their jobs are.

The public doesn't associate kindness with cops, but believe me, cops are among the most compassionate people I know. Their kindness to me is overwhelming. I've lost track of all the cards, gifts, candy, even stuffed animals, that have been sent to Will. Since very few things are allowed in an ICU room, Myrtle has taken them all to my brownstone and put them in my small guest bedroom which now resembles a gift shop.

Before I can make it to Jacoby's office, Javy comes up to me, smothering me in a massive hug. He introduces me to his temporary partner, an older man named Jackson, who looks as if he's seen it all and doesn't like what he has seen. His handshake is bone-crushing.

I pull back from the hug and ask Javy what he thinks the shooter meant when he said 'Your little bitch lost is as good as dead. You should have stayed out of my business.'

I tell him my suspicions about the possibility that one of Will's informants has been found out and has gone missing. "Maybe the shooter was referring to one of Will's street people. Can you check all Will's CIs, especially the female ones? Might get a lead."

"I'll check on them, Cate. I don't think I know all of them, though. You know how it is. Sometimes we have a few CIs we keep only in our own confidence. But I'll check, believe me."

His temp partner looks at his watch and tells Javy they have to go. Then, turning to me, he tells me not to worry, "We'll get this cop shooting fucker. Benigni's a helluva damn good detective. You tell him I said that, you hear me?"

I finally arrive at Jacoby's office and he greets me at the door. "Come on in, Cate." He glances down the aisle of detectives' desks and grimaces. "Shit. It's not the same without him here. He's one of the best, if not the *absolute best* detective, working here. And he's my friend, a damned good friend. God help me, I need him back here."

I hug Jacoby. "I know, Joe." He hugs me back tightly.

"Listen Cate, when the witness told me the shooter said, 'Your little bitch is as good as dead,' for one agonizing second I thought he was talking about you. I wanted to send a group of cops over to where you were to protect you. But then I thought about it. What he said after, the part about that Will should have stayed out of his business, I knew it had to be someone else. Someone Will had had contact with, someone maybe he was trying to help. I don't know. I'm working on it. It had to be a woman. A hooker in danger or one of Will's street snitches?"

I shake my head. "I have no clue here, Joe. But we're going to find out."

He nods, pats my shoulder, then grabs a folder off his desk and hands it to me.

"The two witnesses are in room three. This folder has their statements. I'll walk you down there."

Room three is where police psychs usually talk to traumatized kids. There are toys, puzzles, an old-fashioned chalk board, and children's books. It also has four old, but comfortable chairs, grouped around a table. Through the two-way glass window, I see a man and a woman sitting in two of the chairs, both holding vending machine cans of soda. They're sitting so stiffly they appear to be mannequins. In another chair is a sweet-faced psychiatrist, Dr. Lara Evers, a violent crimes counselor and trauma expert, whom I've met a couple of times. If anyone can calm these people down it's this woman. This was the best place to put them.

Jacoby knocks lightly on the door and we enter. "Lara, you remember Cate Harlow?"

"Yes, of course I do," she says rising from her chair and coming over to me. "It's good to see you here, Cate. Captain Jacoby has been keeping me apprised of everything. If you want to grab a coffee or something with me later, I'm available. I'd love to hear all about your trip to New Orleans."

She doesn't give a damn about my trip to New Orleans. In her gentle way, I understand that she's telling me that if I need to talk to a professional shrink about how I'm dealing with Will being shot, she'll be here for me.

"I've got a pretty full night ahead of me, Lara. But thank you."

"Another time then."

She smiles and gently presses my hand. Telling Mr. and Mrs. Flanders, good-bye, she grabs her handbag and leaves.

"Cate, this is Ariel and Philip Flanders," says Jacoby filling the awkward pause. "Mr. and Mrs. Flanders, this is Cate Harlow, she's helping us with the case. Cate would like to ask you a couple of questions."

I admire the way Jacoby introduces me. No mention that I'm a private investigator. For all they know I'm a police consultant, someone who works in the department and does in-depth studies of cases.

"Hello." I speak softly and distinctly, my voice low and smooth. Keeping eye contact with them, I place the folder on the table and pull a chair into a position directly across from them.

The wife is slim and small with trusting-looking eyes behind designer frame glasses. Her husband, who's also wearing glasses, towers over her, even while sitting down. He puts a protective arm around her shoulders. Both look as if they spend more time indoors than out. Possibly academics. The shooting must have been a true terror for them to witness, especially close-up.

"As Captain Jacoby said, I'd like to ask you some questions. I know this whole incident has been horrible for you, but anything you can remember or tell me will help us find the person who shot Detective Benigni that much sooner." I pause, looking at each one in turn. "Is it all right if I begin?"

Ariel Flanders flinches when I say the word 'shot,' but she looks at her husband and nods. "We want to help as much as we are able. We don't know Detective Benigni very well except to say hello and chat a little. But he was so nice when we moved in a few months ago. He helped Philip carry boxes to our condo. There were so many boxes and Philip was having a real time of it."

I don't say anything. Mistaking my silence for not understanding why they had so many boxes, she explains, "We're antique book archivists for the City University."

This time I nod in understanding. I was right about them being academics.

"Captain Jacoby has been keeping us informed of his progress. He says we're not to talk to anyone about this. We're living with two police officers outside our door." She looks at me fearfully. "But, please, I have to ask. The detective? He will pull through, won't he?"

CHAPTER 11

HER QUESTION TAKES ME off-guard. Under the table I dig my nails hard into the fleshy inner part of my right thigh. It hurts like hell but the pain centers me. I am here to do a job and I can't do it if I allow myself to get emotional. I respond calmly.

"According to the medical team at Lenox, yes, chances are good."

"Oh, thank you. We were so worried!"

I will myself to believe what I just told her as I open the folder and read over their statements. I remind myself to put emotion aside and concentrate. My professionalism and expertise as an investigator will help Will much more than my fears.

"Mr. and Mrs. Flanders, according to both your statements, you were outside the building waiting for an Über when you say you saw Detective Benigni walking toward you from where he had parked his car."

Mr. Flanders adjusts his glasses. "Yes, we were going to the theatre. Detective Benigni was walking toward our building and he waved at us."

"He asked us where we were off to." says Mrs. Flanders. "We only spoke for a few minutes because Detective Benigni said he was meeting some friends for dinner and was already running late."

"Okay, Mrs. Flanders. Good, you're both doing really well here," I say encouragingly. "When did the shooter appear? Was he waiting for the detective? Did you see him waiting?"

"No, he wasn't waiting. We were alone outside the building. But—he seemed to appear almost immediately. Almost as if, yes, almost as if he was following the detective."

"Can you recreate the scene of the shooting from the moment you saw the man who shot Detective Benigni? Right from the beginning. Did you see him approach? Did he come up from behind the detective or approach him from his right or his left? Remember, anything, anything at all, no matter how small or inconsequential it may seem to you, can really help a case."

"It all happened so fast," says Mr. Flanders, adjusting his glasses again. "As we told Captain Jacoby, one minute we were talking and the next minute this man came out of nowhere and hit the detective in the back of the head."

"Did Detective Benigni—Will—did he go down onto the ground immediately? Was he knocked-out?"

Mr. Flanders looks at me sadly. "Oh, no. He actually spun toward his assailant. He was reaching into his jacket as he turned. That's when the man shot him."

If Will was reaching into his jacket that means that he was reaching for the service weapon inside his hip holster. Will turned toward his assailant, not only because he was trying to see who had smashed him in the back of his head, but he was also trying to protect the two people now sitting in front of me. Protect and serve. Will takes those words very seriously.

I sigh so deeply that I startle Mr. and Mrs. Flanders. I can't help thinking that if Will had fallen to the ground after being hit on the head, maybe he wouldn't have been shot. The assailant might have assumed that he had killed him with that blow. But, then again, it's more than likely the bastard would have shot him while he was down on the ground.

"Your description of the shooter is that of a man, a muscular male, shorter than the detective, dressed in dark clothes and wearing a hat and sunglasses. You said he ran to a black or dark SUV or van and drove away but you couldn't see the license plate. Did you see in what direction he drove after he got into the vehicle?"

They both shake their heads no, and the husband says, "I think it was straight, which would be east, but our attention was focused on getting help for the detective."

I am frustrated, but I understand. Cops, PIs, anyone in law enforcement, are trained to look for details. Even in a sudden crisis, we observe as much as possible. Civilians panic and the fear of a situation makes them miss crucial details.

Everything they've told me matches up with their original statement so I turn to the wife with the last question I have. "Mrs. Flanders, Captain Jacoby told me that you called today because you remembered something that the shooter said to Detective Benigni just after he shot him. Can you repeat to me what you heard?"

There's that visible flinch again when I say the word 'shot,' but she pulls herself together and sits up straight. She reminds me of a child in school who has to recite a difficult poem and is determined to do her best.

"Yes, the man, the—shooter—right after he shot the detective, he said, 'Your little bitch lost is as good as dead. You should have stayed out of my business.'"

"You're absolutely sure you heard him say those exact words, Mrs. Flanders?"

She sits up straighter and looks into my eyes. "I am absolutely certain he said those words. I will remember what he said forever. He said it in such a vicious, angry tone."

"Do you remember anything else? Anything at all?"

"Sorry, I guess we weren't that observant."

"No, really, you observed more than you think you did. And you saved the detective's life by immediately calling an ambulance, Mr. and Mrs. Flanders. Okay. Thank you both for being so kind and patient in going over all this again. I know it's difficult for you. Before you go, can I get you anything? Another soda or coffee? No? Then, I'll get a uniform to walk you out."

"Ms. Harlow," says the husband hesitantly. "Will we have to testify in court? I mean if you find this shooter, will we be required to go into court and tell the judge what we witnessed and heard?"

They're afraid, I know, so I respond very gently and reassuringly to them.

"Yes, Mr. Flanders, when the police catch this person, and you can be *absolutely certain* that he will be caught, you will have to testify. But, you'll continue to have twenty-four hour police protection until he's convicted and locked away."

He and his wife look at each other, frightened but resigned. They're the type of citizens who will do their civic duty no matter how terrified they may be.

I go to the door and signal a young cop walking past. "Please escort Mr. and Mrs. Flanders to the front desk. Tell the desk sergeant to arrange to have a uni drive them back to their home."

As they're walking to the door, Mrs. Flanders stops and touches my arm.

"Yes, Mrs. Flanders?"

"You said if we remembered anything else about this assailant, no matter how small, we should tell you?"

I'm on alert. There's a reason that law enforcement has more than 'one go' at witnesses to a crime. There's always the possibility they might remember something they forgot, but which can be pertinent to a case.

"Anything, no matter how small, Mrs. Flanders," I say. "What do you remember?"

"Well, it was a smell."

"A smell? What kind of smell?"

"I can only describe it as minty garlic."

"Minty garlic?"

"Yes," says Mr. Flanders, looking at his wife. "I smelled that, too, Ariel."

"It's like when you eat a pasta dish that is heavily seasoned with garlic," explains his wife. "Then you chew mints or a mint-flavored gum to disguise the smell. Minty garlic, that was what I smelled when the assailant spoke. Is that helpful, Ms. Harlow? I mean it doesn't seem all that important."

"It *can* be important Mrs. Flanders and it is helpful. If you remember anything else, please call Captain Jacoby. Or, here, give me your phone." She looks at me, but hands it over. I quickly key in my private number. "This is my personal cell number. You can call me anytime."

I don't give them my business card as I don't want them to know I'm a private investigator. Jacoby let them assume that I work for the police department and I want to keep it that way. Opening the door for them, I stand to the side and we say good-bye. Then I wait until they're out of sight before walking back to Jacoby's office to talk to him about my interview with the witnesses.

Minty garlic smell. That can describe just about anyone who has eaten in a variety of restaurants where the food is spicy. But it's a start.

⸺∝⸺

I check my watch as I walk out of the police station. It's almost nine o'clock. I want to get back to ICU and Will, so I jog quickly toward my car.

In the visitors parking lot, a woman, who is one of the toughest police lieutenants I have ever met, calls out to me and walks over. She hands me a small stone with a green shamrock embedded in it.

"This is for Will. My lucky stone. I want him to have it. Give it to him, okay?"

Before I can say more than thank you, she walks quickly away toward the precinct door. I see her take out tissues and know that she's wiping away tears that she doesn't want me to see.

Will, with everyone pulling for you, how can you not come out of this alive and well?

CHAPTER 12

T HERE'S HURRIED ACTIVITY on the ICU floor. My heart thumps wildly in my chest. My first thought is Will, something's happened to Will, and I run to his room. I open the door to find a nurse making a notation on his chart. She turns at my entrance and smiles at me. I breathe out slowly.

"All is good, Ms. Harlow. Normal for his condition, no change. How are you tonight?"

"I'm fine, thanks. There seems to be a lot of action going on here." I gesture toward the hallway where nurses and doctors seem to be searching for something.

"Yes, we had a good Samaritan come in and say there was a barely conscious woman outside the emergency doors. He said he witnessed her being hit by a car. But when a doctor and attendant went outside, there was no one there, no injured woman, no one needing medical assistance. The man who reported it tried to help find her, and ended up on this floor saying he thought she'd be brought to ICU."

"I didn't see any cops near emergency. The hospital is required to call them for a hit-and-run."

"We did. They were here, but they left when we couldn't find the woman. The ER was pretty full tonight, but we looked all over for her. We're still looking."

"Did you search the parking lot? Cameras?"

She nods. "We had security check that also. There was no sign of her."

"Cops have any information on a hit-and-run?"

"As far as I know, they didn't. No one had called it in. It's strange to say the least. The guy who reported the hit-and-run victim to us disappeared too, so they weren't able to question him for details about the accident."

I want to ask another question when Will stirs a little, moves his lips, and makes a sound. I hear something that sounds like, "kree, I, shuh."

I move to his bed. "Is he trying to say something?" I ask the nurse.

I hold my breath as she leans over him. We both listen intently. Then she straightens up.

"It's possible," she says kindly, "but it may have just been some gas from his stomach gurgling up to his throat. You know kind of like a burp. That happens."

She does one more check on the fluids flowing into Will, smiles a good-night to me, and leaves.

I walk over to Will and, as I do every night, place my phone on the stand next to the head of his bed and play music. Myrtle read that music causes a reaction in people in a coma because the brain processes songs differently than spoken language. The region of the brain responsible for song is not only soothing to the patient but it helps heal the body. I will try anything to help him heal, no matter what it may be.

Then I lean over the bed and snuggle my face next to his and talk to him. I tell him about my visit to the precinct, how everyone is rooting for him to get back to work as soon as possible, my talk with Jacoby and interview of the witnesses, my entire day including my missing spouse case. I end with, "Hey, Will, baby? Dr. Charles is going to start the wake-up process really soon. Hopefully next week. When he reduces the meds keeping you in this coma, you'll be awake in about 48 hours. Soon you'll be coming home. Isn't that great news?"

I keep talking until I can't talk anymore. Then I drop into the lounge chair next to his bed and fall asleep. I dream of a black shadow of a man coming toward me. He has a gun. In my dream, I stand frozen like a deer in the headlights of a car. I can't move. Miraculously, just as the shadowy man shoots the gun, Will pushes me out of the way. The bullet hits him in the chest and he drops down at my feet.

∝

"Good morning Catherine."

I open my eyes to see Giles standing in front of me. He's smiling that gentle smile he always has reserved for me. I squint at him and then at the window. The light filtering through it illuminates the room and lets me know that it's early morning.

"What time is it?"

"It's going for 6:30. I came to get you for a special treat. You need a good, homemade breakfast. I took the morning off and I don't have to be in the ME's office until 1:00 this afternoon. What do you say I follow you home in my car and, while you take a shower and change clothes, I whip up my famous cherry cheesecake pancakes with a nice side of Applewood smoked bacon?"

I sit up surprised and guiltily pleased. Guilty because I will be able to enjoy a good breakfast when Will is existing solely on liquid nourishment dripping from a tube inserted in a vein in his arm. But I know Giles is only trying to make a bad situation better.

If Myrtle's Harry is the king of yummy desserts, Giles is the pancake and breakfast prince. When we were together I would wake up to the wonderful aroma of all kinds of pancakes or waffles served up with a nice side of bacon, sausages, or Taylor Ham. It was one of the ways he showed his love for me. The fact that he wants to make breakfast for me now is overwhelmingly sweet.

He walks over to Will to check his pulse, and his heart rate. Then he monitors the endotracheal tube helping Will breath. Giles turns to me and gives me a thumb's up.

"Come on, Cate. Let's get you home for a couple of hours. You need a break. Staying here is making you antsy and anxious. I know you, Cate. Patience is something you have very little of but you need to be patient now."

I swing my legs over the side of the lounger and, bending at the waist, stretch to the floor, getting the tight kinks out of my body. My body feels sluggish.

"Okay. Give me a few minutes with Will. I'll be right with you."

Giles nods at me and, as he leaves the room says, "I'll be in the waiting room, Take your time."

I kiss Will good morning and talk about what I'm going to be doing today. I even tell him about my breakfast date with Giles and I swear I see a grimace. Jealousy and rivalry between Giles and Will. All for the fair hand of Cate Harlow, PI. I laugh at what I'm thinking.

Will makes a noise in his throat, and I listen closely but all I hear is a "kr-shuh" sound. More than likely gas from his stomach as the nurse said last night. I kiss him and snuggle against him. "I love you, baby. I love you."

Then I gather my things and go to meet Giles in the waiting area.

CHAPTER 13

A GOOD, LONG HOT shower makes me feel almost normal again. I throw a short summer robe around me and follow the familiar smell of Giles's breakfast specialties into the kitchen. Little Guy and Mouse are happy to see me, even though they show it by simply sitting on the counter next to me while I drink my coffee and gently butting their faces against me. Cats are not like dogs, who will run circles around us to show their happiness at our return. Cats take a subtler, but no less loving, approach to a reunion.

The aroma of the cherry cheesecake pancakes and Applewood smoked bacon is as delicious as it is comforting. I watch Giles carefully plate the pancakes and bacon onto two of my best china dishes. He places the food on the counter, then expertly mixes champagne from a small bottle with orange juice, making us mimosas. Of course, he's using champagne flutes from my Baccarat crystal. I rarely use any of those glasses, which were given to me by my wealthy, elderly aunt for my bridal shower. But they are beautiful and I'm glad he used them.

"Here, Catherine. Take a sip and relax. The bottle is a demi size so there's only a small amount of champagne in the orange juice. Just enough to release tension."

We clink glasses but don't toast anything. I guess we could toast to the fact that Will survived both being shot and the subsequent surgery, but I'm too superstitious. I don't want to tempt Fate and have it bitch-slap me later with something bad.

"This is great, Giles, thanks." I dig into the pancakes and sigh. Giles smiles at me. Little Guy and Mouse come up on the counter again and sit patiently waiting for a piece of bacon. I break some of my bacon into little bits and hand-feed each one.

"That's it, babies. No more. People food is not good for you."

When they see that they're not getting any more goodies they jump down from the counter and walk over to the window seat where they begin to lick their paws and clean their faces.

Giles pours orange juice and the rest of the champagne into our glasses. Then he leans back and looks at me. "How're you feeling, Catherine? I know this has been a tremendous strain on you mentally as well as physically. The body's reaction to intensified stress is fight or flight. That's built into our primitive DNA. Are you getting enough sleep? Sleep and nutrition are necessary for you right now. If you need any help sleeping I can give you something very mild, just to take the edge off."

"No," I shake my head. "I need my edge. I want all my senses alive and working up to par right now. I sleep okay. I'll be fine. And, as for nutrition, between you, Melissa, Harry and Myrtle, I'm eating just fine."

I finish the Mimosa and sit back to look out my window. There's the usual traffic going by, both of walkers and cars. Life hasn't stopped because I have a crisis in my own life. It goes on as it always has and always will. Perhaps the cruelty of life is that no one really matters enough for it to stop. Then again, maybe that's also the compassionate reality of life. History has shown us that life has to continue even under the most horrible, traumatic events.

I remember what Marc Crofts said to me. Marc Crofts, the man I think of as the assassin-with-a-heart, the man who helped me find, and save, my client after her husband had buried her alive in Potter's Field on Hart's Island. He said, *"We make our own justice in this world."* I know *he* certainly adhered to what he said.

Crofts worked outside any, and all laws, dispensing his own brand of justice, whether good or bad.

For someone like me who has always questioned authority and has downright worked outside the legal limits myself, having been married to a police detective might seem strange. I think of Will and how he believes in the justice system. But truth be told, Will, for all his being a stickler for the law, has no problem working outside of it either, if he thinks the ends will justify the means. He has done things that can technically be said to be illegal but, by doing so he has brought murderers and other degenerates to justice. We don't talk about it much. But, from the few things he has said to me, I know that, when it comes to working just outside the legal limits, as long as what he's doing is *against* the criminals and *for* the victims, then he's fine with it.

Giles places a mug of coffee in front of me. His voice takes me out of my thoughts.

"Any news from Captain Jacoby?"

"Some," I say as I grab the mug and inhale the delicious scent of hazelnut coffee and cream. I tell Giles all the details about the type of gun and bullets crime analysis says the shooter used and about my interview of the witnesses.

"'Your little bitch lost is as good as dead. You should have stayed out of my business.' That's what the female witness heard? That's interesting right there, because it means that the person knew Will, right?"

"Yes, it does," I say nodding in agreement so vigorously I almost spill my coffee. "And it also means that the person who did this had a personal beef with Will. He must have thought that Will was interfering in his activities in some way. That points to a criminal, someone who doesn't want anyone in the law to screw up what he's doing."

"Does Jacoby have any clues as to who it might be? Anyone he knows with whom Will might have had a run-in?"

"Not really," I say. "But there was this domestic violence case that both Joe Jacoby and Will's partner Javy, had mentioned. But Javy checked Will's cases and his files, and found nothing. That's a little weird, that there's no trace of that case."

"That is strange. I'm pretty sure that Will is as meticulous in documenting his cases as I am. We actually discussed that when I did the autopsy on his case about a homeless man. Both of us are sticklers for keeping regimented legal files, both hard copies and digital."

I look at him. Whatever their personal differences concerning me, Will and Giles can work together easily. They're solid professionals. I admire that.

"That case file might be able to lead the police to who shot Will. There's a reason it's missing and whoever took it, or got rid of it on Will's computer, has to be found out. The questions are who did this and why?"

"Both good questions. Hopefully, Will's partner and his captain will be able to find out the answers."

"I sincerely hope so, Catherine."

We continue to talk while we finish eating. I'm so happy that we're able to be alone together in such an easy, companionable way. After all, we *were* lovers, in the truest sense of the word, in this very brownstone. In the bedroom, in the living room, even in the kitchen! I lower my head at the memories and pull my robe closer around my hips.

Giles pours a second cup of coffee for me and then begins to clear the breakfast nook table. Glancing at the clock on my stove I see that we've been eating and talking for almost four hours. Giles did say he had to get to the ME's office by one o'clock.

My protest, insisting that he leave everything on the counter, and that I'll put them into the dishwasher later, makes him laugh. I laugh too. Domestically challenged that's me. Giles faces me with a boyish eagerness and a smile that touches my heart.

"Catherine, you always say that. I've awakened here too many times to find the dishes from the night before are stacked on the counter still waiting to be put into the dishwasher. I'd come out of the bedroom and there they'd be. Believe me, it was never a problem for me to get them done before you woke—"

He stops abruptly. The mentions of his 'having awakened here' and 'come out of the bedroom' brings an awkward moment into an otherwise easygoing morning. Giles quickly avoids looking at me by bending to stack the rinsed dishes into the dishwasher. When he straightens up, the boyish grin has been replaced by a sad smile on his face.

I begin to cry and, after a few moments, Giles comes over to gather me in his arms. I put my head on his shoulder and let the tears come. Tears of exhaustion, of stress, of my fear for Will. I even cry over the happy memory of Giles and me together here at my brownstone. He lets me cry myself out, murmuring comforting words into my hair.

"Shhh, Cate, it's okay. You're overwhelmed by everything, that's all. It's okay. Shhh, sweetheart."

His arms are so strong and I can feel the warmth of his body through my thin robe. Sobbing, I turn to look up at him. His face is so close to mine. With only a slight hesitation, he begins to kiss my lips, softly, tentatively. I lean into the kiss, eyes closed, lips parted. His once-familiar lips are sweet with the taste of cherry cheesecake and pancake syrup and we kiss with an urgency of remembering. It's so warm, so familiar to be like this with him. I kiss him with a remembered passion and love. I need this warmth, this strength and comfort. Giles pulls me closer into the kiss and I feel as if I can willingly drown in his arms. Sweet, gentle, passionate Giles.

And then—just as suddenly as the kiss began—it is over. Gently, we both pull away from each other.

Holding me at arm's length, Giles, smiles that sad smile again and murmurs, "It's okay. It's going to be okay." Then he walks back to the sink.

"Just sit there and finish your coffee, Catherine. Then go about your day. I'll see you at the hospital either later today or tomorrow. Just relax, everything is good, believe me, it's good."

He turns to the sink to hand wash the Baccarat crystal glasses and I look out at the busy traffic moving down my street. Good. Everything is good.

CHAPTER 14

I STOP BY THE office of *Catherine Harlow Private Investigations* instead of going straight to the hospital. I texted Dr. Felicia Hayden and her quick response was that Will's condition is "still stable and unchanged."

Please, I think wistfully, just once, it would be so good to have someone lie to me and tell me he's miraculously awake. But I know they only tell the truth, like it or not.

The kiss with Giles, brief as it was, is still on my mind but I 'Scarlett-O'Hara' it and tell myself that I'll think about it tomorrow. As Ms. O'Hara was fond of saying, *"I can't think about it now or I'll go crazy. I'll think about it tomorrow."* Gotcha there Scarlett, I can't allow myself to go crazy right now.

A call to Myrtle lets me know that she is picking up some yogurt and cream for coffee to restock the small fridge we have in the office, so she'd be a little late. That's okay. I need some time alone to check out the minute bit of information from my client, Eric Wigand. I'm going to start with names of doctors, past and present, who practice in the area of Rural Valley.

But before I do that I'm going to try to get in touch with Will's mother once more. Her cell phone rings four times before I hear her Ivy League college voice. "You've reached Francesca Sutton

Benigni. Please leave a message with your name and call-back number. Thank you."

"Hi, Francesca. It's me, Cate, again. Please call me as soon as you get this message. I really need to speak with you." I leave both my cell number and my office one.

Francesca Sutton Benigni. I close my eyes and remember when I found out that she was Will's mother.

⌒∝⌒

"Francesca *Sutton*? *The* Francesca Sutton? She's your *mother*?!"

We were lying on the large chaise lounge in Will's loft apartment, lazy and in love on a Sunday morning. We'd been together for almost six months and talks about marriage were beginning to take tenuous shape.

When Will got up to put on the Bose system, I idly glanced at the *New York Times Arts* section. Celebrities at glittering events for a new exhibition, book launches, a new wing at the Whitney; all the glamorous doings of the glitterati who live lives so different from my own. I like living vicariously through them. I lay back relaxing and reading.

A second later, I had pushed myself up to a sitting position and was staring at the page. A picture of a handsome, tuxedoed Will, at an event for the Cloisters last month, standing with an older, very beautiful woman, stared back at me. The words 'mother and son' catch my eye and I gasped out the woman's name. Will looked at me curiously.

"Francesca Sutton *Benigni* is my mother, yeah, why?"

"Seriously? You don't know why? I mean she's famous! Why didn't you tell me Francesca Sutton is your mother?"

Will comes to look over my shoulder at the picture. His only comment is, "That's an old picture, taken three years ago. You'd think they'd use a current one. And that reception was boring."

"Will! Your mother is Francesca Sutton! I mean, you didn't think to tell me this bit of family background?"

"Francesca Sutton *Benigni* and I didn't think it was important. You'll be meeting her in a couple of weeks, so what's the big deal? She's my mother, end of story."

"She's also the woman who brokered the biggest art deal in decades. She was able to purchase the *Madonna and Child* by the early Renaissance master Duccio di Buoninsegna, for the Metropolitan Museum of Art. It's a masterpiece! The museum paid $45 *million* for that work. *$45 million!*"

"And you know this how?" Will smiles with interest at my excitement.

"Arts and Humanities 101 at NYU. My professor took a group of his students there to see it. He was enthralled by it and he told us the incredible story of how the museum came to own it. All the behind the scenes intrigue, the bidding wars, everything. The painting is only an 8 by 10, but it is breathtaking. Do you know how many museums had tried to get that painting?"

"Not off the top of my head, no," he says, laughing. "How many?"

"Most of the ones in Europe and many of the ones in Asia. But Francesca Sutton was determined to get it for the Met." I look at Will a little annoyed. "You said your mother worked for a museum."

"She does. She works for the Metropolitan Museum of Art."

"Oh, my God, Will. I thought she was a docent or worked in public relations or something at some small museum. You didn't say that she was a collections curator for the Metropolitan Museum of Art, for God's sake!"

Will comes back to the chaise and lifts the hair on the back of my neck, kissing a very sensitive part, and running his tongue behind my ear. It makes me shiver with anticipation, but, I'm determined to continue the conversation and I pull away.

"She's a collections curator and she possibly brokered the biggest acquisition of the century and you don't think that's important enough to tell me?"

When he doesn't answer, I continue. "She outbid and outwitted curators from around the world! She made sure that the Met got that coveted painting. And, to make sure that the painting went to the Met, my prof said that Francesca Sutton donated a hefty amount to the museum to ensure the purchase."

I stop, embarrassed, but Will doesn't seem in the least bit concerned or annoyed at my comment about money.

"Francesca Sutton *Benigni*," he says again, wickedly winking at me. He lies back on the chaise and pulls me into his arms. "And it was my grandfather who donated a hefty sum, as your professor so rudely stated, not Francesca. However, the donation had nothing to do with the acquisition of the painting. It went for some much-needed repairs to the museum, especially the members-only dining room. The old gentleman loves to dine there with his cronies!"

"You call your mother Francesca?"

"When you meet her, you'll understand why I call her by her first name. She's too stunning to be called simply mom or mother. She *is* Francesca."

"Oh, God, and you want *me* to meet her? Now I'm scared!"

"Don't worry. She'll absolutely adore you. She always tells me that all she wants is for her baby-boy to be happy. And *you* make me happy." His hands travel down the back of my shorts as he kisses my neck again. "Now come here and give Francesca's baby-boy some sweet love."

A couple of weeks later, I met the beautiful Francesca Sutton Benigni who was charming, sincere, and made me feel so welcome. She told me to call her Francesca and I remember thinking that Will was right. She's too stunning to be called by anything but that classic, sophisticated name. She is the epitome of the elegant name Francesca.

I stare at the screen on my phone. Somehow, I'm hoping that my memory of the day I found out she was Will's mother will trigger a telepathic response from Francesca and she'll immediately return my call. Rationally, I know it's not going to happen and after a few minutes I turn away from the phone and click on my computer. I've got to start the day.

CHAPTER 15

HIDING IN PLAIN SIGHT is something prey in the animal kingdom learn to do to protect themselves from their predators. I watched a documentary about it on a hot summer night last year, when sleep eluded me. It was fascinating. Instead of putting me to sleep, as I'd hoped it would, it had the opposite effect. It got me thinking that humans are animals too, and perhaps those people who are declared missing, are really just hiding in plain sight. Perhaps their camouflage is so good that they won't be found. Maybe that's what Wendy Wigand is doing.

I have no reason at all to think that Wendy is in hiding or that her husband is a predator. He seems genuinely sincere in having me find her. There's a loneliness in his voice that is touching. He's probably just a gruff guy who's socially awkward. Maybe he has a hard time communicating with people, especially women. Maybe Wendy was the only woman with whom he felt comfortable. I don't know, but what I do know that I have to start earning my retainer.

Even though Eric Wigand told me his wife didn't go to doctors and that the only one she had ever visited was now retired, I decide to do an online search for doctors or medical centers in

Rural Valley. Someone had to know this woman.

There are three doctors listed in Rural Valley, Pennsylvania and one Medi-Clinic. I print out the information from my Google search. Glancing at the clock, I figure I'll give myself another hour before I leave for the hospital.

The office of the first number I key into my phone is answered by an automated voice that tells me the number is no longer in use. The second number, that of a Dr. Paul Learner gets me a busy signal.

I try the third one, get put on hold for ten minutes, and when I finally get to speak with Dr. Jeani Rector and describe my client's wife, I find out that the doctor has never met nor heard of Wendy. I have the same result with the Medi-Clinic. No one there knows her.

I go back to the second number and key in the phone number of Dr. Paul Learner. The call is answered on the second ring.

"Dr. Learner's office." A warm motherly voice answers. "Can I help you?"

"Yes, good morning. My name is Cate Harlow and I'd like to speak with Dr. Learner if he's available."

"Is this about a test or medical procedure you've had done? I can help you with that."

"No, this is a private matter, a confidential one, that I need to discuss only with Dr. Learner. I can hold or I can give you my number and he can call me back when he's available."

"Well, excuse me, is it Miss Harlow? Mrs. Harlow?"

"Just call me Cate."

"Well, Cate, he's seeing patients right now. It's a busy day and we're kind of booked until this afternoon. Are you sure there's nothing I can help you with? I'm Bev Vesterholt, Dr. Learner's nurse practitioner and anything you need to know or ask is as confidential with me as it is with him."

I debate waiting to speak with the doctor, or saving time and asking questions of his nurse practitioner. I want to get to the hospital and Will, so I go with asking questions of the woman on the phone. She might know about Wendy Wigand.

"I'm a private investigator and I've been retained to find a woman named Wendy Wigand. About five-three, average build. I'm sorry but that's all I have as a description. She went missing about a year ago. One important fact is that her husband said that she had had several miscarriages. Has anyone by that name, or anyone having had miscarriages, been to see Dr. Learner?"

"We do get women who are pregnant. Dr. Learner is a general practitioner and he does all areas of medicine. But, I don't feel comfortable talking about our patients with you. Can you fax me your credentials? I'd feel more comfortable seeing them. However, even then, I can't give out any medical history, you understand. Just generalizations."

I walk over to my fax machine and take out my PI license and business card. "I'm faxing you a copy of my state license and my PI business card. And all I want to know is if a woman I described, with the name Wendy Wigand, has ever been to your office. I don't want her medical information. She's missing from Rural Valley and her husband is frantic to find her."

We chat for a few minutes and I hear the whirr of a machine over the phone. Bev Vesterholt asks me to hold while she checks my license.

"It certainly looks legit, Cate. New York City, my goodness. We just have to be careful here. There are a lot of women who come in here who have real problems, medical and otherwise. I can tell you that I have not ever met a woman named Wendy Wigand. Let me check the files. Give me a minute."

I hear the sound of a chair rolling across the floor. Then I hear what sounds like old metal cabinet drawers opening. Obviously the doctor doesn't believe in computer filing.

"Cate? No, I checked and no one by that name has ever been a patient here. We do have women who, I guess, match the description you gave to me but, only one of them has been pregnant, three times, and no miscarriages. Do you have a picture you can fax to me?"

"No, no picture. I know this sounds odd, but it seems that she took all pictures of herself with her when she left. Her husband is looking for one that she might have missed."

"Well, now, that is strange! Seems as if she just wanted to get away from her life here, doesn't it? Anyway, I'm sorry that I couldn't help you more."

"That's okay. But listen, I'd appreciate it if you could ask around the office if anyone may have met a woman named Wendy Wigand. If someone does know of her, can I ask you to call me at the number on the business card?"

"I will do that if I hear anything. I'll ask around."

We say our pleasant good-byes and hang up.

But, as I prepare to do a few more online checks, I can't help but think about Bev Vesterholt's words, "Seems as if she just wanted to get away from her life here, doesn't it?"

I think it's time that I met Mr. Wigand in person. I make a note to place a call to him to set up a meeting. Looks like I'm going to Philadelphia.

CHAPTER 16

"**S**OMEONE IS WORKING HARD," is Myrtle's cheerful greeting as she comes through the office door, juggling several shopping bags. I'm seated at my desk checking out the time it will take me to get to Philadelphia.

"Put the bags on the floor, Myrtle. I'll put everything away. Just finishing checking something online for that Wigand case."

"Nonsense, Catherine. I'll do it. You have no idea where anything goes. Besides, I'm not as ancient as you might think!"

"Myrtle, my darling, there is nothing old or remotely ancient about you. I've played tennis with you, remember?"

I get up from my chair, stretch, and walk over to the bags Myrtle has settled on her desk while she begins to empty them.

"Anyway, I believe I know where the cream and yogurt should go. Ummmm. In that cold thing, right? What's it called again?"

I jokingly point to the refrigerator making Myrtle laugh. I laugh too as I go to put the items in the 'fridge, leaving one yogurt out for a snack.

"It's good to see you making a joke, Catherine. Are you feeling better? A little less stressed about Will?"

"Oh, I guess. Kind of less stressed." Guilt over the morning kiss hits me full-force. "Giles made me breakfast today."

Myrtle smiles at me and says, "That was nice."

"At my brownstone. He made me cherry cheesecake pancakes and Applewood smoked bacon just like he used to do when we were together. He had everything ready by the time I came out of the shower and put on my robe. He even made mimosas and—"

Myrtle holds up her hand to stop me. "Honey, stop the guilt-ridden disclosure. You don't have to feel guilty over the fact that a very good male friend made you breakfast in your brownstone. This isn't Victorian times, Catherine. Being alone with a man in your own place won't sully your reputation."

Flopping onto the couch I grab the pomegranate yogurt I placed there for a quick snack.

"How did you know that I felt guilty? I mean, not guilty-guilty about breakfast, just a twinge of guilt. Just a little bit over something he said." I relay what Giles said about "having awakened here" and "come out of the bedroom."

Myrtle goes over to the Keurig to make coffee. She comes back to sit on the couch and face me.

"Catherine, that's just a sweet memory that he shared with you. Nothing wrong with that. Don't give it a second thought."

"But I remembered it too and that's where the guilt-twinge comes in. I *liked* the memory. It made me smile."

"Honey, you're human. Memories that are good shouldn't be forgotten. You have every right to like a time that was pleasant for you and Giles. That was a good part of your life. It is a happy memory that involved both of you" She pats my shoulder. "Keep it in your heart but don't dwell on it, Catherine."

"There's something else, Myrtle and this really makes me feel guilty as hell."

"All right, Catherine, tell me what happened."

"I starting crying and Giles hugged me. I don't know why it happened, but it happened. He kissed me and—I kissed him back. I kissed him back! I mean, it was only for a few seconds and we both backed away before it went any further, but still, with Will in a drug-induced coma, I *kissed* Giles. What kind of a person am I? I am a horrible person, right?"

Myrtle doesn't blink an eye over my confession, just looks at me directly.

"Catherine, what happened between you and Giles is natural and I'm sure, on his part, it was to offer comfort. On your part, you needed comfort. You're not a horrible person at all, you're vulnerable and scared. Those are two powerful feelings.

"The way I see it, you both had the common sense to not let that kiss lead to anything else. My advice to you is to let it go and to not let it happen again. You're a good person, Catherine, never doubt that."

I think about what she has said and, after a few guilt-ridden minutes, decide that, once again, Myrtle makes sense of what is happening in my life. She's my rock-solid, practical conscience.

"I guess you're right, Myrtle. The memory was of a pleasant time, a good time in my life. And the kiss was sweet but, I know both Giles and I will never let it happen again. So—how do I get rid of the guilt?"

"You don't. You just live with it. But, as I said before about the memory you and Giles shared, you don't dwell on it. It happened, it's over, and that's it."

"God, I love you Myrtle!"

I get up to throw away the empty yogurt cup and grab some coffee.

"Anyway, I'm glad you came in before I have to leave for the hospital. I'm going to call my client, Eric Wigand and make an appointment to meet him in Philadelphia on Friday. Since it's almost definite that he won't be coming to New York City, I'm going to meet him on his home turf."

"What do you need me to do? Anything special?"

"Take care of things here as you always do. Any new cases that come in, older cases that might need me to review new evidence. And, you know, Will."

"Honey, Will is at the top of my everyday to-do list. Don't worry about that. Between Harry, Melissa, Giles, and me, we've got it all covered."

"I know," I say tearing up. "All of you are so damned good to me."

Myrtle comes over to me and wraps her arms around me.

"Catherine, we're family. Never forget that. You don't have to be related by blood to be family. Heaven knows, I have some so-called blood relatives that I don't *want* to consider my family."

I smile and hiccup through tears.

"The truth is, Catherine, sometimes the people we meet in our lives may start out as strangers, but in the end, they become our real family. You, Harry, me, Melissa, and Giles; like it or not, honey, we're all family."

"I like it, Myrtle. I love all of you."

"Good. Now, go wash your face and get on the phone. You've got a missing person case to solve."

Myrtle is the absolute best.

At my desk, I turn and look out the window to the street below. Again, there's the feeling of being watched. It's spooky. Jacoby has got to call off his dog, that discreet detective who has been assigned to follow me.

CHAPTER 17

HARRY MEETS ME in the waiting room of Lenox Hospital. It seems he's brought boxes of his home-baked goodies and has been giving them to anyone, staff and all, who comes in here.

"Cate!" He puts down the open box of cannoli and envelopes me in a bear hug. "How are you? We keep missing each other here. Melissa is in Will's room. Do you want me to tell her you're here?"

I gently extricate myself from his hug. "No, I'm going to his room now." I look at the boxes, one filled with cannoli and the other box loaded with a new cream-filled pastry called sfingi di San Giuseppe, which literally translates to St. Joseph's Sphinxes.

"How about a cannolo or a sfinge?" Harry offers pastries as comfort.

"No, thanks, Harry. I had a big breakfast. Later though, okay? Put one aside for me."

I walk down the hall to Will's room. The two uniformed cops are there and they greet me with a tip of their caps. Looking through the window to Will's room, I see Melissa and she waves to me. Just as I'm about to go in, I hear my name called. Dr. Charles is coming down the hall and I stop to wait for him.

"Cate, do you have a moment?"

"Yes. Is everything all right?"

"All is going well so far. I wanted to tell you that I'm going to be doing a complete exam on Will in a few hours. Then, if all signs are good, as I hope they will be, we'll seriously consider the process of bringing him out of the coma."

"You said that it usually takes twenty-four to forty-eight hours for a patient to come to full consciousness, right?"

He nods as he scribbles something on a chart he's holding. "Usually yes, but that's a ballpark figure. I've had patients fully awake after eighteen hours and others regain consciousness an hour or two past the forty-eight-hour mark." He looks at me and gives me an encouraging smile. "Will is a healthy, strong young man, Cate. His condition is stable. I expect a good response from him."

"When are you going to start decreasing the meds?"

"As I said, I want to do a thorough exam of Will first and make the decision based on my findings. But to give you an estimate of when, it will most likely start next Wednesday. For now, if you have something you need to do or somewhere to be, it's all right if you leave. He'll still be as he is now."

I think about my morning phone call to Eric Wigand. He's agreed to meet me tomorrow in the late afternoon in Philadelphia.

"No, I don't have to be anywhere today. Tomorrow, I'm meeting a client out of state, Pennsylvania, Philly. For today, I'm just going to go between here and my office."

"Of course, do what you need to do." He glances at his watch. "I have a surgery in an hour, so I have to leave now. I'll see you later if you're here."

I watch Dr. Charles hurry past me toward the elevator and I push open the door to Will's room, where Melissa is waiting for me.

"Thanks, Melissa. How long have you been here?"

"About four hours." She gets up and stretches her arms in a full reach toward the ceiling, as delicately as a cat. "Good news from Dr. Charles?"

I tell her about the conversation we just had. Then I debate telling her about the kiss Giles and I shared, but decide against it.

Who knows what Will can hear? Besides Myrtle told me to put it out of my mind and I will—for now.

"Oh, darling, that is good news! You'll see, next week Will's going to be awake and, hopefully, soon leaving the hospital." She pauses and shakes her head. "He can't go back to his condo, though, Cate. I don't think he should be alone after all this."

"No, he won't be alone. He'll come back to my place. It's familiar and comfortable."

"Good. And you know we'll all be there for both of you."

"I know. All of you have really helped me a lot. I'm overwhelmed with gratitude." I stop. Every time I think of how wonderful my friends, the people Myrtle calls my family, have been in this crisis, I want to cry.

Melissa blows me a kiss from where she is sitting and smiles. "I'm going to grab some coffee at Timothy's Coffee Emporium on the way home. I'll be back later. Call me if you need anything."

She stands and takes something out of her handbag. It's a small vial containing a blue liquid. Opening the stopper, she dabs a little of the liquid on her finger, and bends over Will. Then she slowly and methodically traces a circle on Will's forehead. Her lips move in a soft whisper. Touching her finger to his lips, she closes her eyes and murmurs the words, *"Tous soient bien, les plus puissants. Je crois."* Oh powerful ones, let all be well. I believe.

A delicate, pleasing smell, that reminds me of hyacinths in the spring, seems to be in the room. I see Will's body move slightly.

Then Melissa gathers her things and walks toward me and we walk to the door. My curiosity is piqued and I want to know what's in the bottle. I have to ask.

"What's the blue liquid, Melissa?"

With her hand on the door handle, she turns to me and smiles mysteriously. "It's another powerful gift from Tante Anjali. She made it herself specifically for Will. It helps memory."

Kissing my cheek, Melissa then walks out the door and disappears down the hall.

I stay with Will for a couple of hours, then head to the waiting room where I am allowed to use my laptop. The rest of my morning is spent making two more calls to Francesca, and getting the same recorded message, and working on the Wendy Wigand case. I peruse places in Rural Valley where Wendy might have been seen and check the news online for any mention of someone fitting her description.

A small online article catches my eye. It's about an Amish produce farm that has won recognition as the oldest family-owned farm in Pennsylvania. The farm, owned by a family named Hochstetler, has been supplying Farmers' Markets in the area with high quality fruits and vegetables for over sixty-five years. They travel from market to market and they will be in Rural Valley on Wednesdays and Fridays. Their specialty, states the article, are "huge, sweet-tasting tomatoes," the kind Eric Wigand said he liked. The ones he and Wendy bought at a Farmers' Market. Maybe they bought them from the Hochstetlers.

The meeting with Eric Wigand is tomorrow, which is a Wednesday. Scratch going to two places that far apart in one day. Okay, maybe I can make the trip to Rural Valley and the Farmers' Market on Friday. There's a chance that someone at that market just might remember seeing Wigand and his wife there. I wasn't looking forward to making two trips to Pennsylvania in one week but, that's part of my job.

Late in the afternoon, Dr. Charles tells me that his cursory exam of Will confirms that he can start to decrease the barbiturates and slowly bring him out of the drug-induced coma as early as Monday next week. I spend the night with Will and leave early the next afternoon to go home, shower, and change my clothes.

Philadelphia, here I come.

CHAPTER 18

A LTHOUGH PHILADELPHIA IS ONE of the most historic cities in the United States, it is also considered one of the most dangerous. Each year, people who plan to move to this city, worry about their safety and rightly so. Crime runs rampant in certain neighborhoods and only fools, or someone with a death wish, venture into dangerous areas. Even then, the names of the neighborhoods give a false sense of safety. A good example of this is a neighborhood named Strawberry Mansion.

With a name like Strawberry Mansion, you could easily think this neighborhood was full of lavish homes and expensive lifestyles and, at one time, it actually was. Strawberry Mansion was home to a number of Philadelphia's wealthiest families in the 19th Century. The neighborhood takes its name from a restaurant which was famous for its strawberries and cream concoctions and catered to the upper class. However, as with most wealthy areas over time, the neighborhood was struck by economic decline and urban decay.

Large in population, Strawberry Mansion is difficult to police, or even to maintain, due to historically inadequate city funding. Modern Strawberry Mansion has acquired a reputation as the most dangerous, and run-down area, in Philadelphia. It is ridden with such violent crime that it has gained national attention. Gang violence, and rule, run wild here.

And, of course, this is the neighborhood where I'm meeting my client, Eric Wigand.

After canvassing the area for what I can possibly consider a safe place to park, I settle on a fairly well-lit lot on the outskirts of the neighborhood. It has a guard and, I count three security cameras. I walk to our meeting place.

I'm dressed, and prepared, for the occasion. Ratty-looking jeans, dirty running shoes, and an old sweatshirt of Will's with the hood pulled up to cover my hair and the sides of my face. I keep my hands inside the pocket of my sweatshirt with the right hand firmly on my Smith and Wesson. For added protection I have a Derringer in an ankle holster and a small Taser called a Jolt Mini Stun Gun, in my jeans pocket. The stun gun was a gift from Melissa who carries a similar one on the off chance that one of her 'clients' gets out of line. She told me that she's never had to use it, but carries it 'just in case.' In true Melissa fashion, the Taser is a hot pink color. I would've chosen black but, hey, as long as it works, color doesn't matter.

I walk with a tough determination, hoping that I blend into the area and don't arouse too much unwanted attention. The area is alive with a primal fear. You can feel it. Life is worth nothing here. If someone wants what you have, they'll take it. You can lose your life for a coat, a pair of shoes, or even for a damned cup of coffee. Killing someone is an everyday occurrence and getting arrested is just part of life—if the cops can find you, that is. Why my client chose to meet here is a mystery to me. Since he lives in Philly he should know that there are better places to meet.

The name of the restaurant where we are to meet is called Pot Luk, a Chinese place, and it is as rundown as the neighborhood where it is housed. I find it almost unexpectedly. The heavy smell of overcooked, greasy food alerts me to it. It's hidden between two alleyways and the only way you know it's there, besides the smells, is the dull blinking neon sign above the door that is missing the P and t in Pot and the L in Luk. The remaining letters, 'o, uk,'make me think of the words, 'Oh, yuck!' the perfect exclamation someone would make upon seeing this place for the first time. I laugh. Glad to see that my sense of humor is still working.

A host of odors hits me as I open the door. All kinds of strong seasonings, mingled with a heavy smell of congealed grease, assail my sense of smell. From the doorway I can see into the kitchen. A large metal can near the cooking area is overflowing with old wilted vegetables, obviously well past their sell-by date. The rancid odors make me have to stifle a gag. The room is hot and the constant steam from cooking spreads a heavy layer of humidity over everything.

I try to close the screen door but the bottom hinge is broken and the door hangs slightly lop-sided. Inside there are three old tables that, upon a closer look, are crusty with old food. The legs of the wooden chairs by the tables don't look all that sturdy either. Some of them are duct-taped to the seats.

A tired-looking woman with a menu comes over to me. Her top is stained.

"Eat here or in dining room," she says robotically. It's a statement, not a question.

There's a dining room?

"I'm meeting someone here," I say. "I'm early." I look around the small room and don't see another area where you can eat. "Where's the, um, dining room?"

"In back. Follow me." She beckons me to follow her and we move from the small room through the kitchen. No one looks at us as we pass through. It's so crowded that I keep my arms close to my body for fear of bumping into someone lifting a heavy pot with boiling contents.

In the back of the kitchen is a door and the woman opens it wide for me to enter. It's larger than the room out front and from what I can see as I walk inside it, cleaner and neater. There are no other customers. The woman tells me I can sit at any one of the five tables. I take the one farthest from the kitchen.

"Okay, thanks. I'm going to wait out front for someone. But we'll be eating back here."

She simply places a menu on the table and walks out ahead of me. I follow and position myself near the broken outer door. I like to be early when I'm meeting someone on a case. It gives me a chance to watch the person approach unobserved. I watch their body language, how they walk, hurried or relaxed. A person who hurries is anxious and that means they may not be thinking clearly. I also check out where they're looking as they're coming towards me. If the person looks back or constantly checks the area, it means they're either being followed or they're bringing someone else with them to our meeting. I don't like surprises; I want to be prepared.

Very few people seem to come past this restaurant. The ones who do walk fast as if they know the dangers that can occur in the area. I glance at my watch and see that my client has another ten minutes to arrive. I hope he's not late. This area is scarier than the New Orleans cemetery I visited at midnight on my last case. Not so surprising, since we have a helluva lot more to fear from the living than from any ghosts. This place produces a fear that heightens your senses to a limitless degree.

From my vantage point in the doorway, I scope out the neighborhood. Though it's still not evening, the area is dark and gritty-looking. This is definitely not the place where you would find Mr. Rogers, the kindly icon of my early childhood television viewing. I find myself humming *It's a beautiful day in the neighborhood,'* and shake my head sadly. I can bet that it's been a long time since this neighborhood has had a beautiful day.

A man crossing the street walks into view. He seems to be headed towards the Pot Luk. If he's my client, he's a few minutes early which is a good thing. I observe the man. He's bulky, a little bit taller than my 5'5" and somewhere in his late forties. Average if tough-looking face, dark, thick hair, that appears wet and slick, but is just combed back with some type of greasy gel. Big rough, hands. He's wearing a suit jacket and a tie which he has loosened. His shoes look comfortable. If I'm not mistaken they're some type of comfortable walking shoes from Rockports, the kind favored by cops and anyone who does a lot of walking. His job must require him to be on his feet most of the time.

I stand aside to let him enter and he gives me a steady look. "You're Cate Harlow." I'm easily identifiable from the picture on my PI website.

"Yes, I am. You must be Eric Wigand. I've gotten us a table in the back room, the, um, dining room."

"Good. Let's go back there to eat. We can talk while we eat, okay with you? I had a busy day."

CHAPTER 19

THE TIRED-LOOKING WOMAN appears again, almost as if out of nowhere, carrying two bowls filled to the brim with soft Lo Mein noodles. A young boy, hurrying behind her, carries a large basket of fried wontons. After both are set on the table, they leave and Wigand begins to eat ravenously. He nods toward my bowl inviting me to eat. I inspect the spoon and fork next to my bowl to make sure that they're relatively clean. They look chance-y at best as do the plastic chopsticks laid across my plate.

"No thanks. I'm really not hungry."

"Sure? Okay. Suit yourself."

"You must come here a lot," I say, playing with the chopsticks. "Or did you order ahead today. They seem to know what you want."

"I come a lot. The food's pretty good and it's filling. I don't like to eat in my apartment alone."

"Right. I understand. Sometimes you just need to get out."

"You got that right. I don't like being alone all the time. What about you? You got a boyfriend?" He gives me a lop-sided smile. The question is abrupt and straightforward. I don't like the personal aspect of it.

"We're here to talk about your missing wife, Mr. Wigand. Let's do that, all right?" I say firmly, all business.

"Sorry, but, you know, a looker like you—I just figured there's a boyfriend involved. Yeah, well, anyway, I was just trying to make small talk. I've never had to hire a PI before. I'm a little nervous and I wanted you to feel comfortable, too."

"Most people are nervous in an unknown situation. But I'm here to help you, Mr. Wigand and the more I know about your wife, the better I will be able to locate her whereabouts for you. So don't be concerned about making me feel at ease. I'm fine. I'm a professional and I need facts to solve this case." I take out a small notepad and pen from my sweatshirt pocket and look at my client. "Let's begin with this. Were you able to locate a picture of your wife Wendy?"

"I have one, but it's really blurry. Looks like someone didn't know how to use a camera. But it's the only one I have. I found it in this old jacket of mine. Taken two summers ago at a Farmers' Market."

He stops eating long enough to reach inside his jacket pocket and hand an envelope to me. I open the envelope and look at the picture inside. The picture is crumpled and it is definitely out of focus but I can make out most of it. The woman in the picture is wearing a long-sleeved dress and has a scarf wrapped around her head covering her hair and part of her face. A hat is clamped over the scarf and large sunglasses hide her eyes. Eric Wigand is standing next to her with a protective arm thrown around her shoulders. He's smiling, but she's not. Maybe even then she knew she was getting ready to leave.

This photo could be a picture of any female who is five foot three with an average build. Not much to go on here, but I put it back in the envelope and put that inside the back page of my notepad.

The man can eat. He goes through the Lo Mein, the fried wontons, and after asking me if I'm *really* sure I'm not hungry, starts on the bowl of noodles in front of me. In-between mouthfuls, he orders a large portion of General Tso's Chicken. I glance at my watch. I don't want to be in this area after dark and it's already after 6:00 pm.

"Mr. Wigand, you told me that your wife, that Wendy, didn't work. What did she do during the day?"

He slurps up the noodles and wipes his mouth on a paper napkin. "She had a couple miscarriages. She was supposed to just rest and conserve her strength. She watched TV, read, and pretty much stayed in the house. And she did crafts, you know, things that all you women like to do."

Not all women like to do crafts, Mr. Wigand, I think, but don't say. Personally, I'd rather get dropped in a volcano than do crafts. This guy is a throwback to the 1950's with his antiquated ideas of what 'all women' like to do.

"Anyway, we both were waiting for when my wife would be well enough to try to get pregnant again. I mean, that's what she wanted."

"I know you said that her doctor has retired. What about a dentist or a hairdresser? A nail salon, maybe?"

"Look, Ms. Harlow. My wife was a, a, you know, a very private person. She pretty much kept to herself. Basically it was just her and me. We both liked it that way. Or at least I thought we both did. But she didn't go to a hair or nail salon and she hated dentists. Bad experience as a kid, I think."

I write all this info down. "And you and she lived in Rural Valley, Armstrong County, prior to her disappearance, right? Had you lived there your entire marriage?"

"Yeah, we did."

"Near neighbors? Anyone she spoke to during the day?"

A strange look passes over his face when I ask that part about neighbors. I can't describe the look, but it almost seems as if he is angry at me for asking.

"My nearest neighbor in Rural Valley was a mile away. As I already said, my wife was a private person. She liked her privacy and she kept herself busy."

"Okay." I make note of the fact that he said 'my' nearest neighbor, instead of saying 'our' and continue asking questions. I use his wife's name to give her an identity. "You mentioned that Wendy did crafts, and the picture you gave me is one of the both of you at a Farmers' Market. Did she sell her crafts there or, were you there so she could get supplies for whatever she was crafting?"

"We just stopped there to get tomatoes. Like I told you, I like those big, juicy tomatoes they sell. She didn't need anything. My wife made things out of wood. Lot of old fallen trees and dead branches in Rural Valley near the house. She made do."

"Did Wendy interact with anyone, talk to someone? Look at any crafts?"

A flat "No," is the only answer I get.

"Okay, Mr. Wigand. There's not a lot to go on here, but I'll do my best. Oh, and do you have the missing person's report from the police?"

"Uh, yeah." He reaches in his jacket pocket again and hands me a folded manila envelope. "It's all I got."

It's a basic police report, nothing more. The report officer's name is J. O'Hanlon. Again, there's nothing much to go on. The police report ends with the statement, 'No evidence of foul play or intruders—summation is that one Wendy Wigand left of her own volition.'

I ask a few more questions, mainly to observe how Wigand reacts to them.

"Would you say that you and Wendy had a happy marriage?"

"Yeah." He answers quickly and doesn't seem fazed by the question.

"Any old boyfriends or the possibility of an affair?"

"No."

"*You* have an affair?"

My question produces a brief look of pure rage before he answers no.

"Did you have a major argument with Wendy just before she went missing?"

"I don't need to argue with anyone."

His answers wouldn't necessarily set off alarms. He answered my questions without pause. They're short and to the point. The way he answers questions reminds me of something Will once told me about the police academy training sessions. Cops are taught to answer questions in short, non-committal sentences.

As for Eric Wigand and his short answers, I have to think that he's a lonely guy who likes to keep to himself and has limited social skills. Maybe he married Wendy because he thought she was the same way.

And maybe she was okay with their marriage and social isolation at first. She was trying to get pregnant, after all. Some people do separate themselves from all social contact when they're going through intensely personal situations. But, maybe she got tired of the loneliness of her situation, tired of the marriage, the miscarriages. Eventually she became tired of Eric Wigand and left.

I tell Wigand I have no more questions.

CHAPTER 20

T RAFFIC IS LIGHT ON I-95 and, even with a heavy rain, vehicles move relatively easily. There are some idiots who race by at dangerous speeds even on this rain-slicked highway, and very few do the actual speed limit, but I've been surrounded by reckless drivers before. I drive defensively and figure I'll be back in New York City by eight o'clock. At least that's what my GPS indicates. I keep my wipers on high as I see the rain increase, and maintain a decent speed.

My client walked me back to within two blocks of where I had parked and then headed back to his apartment. Once again he asked me if I had a boyfriend.

"Mr. Wigand, I already told you this case is about Wendy and me finding her. I don't discuss my personal life, so don't ask me again."

"Yeah, sorry, I forgot." He stops and sizes me up. "It's just that I really need to find Wendy. I'm going crazy thinking about where she might be and what's going on in her life. I figured that maybe you had a boyfriend in the same business as you. You know another private investigator or maybe even a cop. Figured maybe they helped you with your cases or something."

"I don't need help, Mr. Wigand. I do very well by myself."

"Yeah, I can see that. Anyway, cops make lousy boyfriends—or so I've heard. A woman like you, you'd always be worrying about a boyfriend who was a cop. You know? The danger he'd face."

I say good-bye and make it safely the rest of the way to the parking lot, pay my ticket, and head toward the interstate and home.

As I drive I think about my interview with Eric Wigand. The info is pretty vague. The two things that stick out in my mind are, one—Wigand is anxious to know where his wife is, and two— he never once mentioned her by name. He always referred to her as 'my wife.' That way of speaking can show possession in the same way some people will say my dog, my house, my car. I remember one time when Will and I were out to dinner and he met a former college classmate. The classmate introduced the woman with him as 'my wife.' Will smiled and then said, "And does she have a name?" We all laughed, but it was very telling of how Will sees women as equals. This is one of the reasons we're good together. Each of us has an identity and aren't just an appendage of one another.

Getting back to Wigand, was he so possessive of Wendy that she left him for that reason alone? Maybe, but then again, the possessive way he talked may mean nothing at all. It is simply a way of speaking for some people. But, still, there's something very strange about this guy.

I turn the radio on to the news station and listen to various stories being broadcast about the government, city crime, a massive fire on the Jersey shore, and other unpleasant happenings. After ten minutes of this, I switch over to music, settling on a station that plays oldies as well as present day songs. Cyndi Lauper's "Girls Just Wanna Have Fun" comes on. I smile, it's one of my favorites, and I sing along loudly.

'I come home in the morning light, my mother says when you gonna live your live right,

Oh Mother Dear, we're not the fortunate ones, and girls they wanna have fun, oh girls just wanna have fun...

The phone rings in the middle of the night, my father yells what you gonna do with your life, Oh Daddy Dear, you know you're still number one and girls just wanna have...'

Bam! I feel the jolt from the impact of being rear-ended. My seatbelt tightens and my head rocks forward toward the steering wheel, then backward. My foot slams down hard on the brake and I fishtail toward the cement divider. Bam! Once again I'm hit and the force of this one sends my vehicle into the center lane. Cars swerve into opposite lanes cutting off other drivers and blaring their horns in anger and the fear of hitting my vehicle. No one wants to be part of an interstate pile-up.

In my left-view mirror I see a large dark vehicle, but the heavy rain makes it hard to tell the type and make, other than that it's not a sedan. It quickly pulls around me and shoots forward. That has to be the one that hit me. I sit frozen for a minute but then my instincts kick in. I need a plate number.

But as much as I strain to see it through the downpour, the dark vehicle is too far ahead for me to get the number. The license plate also seems to be covered with something dark. As shaken as I am from that slam into my Edge, I am so tempted to speed up and follow the bastard who hit me. This was no accident, this was deliberate. Some goddamn yahoo kids out for their version of 'fun?'

But whoever rammed me is far gone and, probably also far gone off one of the many exits on I-95. Shaken, I signal right and try to get over to the side of the interstate. After two speeders zip past me on the right, I floor the gas pedal and make it to the off lane by the guard rail. Once there I close my eyes and try to breathe slowly. Then I hit the call button on my dash and press the number 9 for 911.

"911. What's your emergency?"

"I was involved in a hit-and-run on I-95 going north towards New York City. A large dark vehicle rammed me and then sped off. I'm just outside Bristol."

"Are you in need of immediate medical assistance?"

"No, I don't think so." My neck feels ache-y and I think of the word whiplash. "I'm just shaken up."

"Your name? Spell it, please."

"Cate Harlow, C-a-t-e, H-a-r-l-o-w. I'm a private detective, licensed in New York State. My license number is 420731-6632. I believe my SUV may have been hit intentionally and I need the police to come here as soon as possible."

"Okay miss. A squad car with two officers has been dispatched to your area. They're close by that section of the interstate. Is there anything else I can do for you? Would you like me to stay on the line until the officers get there?"

I see flashing lights in the distance and hear the scream of the police car sirens. That was fast.

"No. Thank you, though. I can just see them coming down the interstate now."

I hang up and sit in my vehicle waiting for the police to arrive.

∽✕∾

The Pennsylvania State troopers are polite, and, once I hand them my PI license, professionally courteous. They take all my info, plus my sketchy description of the vehicle, and put it into the mobile computer in their car. They also verify my PI license and examine my SUV.

"And you say you didn't get a plate number?" asks one of the troopers, a tall woman.

"No, I didn't. The vehicle was speeding away, the rain was heavy, and the license plate looked as if it was covered in something dark."

"Mud, probably," says the second trooper, a man just slightly taller than his partner. "The roads get muddy around here due to lack of trees and vegetation. The wet dirt is splashed up onto vehicles." He points to my SUV whose side is heavily splattered with mud.

"Maybe it was mud, but I think the plate just might have been deliberately covered up."

The two troopers look at me and the woman asks, "Covered up? You mean the driver didn't want you to see it because you might be able to identify the person? You think you got someone trying to harm you, Harlow?"

"I don't think so. There's no one I can think of, anyway. But that plate was covered with more than mud."

"You're licensed in New York State. What were you doing in Pennsylvania? Business or pleasure."

"I met with a client who was unable to come to my New York City office. I will go to other states to meet someone whose case I'm handling. It isn't uncommon for private investigators to do that, you know."

I know that they're only doing their job and that I sound defensive, but I am the victim here. It was my SUV that was deliberately hit twice.

"Just asking questions, PI Harlow," the male trooper says, addressing me formally and courteously. "Free country. You got a right to meet clients anywhere. Anyway, we have your contact information and if we find the driver of the vehicle that hit you, we'll be in touch. Probably just some college kids, though. We get them speeding through here a lot. Damn idiots."

The female trooper walks around to the back of my SUV and inspects it again. "Get your bumper looked at, Harlow. It's pretty damaged and you don't want it falling off as you're driving. Also, have that left rear wheel checked. Looks wobbly. Get home safe. Good-night."

They wait for me to pull out onto I-95 before following me down the highway where they get off at the first exit.

Heading home. I can't wait to get back to the familiar sounds of the congested city streets. Streets in that overcrowded civilization called New York City that inexplicably make me feel safe.

CHAPTER 21

MY EDGE IS DAMAGED but not so badly that it can't be driven home—slowly, very slowly. I know because I drive in the slow lane the entire way on I-95 listening to the bumper rattle and feeling the lopsided shift of the left wheel. I keep expecting the wheel to come off.

I know I won't be driving any great distance in it, so, the morning after my trek to Philly, I take my car to a trusted mechanic that the cops use. He's reliable, honest, and gets the job done. The man has satisfied customers.

"I can have it back to you by Saturday," he says after having taken a long look at the damage. "The left rear axle has to be ordered. My supply guy's usually good about quick delivery, if he has the item. So, if he's got the one I need, I might be able to get it done by Friday afternoon, at the earliest. If he doesn't have what I need, then I won't get it done until next week."

Shit! I had planned to go down to Rural Valley tomorrow to check out the Farmers' Market.

"Got a loaner SUV?"

He shakes his head no. "I don't really have loaners. How about the Mini Cooper over there? It's from the police properties yard. Stolen vehicle, had a bullet hole in it, and the owner doesn't want it back. I picked it up for my daughter. She's into economy cars. It runs well and I repaired the bullet hole. Fresh paint too.

You can borrow it."

I look at the car. Seriously? No way am I getting on an interstate in a 'clown' car.

"No thanks. I have to go to a remote part of Pennsylvania and I feel safer in a SUV."

"Got a truck, a Dodge Ram. I'll loan you that."

He points to a truck parked along the side of his garage. It looks huge and safe.

"Stick-shift?" I have never driven one and don't want to learn.

"Nope, Dodge stopped making the shifts on this particular truck after 2008. This one's a 2010."

"Okay. Let me drive it a few blocks and back. I want to get the feel of it. I'll be on I-95 tomorrow then headed into a desolate part of Pennsylvania. It has to be reliable."

He laughs. "This is one helluva reliable truck. These types of trucks are more suited to cattle country than cities. The only people I know who drive these babies are construction workers and garage owners like me. We need them for hauling heavy items. Trust me, this is one safe, solid vehicle."

He walks me to the truck and says that the keys are on the driver's seat. It's a little strange getting used to being this high up from the road but I climb up, buckle up, ease into drive, and go for a twenty-minute drive-around. After my test drive I can understand why some people would buy this truck. The solid body surrounding me makes me feel safe and protected, like a tank.

I jump down from the truck and tell him I'll pick it up tomorrow around eight o'clock in the morning. I ask him if anyone can give me a lift to Lenox Hospital.

"Sure thing. My son will be here in a couple of minutes. He'll take you."

Eight hours since the doctor has begun to slowly decrease the barbiturates in Will's system and there is little change. I know Dr. Charles told me there wouldn't be, but I'm the type who expects almost immediate results. That expectation is not good in my line of work where results are sometimes painstakingly slow. It sure as hell is not helping me now as I wait impatiently to see even the slightest change in Will. If patience is a virtue, it's one thing this unvirtuous girl will never have.

Giles is at the hospital. Surprisingly, seeing him and talking to him wasn't uncomfortable at all. I was afraid it would somehow affect our friendship, that we would try to avoid each other, but we both seem okay with what happened at my brownstone yesterday. I know we won't let it happen again and I'm glad we can move past this.

He brings me a bottle of lemon-lime seltzer and stands next to me where I'm waiting outside Will's room. Dr. Charles and his physician assistant are doing a check on Will. I'm anxious to hear what the doctor has to say before I leave for what I call, 'God's Forsaken Land,' Rural Valley, Pennsylvania.

Dr. Charles finishes his exam and comes out into the hallway. He's smiling as he shakes hands with Giles. Good sign. People don't smile if the news isn't good.

"Well, Cate, all is going as I had hoped it would. Will is reacting well to the sedation decrease and his vitals are very good. So far, so good."

"I know you said that it varies from patient to patient, but how long do you think it will be before he regains consciousness."

"As I said, it's a slow process and really does vary with patients, but, with Will, well, considering his progress, I would think he might become conscious within the next thirty to forty hours. That's what I call a rational, calculated guess."

"I'll be going down to Pennsylvania today, but I'll be back by late tonight. You have my cell if you need to get in touch with me."

"Of course. I wouldn't worry overly much. As I've already said, so far, so good."

He and his assistant leave to go on rounds. Giles tells me that he has an autopsy that has to be done, as well as some lab tests to run. He leans in towards me and kisses me on the forehead. "Have a safe trip, Catherine. And don't worry about—anything. All right?"

The emphasis on the word 'anything' is meant to reiterate that all is right between us. I smile and push open the door to the ICU room.

Will is lying in his bed but his body seems more relaxed, not so out-of-it anymore. I lean over him and place my upper body lightly on his chest, my arms embracing his shoulders in a hug. Then I straighten up and grab both his hands in mine.

"Hey, Will. I love you, Will. You hear me? I love you. Everything is going to be okay. You're going to wake up soon and then, when you're able to leave the hospital, you're coming to stay with me. I'm going to take really good care of you." I feel his fingers move ever so slightly.

"The son-of-a-bitch who shot you had better be really scared. I swear, Jacoby and Javy are doing everything in their power to track him down, and bring that low-life bastard to justice. And, you know what, Will? *They* had better be the ones who find him because, if I find him first, if I know where he is, there will be nothing left of him for them to charge. I will rip him apart, slowly and methodically, piece by piece, all by myself. I will rip his lungs out through his nose. I swear it."

I lay my head on his shoulder, next to his neck, and listen to him breathing.

"I-shhh, kree-i-shh mmm."

I stand up and look at him. He's moving his head slightly.

"Will? Are you trying to say something to me? Will? I'm here, it's me, Cate, I'm here, Will. It's okay."

I stand very still, not daring to breathe, listening for Will to say something. But, minutes pass and he's silent. I think about what the nurse said when she was in here and I thought Will was trying to say something. She said it was just gas from his stomach escaping through his mouth. Just sounds, no words. But I don't think so.

These are not just sounds he's making. These are words.

CHAPTER 22

D ESPITE BOOKS AND POEMS that extol the joy of living in a country setting, away from the city or suburbia, the thrill escapes me. What some people will see as peaceful, I see as scary. Too quiet, too much aloneness. I would even welcome the metallic voice of my phone's GPS which has been silent for way too long a time now. I've only had one tractor-trailer and two beat-up looking cars pass me in the past two hours. It is silent and dead out here.

I called Rural Valley Police Department and asked to speak with Officer O'Hanlon, the cop who did the missing person's report on Wendy Wigand and was told he was out on extended medical leave. Seems he was viciously assaulted late one night outside his own home. No one knows what happened or who did it. He lay outside on the ground until the next morning when his girlfriend came home from her night job at a 7-11. I ask if anyone can help me with the info on Wendy Wigand but the desk sergeant doesn't seem too eager to oblige. Since Wendy Wigand went missing over a year ago, it's considered a cold case and not top priority. I ask him to just see what he can do and give him my cell number. He gives me a reluctant, "Sure, I'll see what I can find," and hangs up.

Usually I like driving alone, it helps me think about any case on which I am currently working. Sometimes I can see things more clearly, almost as if I have fresh eyes that will show me some crucial missed detail. But the desolateness of Rural Valley has an unsettling effect on my thoughts, especially my imagination, making it work overtime, and not in a good way.

As I drive down one lonely country road after another, I think of every horror movie I have ever seen. The houses, spread distances apart from each other, are old, run-down, and spooky-looking. At any moment, I expect to see a mad killer in farmer's overalls, wearing a ski mask and holding a power saw, coming out of one of those houses and running towards the truck I'm driving.

Or, maybe even worse, I will glimpse the mythical Mothman, a creature who portends horrible happenings in the near future. This creature will smash into my windshield, I'll crash the borrowed truck, and then I'll be left for dead until the man with the power saw comes to finish me off.

About two miles down the road I see a hand-written sign announcing a Farmers' Market. I check the digital map on the dash and, if that's correct, I only have a short distance to go to get to the place. I breathe deeply and hit the accelerator.

The GPS suddenly comes to life, scaring the hell out of me. "In one half mile, make a right turn, then, make a quick left turn onto Alben Road. Your destination is ahead on the left."

Obeying the robotic voice, I make the two turns and unexpectedly find myself in a huge clearing that isn't visible from the country road. It is set up with tents and farm stands. The air is filled with the smell of freshly baked fruit pies and tangy brined pickles. Women in Amish dress are bustling around their stands helping customers. A short distance away, I see horses and wagons. The horses, having been unharnessed from the wagons, are left to graze in a grassy area near a stream. The empty wagons are lined up neatly in a smooth line. Laughing children are running back and forth from wagons to stands, playing some type of game. The scene is bucolic and kind of beautiful. The best part of all this for me is there are people here! At least it's civilization.

I have found the Farmers' Market.

～∞～

The first thing I do after parking the truck near other cars not far from the road, is wander the clearing looking for food and something to drink. It's been a long drive. Roaming from stand to stand, I survey what's for sale food-wise. There's a large variety of fresh produce, meats, cheeses, baked goods & pastries, hand-rolled soft pretzels, and homemade fudge. There are even platters full of fried chicken. I settle on a tomato salad with cheese, two pieces of fried chicken, and a lemonade.

I scope out the area looking at the people milling around at the stands and walking the grounds, then take my food over to a small picnic area. As I'm walking, I pass by the parking area and make note of the license plates on the vehicles. New York, New Jersey, a lot of Pennsylvania plates naturally, and a few from Delaware and Ohio. Quite a good turnout for this market place.

Placing my food on a small picnic table, I take out the photo given to me by Wigand. It is out of focus. I study the woman, the way she is dressed in baggy clothes, the scarf around her head and neck, her posture. There's something vaguely familiar about her, something that reminds me of women who go 'on the run' after having committed a crime. God knows I've seen plenty of mug shots of those women. Maybe Wendy is one of them.

I sit, eat, and people watch.

After eating, I toss my trash and walk the grounds, stopping at the stands closest to the picnic area to show the photo Wigand gave me. No one seems to remember seeing either him or his wife.

Wigand said that he and his wife Wendy had stopped at a Farmers' Market in the area to buy tomatoes. Since the ad that mentioned the sweet-tasting tomatoes said they came from a family farm owned by people named Hochstetlers, I go in search of a stand with that name.

But none of the stands have the names of the farms on them. I go to the closest stand and ask where I can find the Hochstetler family's stand. The Amish woman I ask laughs heartily and says, "Many Hochstetlers here. Are you looking to find the family of Jacob or that of Abram? Maybe Samuel or Isaac?"

"I'm looking for the Hochstetlers who sell the sweet-tasting tomatoes I've read about."

"You will find sweet tomatoes at all the stands," she says turning away to cover a pie with a napkin. A customer comes by to look at the pies and the Amish woman walks over to her. Thinking she's ending the conversation, I say thank you and begin to walk away.

"The best ones are sold by the sisters Hannah and Martha Hochstetler. Very juicy, very good."

I stop and come back to the stand. "Where can I find Hannah and Martha?"

Turning from her customer, she points down the row of stands, back by a small copse of trees. "Over there they are. See the man sitting on the barrel? He is their father, Abram Hochstetler."

I remove the photo from my jacket and show it to the woman. She shakes her head no when I ask if she has ever seen Wendy or Eric Wigand.

"No, but I have not been here for two years." She smiles at me. "Babies. Mine seem to come this time of year. All six of them. This year no baby. Maybe next year a new one comes."

To thank her for help, I buy two small pies and head to the stand of Abram Hochstetler.

The two women at the Hochstetler stand look to be in their late teens, both of them very pretty. I wander around the stand looking at the produce. When I come to a wooden bushel overflowing with tomatoes, I stop, pick one up, and sniff it the way my Nonna Rita used to do with the ones from her garden. They smell delicious, warm from the vine.

"How much?" I ask one of the sisters.

"$1.50 a pound."

They smell heavenly and they feel plump and juicy. I ask her to give me three pounds.

"Anything else?" she asks weighing the tomatoes on an old-fashioned scale.

"Oh, um, sure."

I want to wait until her sister is finished helping a customer so that I can show both of them the picture together. I get a box of green beans, several heads of lettuce, and two cucumbers. Then I gather some fruit and other garden vegetables and bring them to the counter for weighing.

"Hannah, come here and help," says the girl weighing and adding up my things.

"Yes, now, Martha, I am coming."

When she comes over to help bag my purchases, I pull out the photo and my ID.

"Do either one of you recognize this woman? I'm an investigator trying to find her. She's missing and her husband, the man in the picture, has asked me to find her."

The two girls stare at the photo for a few minutes. One of them takes the photo from me.

"I think I have seen her. Yes, Hannah?"

Her sister nods her head. "Papa," she calls to the man I was told is Abram Hochstetler, "please to come."

Abram Hochstetler looks like a biblical patriarch with his long salt and pepper beard. He's a big, rugged-looking man, maybe six foot three. His whole body looks as if it is used to hard work. He comes to stand beside his daughters. I pull out my ID again.

"Mr. Hochstetler, I'm an investigator looking for the woman in that picture that your daughter is holding. She's missing, and her husband has hired me to find her. He's very worried, as you can imagine. The picture was taken here two years ago."

"Her family is worried, ya? That is sad."

I nod yes. Family is strong in the Amish culture, so I don't tell him that she has no family except her husband.

The one called Martha, hands him the picture. Abram Hochstetler looks at me sternly, then looks back at the picture. Shaking his head, he says that a lot of people come to his stand.

"For her family and husband, I feel sorrow, but I cannot say for sure I remember her." He turns to his daughters. "What do you say Hannah? Do you remember this woman?"

"I remember her, Papa, because she was so sad, and she looked afraid."

"Martha?"

"Yes, I remember too, Papa," says Martha, "so sad. Even when I gave her a sample of the peach cobbler our cousin brought to us, she looked sad eating it. I wanted to see her smile. It was a hot day and the peach slices in the cobbler tasted so fresh, so clean."

A hot day and she was wearing long sleeves and a scarf? Certainly that shows that she was trying to obscure her identity. She may have been ready to run from something or someone.

"You say she looked afraid?" I ask this question of Hannah who nods a strong yes. "Were you able to notice why she was afraid, Hannah? Did she say anything to you?"

"She never said anything but she walked a short distance away from here to stand in the shade. Over there by the trees." She points towards the copse of trees and vegetation nearby. "Like Martha said, it was a hot day. The man with her was paying for the tomatoes he bought. When he turned, and saw that she wasn't here at the stand, he looked upset. He went to her and said something."

"Could you hear what he said?"

Both women shake their heads no.

"Did he hurt her or grab her?"

"No," says the sister called Martha. "They just walked away and she held his hand. But, she was afraid of something and very sad."

"Thank you for this information. Really, it helps a lot. At least I know for sure she was here. She lived in Rural Valley."

"Rural Valley?" asks Abram Hochstetler. "Very few people like this woman live there. Mostly abandoned farms. She does not dress like a farm woman."

I try to gather my purchases but there are too many for me to carry. Abram Hochstetler grabs the heaviest parcels and we walk toward the borrowed truck. After he loads everything in the back seat, Abram Hochstetler looks at me.

"I was born here. My family has farmed our land for over a hundred years. But many of the English in that valley, they don't farm." I know that the Amish refer to all non-Amish as 'English' meaning outsiders.

"The English come here to hide. Whatever they hide from,

only God can know. I hope you find this woman. We will pray for her and her family."

Driving away, the words 'afraid' and 'English' stick in my mind. Wendy was afraid of something. She and Eric Wigand were both outsiders. What were they hiding from here? Is that the reason she left?

I still have one place to find while I'm here. Using the Google map on my phone I locate the small area where Wigand said he and Wendy lived. It's about an hour's drive from the Farmers' Market. I key in that destination to my GPS and follow the directions.

The road to the Farmers' Market, lonely as it may have been, doesn't even begin to compare to the total desolation of where the Wigands used to live. I am literally out in the middle of nowhere on a dirt road named County Road 7. If this is supposedly what naturalists call God's country, then God has taken a permanent vacation from it. All I see are abandoned shacks and farm buildings scattered vast distances from each other. No people around, not even an animal. I feel as if I'm on a distant planet where I am the only life force.

The house that Wendy Wigand shared with her husband isn't easy to find. For one thing, there are no numbers on properties. They don't seem to exist out here. I have to go by names on mailboxes that are sporadically lined up on the dirt road. When I finally find an old rusty metal one that has the name 'Wigand' on it, I still have to drive the truck about five-hundred feet to get to the front of their house.

The house itself is falling apart. Literally. I park the truck, get out, and walk around the building. It hits me how very alone I am. The quiet, the feeling of isolation would certainly drive me to leave here. I feel sorry for Wendy Wigand and I don't blame her for running away from this.

Despite the 'For Sale' sign on the place, it looks as if the house has been abandoned. That isn't surprising. Many of the houses I passed look abandoned. I wonder who pays the property taxes on these properties. Probably no one. I'm sure that the local tax offices have a hell of a time trying to find the owners and collect overdue taxes. However, if Eric is trying to sell the property, he must still be paying taxes.

I circle the house and walk the perimeter of the property. There's basically nothing but barren earth, some fallen trees, and dried shrubs. Then something catches my eye. An old garbage can, sitting on a patch of earth that looks as if it had been scorched. Walking over to it, I can still faintly smell smoke, and the unmistakable odor of lighter fluid. Inside the can there seems to be a lot of burned items. I tip the can over and gingerly poke through the remains. At first all I see is burned fabric, lots of it but as I continue to separate the mess I see something else. Pictures were burned here.

There's not much to go on, most of the pictures are charred beyond recognition. But there's one. Off to the side of the garbage can are the remains of a shirt and snagged into a pocket there is a picture. I lift it out and see that it is a picture of a woman and a man. Hard to make out with all the smoke damage, but it appears to be similar to the one Wigand gave me. Two pictures taken in the same place. One I have, and one that was almost burned. Who burned the clothes and pictures here? It couldn't have been Wendy. According to Wigand she left over a year ago. This fire was recent.

I take the picture and head back to my truck. Once there, I call the number of the real estate agent listed on the 'For Sale' sign. When the agent comes on, I ask about the Wigand house.

"Oh, that house has been already sold. Haven't gotten around to take down the sign yet," says a cheerful male voice. "Sorry. Actually sold for less than the property is worth— a lot less. It was a quick sale. Really kind of sad. Man's wife died and he wanted to leave the area. Said there were too many memories."

"You say his wife *died*? This is the Wigand property we're talking about, right?"

"County Road 7? Yes, you got it. That's the Wigand place. Sorry, but it is sold. However, if you're interested in buying a place out here I can show you—"

I cut him off. "No, thanks. Just curious. I knew the family."

We hang up. I drive fast down the road eager to get out of this God-forsaken area. A dead wife, huh? Either he didn't want anyone to know his wife left him, or Wigand is playing some type of weird game with me. And I don't like this game at all.

CHAPTER 23

WILL IS NOT IN his room at the hospital. The cops at his door don't know where he is.

"The nurses wheeled him out of here," says one of them, "but I didn't ask where they were taking him. I mean, that's not my business, right?" He's young and he looks scared.

The other cop doesn't know why Will was taken out of his room either. I turn to him.

"Was he conscious? Can you at least answer that?"

"I don't know. I mean, he was all covered up and—"

Covered up? I quickly check Will's room. His bed has been stripped and the poles that hold the tubes and bags of fluid are gone. Please don't let the words 'covered up' mean he's already gone and they've taken him to the— oh, God!

My mind goes over every detail I dismissed when I came in here. Why wasn't anyone in the waiting room? Usually either Myrtle or Harry are there. I didn't give it a second thought as I walked through. I just assumed that whoever had been in the waiting room was in the hospital cafeteria or taking a breather outside and that I'd find Melissa in Will's room waiting for me.

"What about the woman who was with him? Where did she go?"

"I don't know. One of the nurses spoke with her and then she left. That was before they wheeled Detective Benigni out of the room."

What's going on? My confusion turns to gut-wrenching fear when I hear someone over the hospital's communication system say, "Dr. Charles, please return to surgical suite B, stat. Dr. Charles, please return to Surgical Suite B, stat."

I race down to the nurses' station where the only person there is a young woman checking her cell phone. She's not a nurse I know.

"Will Benigni. Detective William Sutton Benigni, ICU room 12. He's not in his room. Did," I take a deep breath, "did something happen? Where is he?"

She doesn't look at me, just keeps checking her phone.

"I'm a temp. I just came on duty to cover for someone." She sounds annoyed. "What is your relationship to the patient? Your name?"

"Just tell me what happened, okay? I'm his, his—" What do I say? Ex-wife? Girlfriend? Friend-with-benefits or sex-buddy? I settle on the word that I think best describes our relationship, personally and kind of professionally. "I'm his partner. My name is Cate Harlow. Now, can tell me where he is?"

"Sure," she says moving in an annoyingly slow manner. Her cell phone rings and, turning away from me, she answers it.

"Miss? Listen I need help here. Please don't turn away from me."

I hear her exaggerated sigh and then hear her giggle into the phone.

"Hello! I need some information here. Get off the damn phone and find out where Will Benigni has been taken."

I hear her mutter something nasty into the phone about 'some crazy lady with no patience,' and that drives me over the top. She just tap-danced on my last nerve. I hoist myself over the counter between us and grab the phone out of her hand, smashing it on the floor. Then I grab her face and make her look at me.

"Listen to me. This is fucking important! I need to know what happened to Will Benigni who was in ICU room 12 and I need to know that right now. Do you understand? Tell me or I swear to God, *you're* going to end up in ICU."

"Oh, my God! You're crazy! I'm getting you thrown out of here." She reaches for the phone and I grab her wrist and slam it, and the phone, down hard.

"You can get me escorted out of here, that's fine, but you *will* first tell me why Detective Will Benigni is not in his room and where he might be. You got it? I am not messing around here. I *will* hurt you if you don't help me."

The utter look of horror on her face makes me stop. Even to myself I sound like a lunatic. But fear for what may have happened to Will is driving me to act this way. Oh God! I release the woman's wrist and apologize. "I'm sorry. I'm just really upset about my—partner, really upset. I wouldn't hurt you, seriously."

She looks at me fearfully as she rubs her wrist. "You hurt my *wrist*. You scared the hell out of me."

"I know, and I am so unbelievably sorry about the way I acted. I was scared too. The patient is more than just my partner, much more." I give her a sad, pitiful look. "Look can you please find out where Detective Benigni is and why he's not in his room?"

"Cate!" It's Melissa, walking quickly toward me followed by Myrtle. I'm sure they saw my meltdown but, except for Myrtle's glance at the woman who is angrily rubbing her wrist, neither of them says anything.

"Where's Will?" I ask without any other greeting. "The room is all made up like it's waiting for another patient. What's going on?"

Myrtle comes over to me and pulls me to the side. "Will's in surgery having a type of an echocardiogram. There was an indication of infection in his wound."

"Why is he in surgery if it's simply an echocardiogram? Couldn't they do that in his room?"

"Catherine, I spoke with both Giles and Dr. Charles. They explained that this happens sometimes. The doctor wanted to take a closer, more detailed look at his heart, so they needed to insert an ultrasound probe into the esophagus in order to do that. Let's go sit in the waiting room. Giles will be coming down soon, honey."

Reluctantly I follow Myrtle to the waiting area. Melissa stays behind, talking to the temp and, I guess, trying to smooth things over so I don't get thrown out of the hospital.

Less than twenty minutes go by before Giles arrives, but it feels like hours. He comes up to me and pulls me into a tight hug. When he lets me go, I see that he's unshaven and looks haggard. Without preamble Giles says that all is good, there doesn't seem to be any major infection and that Dr. Charles has ordered that Will be given antibiotics.

"He's okay, Cate. Will's okay. They're bringing him back to his room as soon as it has been thoroughly disinfected. That's why the room looked empty of all equipment and the bed was stripped. Dr. Charles doesn't want to risk any infection getting in. You'll have to wear a surgical mask for one or two days when you visit Will." He smiles wearily.

"How are *you* doing?" I ask concerned for him.

"I'm fine. Just working late at the morgue. No problem. I'm just trying to keep up with everything."

My heart swells with love for this man. He's been taking time off from the ME's office to check on Will and make sure I'm okay. He is an unbelievably compassionate man. But I've always known that Giles was a different kind of person. Loyal, fair, considerate, and understanding. He is and always will be someone on whom I can count, no matter what we had, and lost, in the past.

Melissa joins us and we sit, the four of us, while I try one more time to get in touch with Francesca Sutton Benigni without success. Then we sit in silence, all of us lost in our own thoughts, with nothing but the normal sounds of the hospital drifting to the waiting room.

Melissa says she's going to get coffee for us from Timothy's Emporium and after ascertaining that Giles will stay with me because, God forbid I should be alone, Myrtle decides to go with her.

To keep me occupied, Giles asks about the Wigand case and I give him the whole nine innings of what's going on.

"Something is so wrong with this case, Giles. This man, Eric

Wigand is outright lying to me and fudging the facts of the case so that I don't get the entire picture of what really happened. He told me that, when she left, his wife took all pictures of herself and all of her clothes, with her. Then, I find burnt pictures and clothing in a trash can in the backyard of their home in Rural Valley. The real estate agent said Wigand sold the house in a quick sale because his wife died, yet Wigand hired me to *find* her. There's something that I'm missing, something that gives me a bad feeling about this man and his marriage."

"The Harlow gut instinct?" smiles Giles.

"Yeah, that's working overtime. But even with that, I don't understand the reason he would lie to me. It's almost as if he doesn't really want me to find his wife or find out what happened to her. Something very unsavory about this man."

We talk for a while longer, with Giles filling me on the procedure Will's undergoing and why it was necessary. Hospitals, says Giles, are filled with bacteria and even with the utmost care and cleanliness rules, infections can occur. Giles laughs tiredly and says, "It's, as Will himself will say, a crap-shoot. You never know."

We're too tired to keep talking and so Giles and I sit, holding hands and wait for Will to be brought out of surgery. After a few minutes, he leans his head on my shoulder and closes his eyes. Cradled there, between my shoulder and neck, he falls asleep. His arm falls across me and I snuggle into his warmth, closing my own eyes.

∽∝

"Catherine! Catherine, wait up, honey!"

Someone is gently shaking me awake and my eyes open slowly. I see Myrtle standing next to Dr. Charles. He coughs discreetly and I quickly untangle myself from Giles's arms. I must have dozed off myself. Giles and I both look up little unsteadily.

"Well, Cate," says Dr. Charles, "I came to tell you that Will is going back to his room in about an hour. The probe showed nothing major. There *is* a slight infection and I've ordered antibiotics. The wound has been thoroughly cleaned and he's doing very well. He's tough. You can see him after we've done a few tests. I suggest you go get something to eat and come back later. You will have to wear a surgical mask, but I'm sure Giles has made all that clear. I'll check on Will in another half hour." And with that he walks off, briskly, down the hall.

Giles stretches his arms over his head and yawns. I sit and stretch forward, popping the tight, aching discs in my spine as I do so. Containers of undrunk coffee are on a table near us.

"How long have we been sleeping?" I ask Myrtle.

"About two hours. Melissa went home for a little bit. She's coming back with Harry later."

She looks at me and pats my shoulder. "It's okay, honey. Everything is fine. Go get a sandwich at the Panera across the street. You'll feel better. Go ahead, now, both of you. You need a break. I'll be here. Later we'll have Harry's pastries. Now go!"

Myrtle's blessing seems to be the push Giles and I need to get up and moving. I am absolutely starving.

CHAPTER 24

I T'S PAST ELEVEN O'CLOCK at night by the time I make it back to *Catherine Harlow Private Investigations*. After picking up my completely repaired SUV, I spent most of the day with Will. I try to stay with him as much as I can, especially after that scare I had when I came to the hospital and he wasn't in his room.

I make a habit of making sure he's still in his room. Every time I call Melissa, Myrtle, or Harry, I ask, *"Will's still in ICU, room 12, right? Okay, thanks."* I know I drive them crazy, but they've been nothing but kind about my fear-phobia of not finding Will.

The barbiturates that have kept him in a drug-induced coma have been completely decreased, but Will's still not fully conscious. He drifts in and out of sleep. Until tonight I'd been sleeping on a couch in his room. His condition is still being monitored carefully, but wearing a surgical mask when I enter his room is no longer required. I feel confident enough about his improvement to go home and sleep in my own bed. I am on the verge of total exhaustion.

But before I can allow myself to sleep, I want to check a file on my computer concerning the Wigand case. There are a few disturbing observations I need to add to the file. Since our meeting in Philly, he's not returning my calls. Though he answered all my questions during our face-to-face meeting, there's still something about Eric Wigand that I don't trust. Nothing overt, but still something not quite kosher, as Myrtle would say.

After I update it, I want to grab something to eat, and go home to collapse on my bed. I am more than thankful that Myrtle and Harry have volunteered to take care of Little Guy and Mouse all these nights. My cats love them.

Running up the stairs two at a time, I stop dead halfway up, my hand on my gun. There's someone waiting outside my door, hiding in the corner. I can't tell if it's a man or a woman. Shit! I curse my own carelessness—I must have left the outer door unlocked earlier when I left to get to the hospital. Stupid of me, I know, and now there's a stranger in the building.

At first glance the person appears to be one of the homeless in this area. There's the wary and huddled stance that people on the street affect in order to survive. Maybe it's a friend of Bo, the homeless man Myrtle and I have kind of adopted. Even though we've asked him not to do it, Bo tells everyone he knows how Myrtle always has doughnuts, bagels, and water for him. Maybe this person is hungry. I feel sorry that anyone should be without food and my momentary impulse is to get him or her something to eat.

But then again, caution takes over; it could be a mugger or a murderer waiting at the top of the stairs. I slowly pull my gun from the back of my jeans.

"Who are you and what are you doing here? This is a private building."

There's no answer so I speak louder and with more authority. "I'm a private investigator licensed to carry a gun which, right now, I have pointed at you. You're trespassing. Who are you and what do you want? Step into the stairwell so I can see you."

The person doesn't move, but a voice that speaks out of the darkness makes me start in surprise. "Hi, Ice Cream."

I don't recognize the lisping, whispered female voice and I don't recognize the person standing next to my door. What I do recognize is the nickname I haven't heard in over eight years. Only one person ever called me that.

Marley Weiner.

My best friend from the Office of the Public Defender.

Marley Weiner who had abruptly destroyed our friendship over nothing but jealousy.

I go slowly up the last few steps taking my penlight out of my pocket. This woman can't possibly be Marley. Who is she and how does she know that old pet name Marley called me?

"Who the hell are you?" I stand up straight with my legs apart. Shining the light on her face, I gasp. At first glance, I think it is someone wearing a crude mask. But a closer look tells me that, standing before me is a woman, and what I thought was a horror mask is her real face.

My trained eyes document the damage. She has the face of a losing boxer who has gone one too many rounds. Her nose is a mass of flesh that appears to have been broken numerous times, the bone under her left eye has been so viciously damaged that the socket droops downward onto the cheek. Cheekbones, that were obviously smashed into permanent damage, leave the face looking lumpy and scarred. Her brown hair is short and sparse, showing a long scar in her scalp. I see missing teeth when she opens her misshapen mouth. Around one wrist and forearm is a dirty ace bandage.

"It's bad, right? I'm sorry," whispers the woman, lisping badly because of the missing teeth. "It's been a while since I actually looked in the mirror, but I know how I must look. I don't see too well out of my left eye. Maybe that's a blessing. But, it's me Ice Cream, it's me, Marley."

I am unconvinced. As sorry as I feel for this woman who has been so battered, I still need to know who she really is.

"Who the hell are you and how do you know that nickname? What's going on here?"

A car door slams loudly and the car alarm goes off. The noise makes the woman in front of me jump. I see her begin to shake almost uncontrollably. Her eyes go wild.

"Take it easy. It's just a car alarm. The slam of the door

probably triggered the alarm."

"No! No!"

"Listen, it's okay. Just an alarm."

"No, no! You don't understand! It's him! Oh, my God, oh my God! He's found me again. Please Cate, help me!" She looks towards the door in absolute animal fear. "He's outside, he's there, I know it! He has already killed and now he's come to get me!"

Her panic is real. Is someone after her? Did this battered woman leave her home and come here to my office looking for my help? My PI ad, listing all the services of *Catherine Harlow Private Investigations* including help for abuse victims, is online. She may have seen it. The terror in her voice makes me believe that maybe someone *is* after her.

"Stay here," I order. "I'll check downstairs."

I hold my gun with two hands and run quietly down the stairs. Listening at the door, I hear nothing but the normal city sounds. Cautiously I open the door, then fling it wide, stepping forward with my gun pointed. There's no one there, and a look outside confirms that no one is around.

The car alarm is still sounding in that annoying series of beeps, honks, and sirens as I click the double-lock dead-bolt on the outside door and go back upstairs. The woman is huddled in a heap in the corner of the hallway. I make the decision that she's not a threat.

"C'mon. Let's go into my office."

Putting my gun away, I take out my keys and open the door to *Catherine Harlow Private Investigations*. I literally have to half-lift the woman from the floor to help her inside. Once we're inside, I do the double-lock bit again, then go settle her on the small couch. But when I go to turn on the lights, I hear, "Oh, please, don't. He'll see me. Please!"

I feel my way over to the windows behind my desk. Pulling the curtains back slightly, I keep out of sight as I look out at the streets. The streetlights show nothing. The woman sitting on my couch is making whimpering noises. She's terrified. I open a drawer in my desk and take out a pair of night-vision binoculars. Looking out the window, I slowly scan the area. Nothing. Even the street people seem to have gone to where they sleep at night. I look back at the woman.

"I don't see anyone." I gesture to the pretty flameless candles in a decorative box on Myrtle's desk. "How about just a small light, then."

She reluctantly nods yes and I turn one on. A soft glow makes it possible to see each other in the dark office.

"Now," I say standing in front this woman, "who are you, really, and what's with you calling me Ice Cream?"

The woman stares down at her hands. "I can prove I'm Marley Weiner."

"Really? How?"

She looks up at me and I find that I have a hard time looking at her damaged face. Someone did a really thorough job of beating the hell out of this woman. Not just once, but over and over again.

"Cate, I can tell you so many things about yourself. We were friends, we were—best friends."

"Look, I doubt that I know you, so anything you tell me about myself doesn't mean a hell of a lot. I'm not a hermit, my life's pretty much an open book. You could've found out facts about me very easily, either online or in print ads that detail my business. Even the fact that I like pistachio ice cream and that's the reason Marley called me Ice Cream. That's not exactly a secret. She was the *only* one who *called* me that but a lot of people would know about that nickname. The question is why did *you* call me that? Anyway, any info you have won't prove you're Marley."

"Yes, but there is one thing, one secret in my life that no one knows, but you. One thing that to which I swore you to complete secrecy. You vowed never to tell that horrible secret."

The muscles in my stomach clench hard. If this really is Marley, I know what she is going to say. Because only Marley and I know the truth about what had happened in her life and I promised to never tell anyone her secret. I never have. Not even to Will.

But I had to pretend that I didn't know what she meant.

"What secret?" My voice came out stronger than I thought was possible at the moment.

"You know what I'm talking about Ice Cream, I know you do. My mother."

I look hard at this woman sitting before me and try to see even the slightest vestige of the Marley Weiner I met over ten years ago. There is nothing of the pretty, vibrant, red-haired woman I knew back then.

"What about your mother?"

"How she died. How I didn't tell anyone, but you, about what had really happened."

"Go on." I sit rigid. "Tell me."

"You remember I took a few vacation days and went to visit my mom in Connecticut eight years ago? She didn't know that I was coming. I wanted to surprise her. It was her birthday weekend and I planned to take her out for dinner. She was so down all the time since my father, that cheating bastard, finally left her, and I thought a night out would make her smile again even if just for a short time.

"When I let myself in through the kitchen door, I saw water dripping from the ceiling. It came from the upstairs bathroom. I figured that one of the old pipes up there had finally broken. She was supposed to call a plumber like I had told her to do, but she didn't.

"I was so angry at her. My mother was letting the house go to shit after my father left. She wasn't doing anything to help herself. She was so damned weak! I went upstairs, calling for her but there was no answer. Then I went into the bathroom." She pauses and takes a ragged breath.

"My mother," she whispered, staring at me with a sadness that cut my heart, "was lying in the bathtub with the water covering her face. Floating in the water was an empty bottle of tranquilizers. She had taken the entire bottle, gotten in the tub, and drowned.

"I didn't let anyone at work know, even you. I took two additional days off. When I returned, I said my mother had had a sudden stroke and passed away in her sleep. I told you the funeral was only for one day and it wasn't worth it for you to come." She laughs bitterly.

"I never told anyone the truth about how she died, except you.

Even then I waited three months to talk to you about what really happened." She looks at me pleadingly. "You remember the night I told you?"

I nod slowly as I remembered that horrible night Marley told me the truth about her mother's suicide. Three months after her mother died, Marley had come over to my brownstone to help me paint. Later, over a lot of wine, she had told me how she had found her mother dead in the bath tub. The horror of finding her, the anger that her mother took her own life, the lies she told to cover it up.

How, with a strength born of desperation, she pulled her mother out of the tub, dried her body, dragged her into the bedroom, then dressed her in a robe to preserve some sort of dignity. She emptied the overflowing tub, cleaned up the water, and called the funeral director.

How she lied and said she found her mother dead on the bedroom floor. The one truth she told was that her mother had severe heart problems and was always forgetting to take her medicine. The man who arrived to transport the body assume it was a death from natural causes. Marley showed him her mother's full bottle of heart medication. A woman with a bad heart who forgets to take life-saving medicine—the death wasn't suspicious, so no need for an autopsy. Marley hid the empty bottle of tranquilizers and what she considered her shame.

"That little town where we lived had already gossiped over my father's affairs and the fact that he left my mother. I refused to give them more gossip about my family," she'd said.

She cried hard and long the night she told me and I cried with her. In one way, our friendship had gotten stronger that night; she trusted me enough to tell me what she considered a shameful, horrible secret. But, in another way, some strange bizarre way, that night was the beginning of its end. Marley became more and more distant from me, as if, now that I knew about her mother, I might see her in a different light, might judge her family. That wasn't the case at all. She was my friend. My heart broke for her.

The memories end abruptly as I hear the woman say, "See? It's really me, Ice Cream. It's me."

"Marley." I say it softly. It really is Marley.

The last time I saw her was right after Will and I got engaged. That was seven years ago.

∝

I had been dating the charming, handsome Detective William Sutton Benigni for eighteen months and I was floating on air back then. Life was good. I was so crazy in love and lust that I didn't notice the subtle changes in Marley.

When I thought about it at all, I probably knew something was not quite right between us ever since the night she told me the truth about how her mother died. If I did notice the changes, I more than likely thought her irritated and snappy treatment of me was because she was dealing with some serious troubles. Even though her mother's suicide was over a year ago, I knew she wasn't over it. Her mother had left an enormous amount of debt and I knew that she was dealing with that, too.

Plus, recently, she had broken off a short-lived relationship with a quiet, work-oriented lawyer in our office. Her reason was that he wasn't "exciting enough, too polite and nice, like Will, you know? I want a little danger in my life."

She may have said that Will was basically too nice and polite for her, but I know she still kind of envied my relationship with him. There was a bit of jealousy there, but I let it go.

Her relationships were always short-lived, usually with men who were risky bets to say the least. She liked rough guys, men who were dangerous. I never liked her choices. But once the relationships were over, she never spoke the guy's name again. It was as if he had never existed. Marley didn't believe in looking back. I don't know what she was looking for in a man but in the time I had known her, she hadn't found whatever it was.

I was in my own little selfish bubble; I know that now. I was happy and Will made me feel special and loved. My focus was all on him and us being together. He made me laugh and the sex was incredible. His hands, his mouth, his tongue—there were times when I wanted to crawl inside his skin, I wanted him so much.

The saying ascribed to female friendships, 'BFF, best friends forever,' implies an intrinsic endlessness, a bond that knows no boundaries and has no time limit, but that's not always the case. Friendships end. My friendship with Marley ended the night I called her to tell her that I was engaged.

We hadn't gone out together or really spoken for a while. My calls and texts were usually not answered for days or went completely unanswered. Whenever I did manage to get in touch with her, she always had an excuse that she was busy or tired and, I was so involved with Will, that I accepted her excuses without question. But that night, I just *had* to call her. She was my best friend and who do you call when you've just gotten engaged?

Will had just left my brownstone after bringing me home from an upscale restaurant called Regina Margherita where he had presented me with a gorgeous three-carat blue diamond. Giddy with wine, and a hot and heavy sexual encounter in his detective's SUV, I called Marley the second I heard him drive away.

"Hey, Marley, guess what? Guess *what*?! I'm *engaged*! Will asked me to marry him and, oh my God, you should see the ring! Whew! I can't wait to show it to you."

There was a long silence on the other end, then, "Cate?" She sounded surprised. "Engaged? Oh. Great, good, I'm happy for you. Congratulations."

Her tone of voice and lack of enthusiasm were sobering. I put my own bubbly enthusiasm and excitement aside.

"Marley? Are you okay?"

"I'm good." She didn't sound right. I couldn't put my finger on what was wrong.

"Look, Marley, seriously, if you're not okay, well, I mean I can come over there if you want. It'll take me all of fifteen minutes, so if—"

"No, no. Don't come over. I'm fine, just tired and, you know how it is with our workload. I brought work stuff home with me. I was just putting some info into my laptop when you called. I didn't check the caller ID and—" There's an awkward pause. "But listen, I'm happy for you Ice Cream, really. Will's special, you know he's— special."

"He *is* special, isn't he? Thanks Marley," I manage to say, knowing in my heart something is not quite right with her and me. That comment about not checking the caller ID for one thing. Did that mean that if she saw it was me, she wouldn't have answered?

"I guess I'll see you tomorrow at the office, Marley. Maybe we can do lunch or something, okay? Or go to that new wine bar."

"Ummm, yeah, sure, lunch, wine bar."

"Okay. So—lunch tomorrow then?"

"Lunch, right. I gotta go, Cate. I'm really tired. Good night."

"Oh, sure. Good..." She hung up before I could get the second word out.

When I came in to the Office of the Public Defender the next day, there was a note on my desk from Marley, canceling lunch. She wasn't at her desk. On my morning break, I went in search of her, but she was nowhere to be found. When I asked the lawyer, with whom she had been working, where she was, I was told that she'd volunteered to take some documents to some judge in upstate New York and would be gone all day.

When she didn't show up at her usual spot near me the next day, I found out that, three weeks ago, she had requested an assignment in the new wing of our office building and had moved her things there before I came to work.

She made herself unavailable whenever I walked over to the new wing where she now worked and asked her to go to lunch, go get coffee, or get a drink after work. After a while, I stopped trying to see her. But the seed of hurt she sowed deep inside me took root.

Finally, one night when I'd had it with all the mystery and avoidance crap, and after consuming a half bottle of wine that fueled my hurt feelings, I went to her apartment and knocked on her door until she reluctantly opened it.

Standing in her doorway, I was a seething mixture of being annoyed as hell *at her* mixed with a serious concern *for her*. Something was so not right.

"Okay Marley," I began a little too loudly as soon as I saw her, "Tell me what's going on here. Why are you avoiding me at work, not answering your phone when I call or text, and too busy to go get a damned, lousy cup of coffee?"

Marley Weiner, my best friend, checked the hall to see if any nosey neighbors were around, shushed me, then motioned me inside. She didn't ask me to sit down, just faced me squarely.

"Listen Ice Cream, let me speak first before you say anything."

"Okay," I said slowly. She looked deadly serious, the kind of serious that comes right before bad news.

"I've made a decision. I mean, I had to make this decision, I really had to make it." She took a deep breath. "I'm not giving our friendship any more energy. I just can't. You make me feel depressed. We're done. I need to move on with my life."

If she didn't sound so serious, I would've thought I was listening to her quote lines from a comedy starring Jennifer Aniston. But this wasn't a comedy and she wasn't trying to be funny. Very bluntly she was telling me that she was ending our friendship.

"What do you mean, I make you feel depressed? What are you talking about? I thought we were good friends, best friends. We shared so much over the last few years. I don't understand. What did I do? Please tell me, because truthfully, I have no clue here. Marley, talk to me."

I was completely bewildered. I wanted to go and hug Marley, telling her that I could help her through anything if she'd only let me. We were best friends. How could she throw that away?

As I stepped toward her, my shin bumped against a table next to her couch making the small, old-fashioned ceramic house on it slide perilously close to the edge. I remember Marley telling me that her mom had made that house years ago when she was a little girl. It was very precious to Marley. I quickly grabbed it before it hit the floor and carefully placed it in the center of the table.

Marley turned away from me and walked to the two small windows that looked out on an alley. "Great view, huh?" She smirked. "Certainly not as nice as the view from your goddamn brownstone, right?"

"You're not going to be here long, Marley. Remember? You said you'd be looking for a new place once you got that raise. I'll help you find a new place. Is this the reason you're upset? Because of this apartment? This is only temporary."

When she didn't answer I babbled on, relieved that maybe she was just going through a period of feeling trapped. Her apartment *was* cramped and shabby. She had always wanted a brownstone, but couldn't afford one.

"I know what you can do! You can stay at my place. Will and I aren't getting married until—"

Marley turned in a flash of unexpected anger towards me. "Do you even know how fucking *lucky* you are? Do you?! You've always had *everything,* everything! Jesus Christ, Cate! You had parents who loved you, a private school education, you won awards for tennis without even trying. That fucking beautiful brownstone you have, the one all you ever do is complain about because it needs some work done? You were able to put a hefty down payment on it from money your parents left you. You have a *fucking* brownstone and you still don't see how lucky you are!

"And me? What've I got? Let's see. Parents who never gave a shit. My mother not only kills herself, she leaves me to pay off her debts; loans that I stupidly co-signed! My deadbeat father has no interest in seeing me, let alone helping me with her debts. But, God, Cate. You? You're one lucky little bitch! You know that?

"And now you've got Detective Will Benigni, the hottest guy around. Good-looking as hell, smart, sexy, charming, comes from a wealthy family, and he *chooses* you! He dated a lot of women but he asked *you* to marry him. The hot bastard chose *you*, the woman who's *already* got so much."

Seeing the stricken look on my face she sighs. "Oh, Christ, it's not that I want *him*. God, no, not really. It's just that you seem to have everything and I have shit. All I ever got was shit in life. Shit family, shit men, and a shitty place to live.

"I *can't* be friends with you, I just can't anymore. Don't you get it, Ice Cream? I can't take your lucky, lucky life staring me in the face reminding me what a miserable one I have."

"Marley...," I step toward her but she puts her hand up to stop me.

"I made this decision to walk away from our friendship and, once I make up my mind about ending friendships, relationships, anything, I leave and I don't look back. You know that about me, Cate. I don't look back."

She walked to the door and flung it so wide it slammed into her wall. A neighbor across the hall opened her own door a crack to see what was going on.

"Just go, okay? Go now and don't call me or come here again. I don't want to see you."

"But..."

"Get the hell out!"

The neighbor across the hall stared at me and demanded to know who I was and why was I making so much noise. Not wanting to cause a scene, or have the police get involved, I left, confused, angry, and hurt.

Ten days later Marley transferred to another section of the Public Defender's office uptown and a few months after that, I heard she had left her job. I had no idea where she went.

Even though I was hurt and angry, I soon found myself caught up in the joy of being engaged and the euphoria of planning my wedding with Will. My happiness with him was so all-consuming, I never even looked for Marley.

She walked out of my life.

And very simply, vanished.

CHAPTER 25

NOW MARLEY WEINER IS sitting on a couch in my office. A Marley Weiner who is so completely unlike my old friend as anyone could be. A stranger, and, except for that shared memory, a person I no longer know.

Suddenly this shattered-looking person reaches out her hands to me and says pleadingly, "Listen to me, Ice Cream, I don't have too much time. He'll find me, I know he will. He's coming for me now. It's just a matter of *when* he finds me. I'm so afraid, so afraid of what he'll do to me this time, but I had to come here, I had to! Especially now. You have to know who killed him."

"Killed? Who's been killed?"

"Will. He killed Will! I'm so sorry!"

"What are you talking about?" I stand up, my heart racing. "Will's alive. I was just with him at the—." I stop before saying the word hospital. "Why did you say Will's been killed?"

"He's alive?!" She sounds shocked. "But he, I thought—no wait, he *did* say it, he said he'd killed Will. He *did* tell me that he— oh my God, oh my God! If Will's alive—if he's alive, then he's still in danger! He won't stop until he kills him."

"What are you saying? Who is going to kill him?" I shout in

anger and fear. I grab my phone and call Melissa who is at the hospital. She answers on the first ring and I take a deep, thankful breath.

"Hi Cate. Everything's good. Will's sleeping. I've got the latest copy of Vogue and I'm catching up on my reading. You have to see some of the new styles that are coming out for Fall. I'll show you when you come back." Melissa's voice is calm and sweet.

"Melissa, listen to me carefully. Are there two cops at the door to Will's room? Can you see them from where you are?"

"Yes, I can see them, why? Of course they're here. Why wouldn't they be here? Is everything all right, Cate?"

She has picked up on something in my voice and she is immediately alert to any danger. Underneath her delicate, sophisticated appearance, Melissa is a strong, incredibly brave, and practical woman. She will trust what I'm telling her without question and completely understand the imminent danger.

"Melissa, Will's in danger. There's a strong possibility that the man who tried to kill him may be coming to the hospital to finish the job. Alert those two officers now. And call Jacoby. Key in this number. 212-555-0320. Got it? Tell Jacoby we need extra security around Will."

"I'm going to the officers standing outside the door and I'm calling the captain now. Don't worry, Cate, I'll stay here."

"Thanks, Melissa. I'll be over as soon as I can."

"Be careful, Cate."

Telling her that I will, I end the call. Then I walk over to Marley, with my hands curled into tight fists of fear.

"Tell me what you mean when you said he killed Will! Tell me!"

At my approach, she ducks her head, covering her face with her arms, and drawing her knees up to her chest. Startled at her reaction I step back. This is the posture of someone who has been beaten over and over again. She's terrified!

If she's afraid of me, she'll tell me nothing. I take another step back and quietly ask, "Who said he killed Will? Who is he and where is he? Can you tell me that—Marley?"

The sound of her name seems to have a strange effect on the

woman. My saying her name makes it personal and lets her know I believe she really is who she says she is.

She mumbles something that I can't quite hear.

"I can't hear you, Marley. *Who* said he killed Will? Do you have a name? Where is this person now? Please look at me. I won't hurt you and I won't let anyone else hurt you. I have a gun and, believe me, I know how to use it. No one is going to come in here and hurt you. I promise you that and, if you truly know me, you will remember that I never break a promise. Now please, look at me and tell me who said that he had killed Will."

Slowly she lifts her head and looks at me, tears streaming down her battered face. "My husband. My husband killed Will. He told me, he said he did it because of me. I'm sorry, Ice Cream, I'm so sorry! Oh God, oh God! Please forgive me. It's all my fault. Will was only trying to help me. He was only trying to help me! Oh, God! I'm so sorry!"

"Okay, okay, Marley you're not going to be able to help me if you don't calm down. I need you to give me some information. What's your husband's name?"

"I can't!"

"A name, Marley, give me his *name*."

She seems to shrink even more, curling herself into a tight ball. I hear her murmur, "He'll kill Will and then he'll kill me for telling you."

I bend down by her and talk as calmly as I can. "Marley, please help me, please help Will. Give me a name and I promise I'll keep you safe. Who shot Will?"

"Will *knows* him!"

"Who does Will know?"

"My husband, Eric Wigand."

CHAPTER 26

I CALL JACOBY AND tell him exactly what Marley Weiner, aka Wendy Wigand, has told me. I'm reeling from the fact that the client who hired me to find his missing wife is not only her abuser, but the man who shot Will.

Having arrived at the hospital within ten minutes of Melissa's call, he's already got the entrances and exits policed and secured. Ten officers are stationed in the ICU alone.

"*Wigand*? Eric Wigand?" says Jacoby repeating the name I have given him. "You sure she said Wigand, Cate?"

"That's the name she gave me, the guy she said shot Will. Why? You know him?"

"Yeah, I do, but Christ, I haven't heard about him in years. Eric Wigand was a dirty cop. Rumor was that he shook down immigrant shop owners, a lot of them terrified illegals, in his own neighborhood. Took bribes from pimps and gang leaders; nothing we could prove, though. Supposedly, he had a stash of serious cash hidden in his apartment. Got it from a drug dealer he was protecting.

"He was a beat cop who took the word 'beat' a little too seriously. One too many complaints about physical abuse, police brutality. He gave the department a black eye, no pun intended, as far as public relations are concerned. What finally got him tossed was that he beat the holy shit out of a teenage boy whose only crime was hanging out in a local park with his girlfriend after it closed at sundown. Made the girlfriend watch while he kicked and pounded the kid. The girlfriend's father was a councilman. Wigand was kicked off the force after that. He skipped town before the department could bring full charges."

"She says Will knows him. I don't remember him ever mentioning an Eric Wigand."

"He ever mention someone named Bluto?"

"Bluto? Like the character in the old Popeye cartoons?"

"Yeah, big, burly, and mean. That's the nickname we gave that bastard."

"I do remember Will mentioning the name Bluto a couple of times. But that was quite a few years ago."

"Exactly. He was officially dismissed ten years ago. I didn't know where he went and I didn't give a fuck. He was a disgrace to the uniform."

"So Will knows him?"

"Yeah." Pause. "You know something, Cate? Now that I think of it? Wigand was the only cop who didn't like Will. Will's a stand-up guy, always has his partner's back. Other cops like him and look up to him, but not Wigand. Hated the fact that Will got to be a detective so young, hated that he went by the book. Called him Detective Preppie. And now you're telling me he's the prick who shot Benigni?"

"Yes, but I don't know why. I can only guess it has something to do with this woman who says she's his wife. I don't want to explain over the phone, Joe. Right now it's kind of complicated. I want to talk to her some more and then I'm taking her with me to the hospital so you can talk to her but, um, you might want to call Dr. Lara Evers to meet us there." I lower my voice. "This woman is in really bad emotional and psychological shape."

"Got it. Come here as soon as you can. I'm putting a BOLO out on Wigand but I don't like you being out there. Want me to send a squad car?"

"Not now, I'm good. Give me a couple of hours, I'll call you if I need you. Doors are double-bolted so no one can get in. Besides, you of all people know I'm not alone," I say subtly letting him know that I'm fully aware he's having me followed by a plainclothes detective. Knowing Jacoby, he probably has a detective named Vic Rollins keeping an eye on me. Will once told me that Vic was the best at tailing someone. He was so good at it that he was never made by any of the people he was following, including other cops. And he was tough. Only a fool would mess with Vic.

"What are—? Hold on." He puts me on hold, then, "Cate, Javy just called me. We might have a lead on something here. Gotta go. Call me in two hours, got it?"

We hang up and I go to sit by Marley. I have a lot to process. Wigand hiring me to find a woman named Wendy Wigand who is in reality, my old friend Marley Weiner. The knowledge that I was hired because of my connection to Will, who is somehow involved in all this. I need to work through all this and put everything together to solve my case.

But before I can make sense of that, I need to know how, and why, Marley Weiner became Wendy Wigand, how she ended up marrying a man who would do these horrible things to her, and how Will is involved in all this.

I take Marley's hand and talk softly, telling her that there's a detail guarding Will. Then I look out the window and see a dark van parked discreetly up the block. That must be Vic. Good.

"And, listen Marley, Captain Jacoby has a plainclothes detective assigned to me, sitting in a car outside right this minute. No one is getting in here, believe me. So we're safe here."

Then I sit next to her and urge her to tell me everything about what happened to her.

"Things never seemed to go the way that I wanted."

Listening to Marley, who once had a strong positive sounding voice, lisp painfully through her narrative, is hard for me.

"I met Eric not long after I broke up with that lawyer in our department. Remember him? I said he wasn't dangerous enough for me, too bland."

I nod my head. I remember it all.

"Guess I should have stayed with bland, huh?" A glimmer of the old Marley struggles through with that comment.

"Where did you meet him, Marley?"

"A bar. I was at a bar in the West Village. I went there a lot to drink. Better than staying in my dump, drinking alone. One night, I guess I was drinking more than I should've been, and I ran up quite a tab. When it came time to pay it, I didn't have enough cash on me and when I gave the bartender my credit card, it was denied. The bartender was kind of nasty about it. I was so embarrassed, I started to cry right there in the bar. I was so broke. The bills my mom left me were staggering.

"Then this guy comes over and tells the bartender that it's okay, and that my bar bill should put on his tab. That man was Eric and I later found out he did security for the bar. They didn't want to call him a bouncer, because the place was kind of snooty, but that's what he was. Anyway, he was very nice to me and I let him drive me back to my apartment. I was too drunk to drive."

"How long before you started dating him?"

"Not long. At first, he was very good to me and good for me. He was kind and so loving. Even now I feel—oh, Ice Cream, I'm ashamed to admit it, but even now, when I remember those days I still can feel love for him. Is that crazy? After all he's done to me?" Her eyes fill with tears and she looks at me questioningly.

"No, Marley, it's not crazy. He was all you had back then and your dependence on him was emotionally charged. I don't know if it's actual love you feel. I think it's more of a nostalgia for how he treated you in the beginning of your relationship. But, tell me, you never noticed anything about him that tipped you off to his violent tendencies?'

"Oh, he was always kind of jealous, a little possessive, but I liked that. I told him all about my mother's bills and how I was desperate for money. I was drowning in debt. Over my protests, he paid off all my mother's creditors. He said money wasn't a problem for him. I thought he was wonderful. He told me he only worked as a bouncer to keep busy, that he'd once been a cop. When I said that he seemed too young to have retired from the force, he told me that he'd left after a few years because there was too much corruption in the police department. Who knew he was the real corrupt one?"

She stops and takes a sip of water from the bottle I gave her. I try not to stare as the water dribbles a little out of her damaged mouth. The anger I feel toward Eric Wigand, over what he has done to her, is overwhelming.

"I would be lying to you if I said there wasn't that element of danger I liked in a man. Eric fit that criteria. You can laugh, but the fact that he wasn't exactly safe was a turn-on for me. As I said, he was very jealous of other men even being near me. A couple of times he broke things in a rage and once put his fist throw a wall, but I found that exciting. He was always sorry after he did those things. I never, never thought he'd lay hands on me." She looks at me for a long second. "You never approved of the men I liked and you were right. I dated dangerous men. But no one is as dangerous as Eric. You have to believe me that he will kill me when he finds me." Marley says this with a sad acceptance of her fate, a finality.

"No one is going to kill you, Marley. I promise. But, listen, I have to ask. When did the abuse start?" She doesn't answer right away and I wait for her to gather her strength.

"It was two months after we got married at a quickie ceremony at city hall. We were still living in my apartment." She takes another sip of water. "I was working for a women's clinic then. A little more money than the Public Defender's office. Anyway, he wanted me to quit my job and move away with him to Pennsylvania. He said the city had too many bad memories for both of us. But I kept refusing to leave. He asked me if there was another man in my life, you know, since I didn't want to move away from the city. I laughed because I didn't think he was serious. He didn't like that I laughed.

"One night I was late coming home. I had stopped for a drink with a couple of colleagues. I called the apartment but there was no answer, so I left a message that I would be late. He was standing in the dark, waiting for me. When I came in, he shut and locked the door. He asked if I liked being a whore, if I liked going to bars to pick up men, the way he said I had picked him up. His voice was low, but it terrified me. I told him to go to hell and turned to go to the bathroom. His fist smashed into the side of my head and knocked me out. That night was the first time he hit me. Later, when I woke up, he beat me so badly that I knew there was no way he'd allow me to go to work for at least a week."

"Marley, didn't you scream, didn't your neighbors hear anything?"

She shakes her head no and looks away. "He stuffed a ball gag in my mouth. You know we had it for—well—I'm sure you can guess."

I don't say anything. I remember, all too well, Marley's graphic descriptions of the S & M erotica she enjoyed. She had absolutely no filters about what she liked.

"Anyway, he was very methodical with his abuse. No loud slaps, just punches and—that night was the first time he broke my nose. It's a sickening thing to feel your nose break. The sound of it breaking, oh my God." She breaks off and begins to cry.

"Okay, Marley, okay. Take a breath and look at me. You're safe here. Okay? Now, how did you get to Rural Valley, Pennsylvania."

"The morning after the first assault, he called my office and told them I had to resign my job because we were moving. I overheard him on the phone and made the mistake of protesting what he was doing. I told him that I'd go to the police. He beat me until I passed out. When I regained consciousness, he beat me again. He told me he would *train* me over and over again until I understood that he was in charge."

A loud whoop from outside makes Marley cringe and she begins to shake. I go to the window and cautiously look out. It's a group of teens just walking past, probably leaving the rec center down the block. They're heading someplace else for fun. The area around my office building is desolate at night.

Going to my bottom desk drawer, I grab a bottle of homemade whiskey given to me by a ninety-something year-old man named Mr. O'Leary who helped me on a case two years. I pour Marley a good stiff shot and go back to her to listen to her tale of terror.

CHAPTER 27

"RURAL VALLEY WAS AS foreign to me as if I had been taken to another dimension. Eric made sure that I was completely isolated. No phone, no contact with anyone. I saw no one but Eric. I did mindless crafts to keep myself occupied. And, then—I became pregnant. I thought that my pregnancy might just be a way out for me. Certainly if I was going to a doctor during the pregnancy, he or she might be able to alert authorities and I could get away from Eric."

"Did you *ever* see a doctor, Marley?"

"Only once, to confirm the pregnancy, but Eric came with me and I had no chance to talk to the doctor alone. A few weeks later, I miscarried. I had said something, I can't remember what, something that made him angry, and he knocked me down the stairs." She laughs bitterly. "After I miscarried, Eric was so kind. He was sweet and gentle. He said that he was sorry for what he had done, but that I had forced him to do it. I almost began to believe that I deserved to be beaten, that it was my fault. Can you believe that?"

"Yes, Marley I believe it," I say quietly. "You were alone, isolated, and you depended on him for everything. You were being brainwashed."

She shivers and takes another small sip of whiskey. "I did try to leave him, Ice Cream," she says looking at me and willing me to understand. "Twice I ran away and twice he found me. What he did to me those times—it was horrible. Because of the abuse, I miscarried two more times but, the last time I became pregnant—that was the worst. The last time I made it to seven months and I went into labor. The baby was born at the house. I-I," she puts her hands over her eyes as if to block out a horrible scene, "I held that baby, it was a little boy, perfectly formed. I begged him not to die, I begged God to let him live but—he took his last breath in my arms. He lived for less than an hour. He was beautiful, even in death. Eric buried him in the backyard, as if he were nothing at all to him. He buried that poor, little innocent boy, without any emotion."

I feel a physical ache in my chest. What horror she has endured from that bastard!

"He beat me for years. I was afraid to run away again." She looks at me sadly. "I'm not like you, Ice Cream, I was never brave like you."

"I'm not all that brave. I get scared too, Marley. I just push through it."

"But you never thought of killing yourself. Death would be my final escape. You wouldn't do that. But me? I wanted to end my life. Just like my mother did."

The lisping intensifies with her agitation and I have to listen carefully to what she is saying.

"How did Will get mixed up in this?"

"I stole a phone."

"You—how were you able to steal a phone?

"I saw a phone left on the counter at the post office and I stole it. That was a little over a year ago. A man picking up some packages, accidentally left it there. He just forgot it and left. I don't know what made me do it, but, when no one was looking, I leaned against the counter and slipped it into my jacket pocket."

At my questioning look, she explains, "Eric had to go to a small post office every two weeks to get his mail. He never left me alone, so I had to go with him, although by that time he knew that

I was too afraid of him to run away again. I don't know what happened that day, but something inside me came alive when I saw that cell phone. I guess I still had a wild thought that I could be free." Tears spill down her cheeks but she doesn't wipe them away.

"Oh, God, I was so scared that Eric saw me take it, but he didn't. I turned that phone off and kept it hidden on the way home." She pauses, remembering her fear, and I wait.

"That night was a really bad night. I accidentally burned a steak I was making for his dinner. He was furious and he hit me so hard that my left ear wouldn't stop ringing. He just kept hitting me and hitting me." Marley begins to sob.

"I couldn't take it anymore. But I knew that I couldn't escape on my own. I needed someone to help me. That night, like almost all nights, Eric drank heavily and lay down on the couch. When I knew he was asleep, I used the stolen phone to call Will. I'm surprised that I still remembered his number, but I did. I was terrified, but I didn't know who else to call and I figured he would help me."

"Will never told me he had contact with you."

"That's because I asked him not to tell you. I was so—ashamed of who I had become."

"How did he help you?"

Marley goes on to tell me that Will gave her two options. He could have the Pennsylvania police arrest Eric that very night. Marley would have to testify, but Will was sure Eric would be sent to prison for domestic violence. He tried hard to convince her to have the police arrest Eric. There'd be an order of protection put in place. But Marley refused. While she was working at the Office of the Public Defender, she had seen too many women, who had those so-called restraining orders, end up in hospitals or even the morgue. There was no real protection. So Will gave her option two. She could go into hiding at a safe house. He'd help her to relocate somewhere where Eric would never find her.

Her story makes it very clear why Javy couldn't find any info in Will's files concerning a domestic abuse case. There was no case. This wasn't official, it was just Will doing all he could to help someone he knew had been my friend. When he was talking to Jacoby and Javy about a domestic abuse victim, and how the courts don't help the victims but helped the perps instead, he was talking about Marley's situation. How she didn't want a court order of protection, how she knew it wasn't worth the paper it was printed on. Her husband could still get to her despite the restraining order. Jacoby and Javy simply assumed he was talking about an old case he'd worked.

"He told me he was coming to get me. I told him that Eric was dead drunk and that made him a meaner person. Will told me not to worry, he'd deal with Eric."

Marley continues, talking in a slow painful way. She tells me that, when Will arrived at the house later that night, Eric woke up and saw her leaving with him. How he drunkenly attacked Will and how Will knocked him flat, punching him really hard in the mouth. Then Will grabbed Marley, put her in his car, and drove to a house in upstate New York. There, he said, she'd be safe.

"I *was* safe. I even dyed my hair brown so no one could identify me as a red-head in case Eric put up flyers describing me in an attempt to find me. I stayed there for almost a year. Will called me every month to make sure that I was okay. Then, ten days ago, I got a phone call and it wasn't from Will; it was from Eric. I don't know how he found my number. He was a former cop, so maybe he had ways of finding out where I was hiding. I was scared out of my mind! He told me that he was coming after me. He said he knew where I was.

"I called Will and he told me to lock myself in and that he would come and get me. He called local police and had them place an unmarked patrol car near the house. When he arrived, Will drove me to an apartment in the city that was used for crime victims, and again, requested to have an unmarked car parked near the building. He said he had to leave because he was going out with you and some friends. Will told me I'd be safe there and that he'd come back in the morning and we'd talk about what I was going to do next.

"The following day I waited for Will. I waited and waited until it was getting dark. But—Will never came. I had no idea why he wasn't coming back. I heard on the news that a cop had been shot. I didn't know that it was Will, but I was terrified to leave that apartment. I stayed in that apartment until today and kept waiting for Will to call me."

She begins to cry again, big, heaving sobs. "This afternoon, my phone rang and it was Eric. He said that he had finally found me. He told me that he had killed Will and was coming after me. I ran out of that building terrified that at any minute he would grab me.

"I didn't know where else to go. Will had told me that you were a private investigator so I came here to you, Cate, I had to! I'm so sorry! Now, by coming here, I put you in danger, too. I should never have come here. Cate, I'm so—"

I interrupt her. "Marley let me ask you a question. Did Eric *know* that you and I were friends? Did he know about Will and me?"

Marley nods her head. "I told him when we were dating. I was kind of nasty about you. I'm so sorry, Ice Cream! I was jealous of you. I told him about you and Will and that you were engaged. I told him how lucky you always were and how I hated you for that. I'm sorry, I'm sorry! Please forgive me!"

I'm starting to make sense of everything that has happened and see inside the cruel twisted mind of Eric Wigand. He hired me to find Marley, aka Wendy, knowing full well that he was going to shoot Will. And I'm pretty certain that, after the shooting, Wigand found out that he hadn't kill Will after all, and that he was taken to Lenox Hospital. As Marley said, a former cop has ways of getting info. My anger grows as the thought runs through my head that he probably took great pleasure knowing that he had me working his case while Will lay in the hospital in ICU. That son-of-a-bitch.

Wigand more than likely knew that Marley might come to see me if she thought I could help her, if she believed Will was—I shake those words out of my mind.

"Okay, Marley, okay, we're going to leave here soon. I'm taking you to the hospital."

She begins shaking her head no. "He'll see me; he'll kill both of us."

"Don't worry, there's a detective outside so we can walk to my car without being afraid. He has a gun and so do I. My car is right outside. Okay?"

She shakes her head slowly. "Why do you want to help me, Cate? I brought all this trouble to you and Will. I broke our friendship. Why do you care what happens to me?"

"Because I *remember* that friendship. I remember what it meant to me and it meant a great deal, Marley. Now, just one more question before we leave for the hospital. Why change your name? Why are you called Wendy?"

"A children's book."

"What do you mean?" I look at her questioningly.

"The name is from a children's book, *Weak Wendy and the Windy Day*. It was about a little girl who was afraid to go outside, afraid of everything. Eric saw that book in a flea market and bought for me. He said that's what I am, a Weak Wendy. He called me that so often, that I became what he said I was. I *am* Weak Wendy."

"No. You're not weak," I say gently. "You're an incredibly brave survivor. You're Marley and that's who you will always be."

She shakes her head sadly. "I don't remember being Marley."

"I'll help you remember. You're Marley, Marley Weiner. Remember that. Your name is Marley."

"Yes, I'm—I'm Marley." She looks at me sadly. "Cate? Why did you ask me if Eric knows we were friends?"

I feel so unbelievably tired. Sighing deeply, I tell her how Eric Wigand played a cruel joke on us all by hiring me to find his wife.

CHAPTER 28

EXHAUSTION CAN TAKE ITS toll on the human mind in many ways. One of these ways is in a depleted lack of concentration and judgment. For me, that means that I have let my guard down and turned off the warning signs of my gut instinct. Doing that can have deadly consequences for a private investigator.

Unlocking the deadbolts, I have just reached for the thick brass handle on the inner door of the building when it is pushed violently inward and then, just as violently, slammed shut. The dingy hall lighting shows me only a shadowy figure and I smell him before I see him. A minty garlic smell, just as the witnesses to Will's shooting said they smelled before Will was shot. The man who shot him is here.

"Well now, Ms. Harlow. I see you found my missing wife. Congratulations. You earned your fee. Too bad you won't get a chance to spend it."

Eric Wigand, standing inside the vestibule, is pointing a gun at me. Marley grabs me around the waist, and holds on so tightly I find it hard to get a deep breath.

"Been eating at the Pot Luk again? Or maybe a pizzeria? Your breath stinks," I say, pretending a toughness it's hard to feel when someone is clinging to you with all their terrified might. "You know the mint gum you're chewing doesn't really hide the smell of garlic, Mr. Wigand. That's something witnesses to attempted murder will be sure to remember."

With his gun still on me, he looks at Marley. "You little bitch. I'm going to beat you to death. I said I would and I never break my word. But you know all about what I said I would do, don't you? You know all about my promises to you. Didn't I always do what I said I would do? You remember what I can do to you?"

"No, no," whimpers Marley. "No, no, no."

"Come here." His voice is calm. "Come to me, sweetheart. Come here. Come on."

She doesn't move and he walks toward her. As soon as she's within his reach, his left hand grabs a handful of her hair and he places the gun next to her temple. I recognize the weapon; it's a Ruger Redhawk Revolver, the same type Jacoby told me was used to shoot Will.

Looking at me, Wigand says, "You move one inch, Harlow and this little bitch lost is dead. Where's your gun?"

I stand perfectly still, my hands, palms out, held toward him in a placating manner. I tell him my gun is in the back of my jeans, under my sweatshirt. Tightening his grip on her hair so that she cries out in pain, Eric Wigand moves toward me and tells Marley to get my gun.

Her hair still being painfully held in a vicious twist, Marley slowly removes my gun. I'm hoping that, once she has the Smith and Wesson in hand, she'll turn and shoot the bastard, but that doesn't happen. She's so conditioned to be terrified of him that she simply does as he tells her and drops it on the floor. He kicks it away into the darkness, out of sight.

"First, you're going to lock this door, Harlow. Then we're going upstairs to your office. Don't do anything stupid," he warns me. "No heroic moves like your boyfriend did. I will blow her brains all over this fucking place if you do. I promise you that. Get going."

I go to the door and, praying he doesn't notice, only turn the locks halfway so that they don't catch. It's a way out for me and a way in for the detective who's been shadowing me.

Wigand motions me up the stairs as he and a whimpering Marley follow. Once upstairs and inside my office, he slams the door shut, locks it, and throws Marley onto the floor beside Myrtle's desk. I wince at the sound of her head hitting the wood floor. Wigand shakes strands of Marley's hair from his hand. He looks at her with an evil smirk and says, "Stupid bitch. I told Benigni you were as good as dead. Big protector, couldn't even protect himself."

While he's looking at her, I take a calculated chance, lunging forward suddenly so that his attention becomes focused on me. "Run!" I shout. "Run, Marley, run now!"

But she doesn't move, just stays slumped on the floor, her arms crossed over her body. She's become an animal who is too brainwashed and terrified to leave her abuser. Looking at Marley, Wigand aims his Ruger at me.

"Marley, huh? She was Marley when I met her. I hated that name. Now, she's just Wendy, Weak Wendy. Weak Wendy, it fits her; sad and helpless." He looks at her crumpled on the floor. "That's right, you pathetic little bitch, you know better than to run again."

Eric Wigand turns his attention back to me. "You're good at this private eye bullshit, I'll give you that much. You don't leave any stone unturned but you missed the fact that you were being followed, didn't you? I've been watching you all this time, Harlow. I've tracked you like a hunter tracks prey. All the while you thought I was in that shithole in Philly, I've been in New York City, following you."

My heart sinks. I thought it was one of Jacoby's best detectives who was shadowing me, but it was Wigand, the dirty ex-cop. Damn it! I wasn't up on my game, not alert enough to what was going on. I am totally on my own here. Shit! I wish I had told Jacoby to send a police car for us. How could I have been so careless? Exhaustion, that's how. Exhaustion and fear for Will. Marc Crofts, the assassin with a heart, told me that loving someone puts you off your game. You stop thinking clearly. The woman he loved paid for loving him with her very life.

"I know your every move, where you go, who you see. I should've tried harder to kill you on that rainy I-95."

I stare at him.

"Yeah, stupid private investigator, you didn't even guess? That was me ramming you from behind. I know all about your nosy little side trip to Rural Valley, too. And I know that do-gooder you're fucking is in the hospital, unfortunately still alive. But that's not for long. I'll be taking care of unfinished business after I deal with my dear, sweet wife, and with you. I tried to get to him the other night. Pretended I saw a hit-and-run. I got up to ICU but there were two fucking cops guarding his door. But I'll get him later. I'll find a way in."

"You had every intention of shooting him after you smashed him in the head, didn't you, you son-of-a-bitch? Didn't you?" I shout this at him in a white-hot fury.

He looks at me with a sneer. "Do you know that that bastard Benigni broke my jaw the night he took this little bitch? That wasn't a fair fight. He wouldn't have been able to do that if my dear, stupid Weak Wendy hadn't pissed me off and I got drunk. Now, the score has to be evened and it's going to be done on my terms.

"And yeah, blondie, I had every intention of killing Detective Preppie after I whacked him in the head. Your fucking boyfriend is a very good and accurate shot—I'll give him that. I wanted to take no chance that he'd shoot me first, so my plan was to stun him with a blow to the head and then finish the job and *shoot* him in the head. But he turned, threw me off my plan, and I went for the heart instead. Thought I'd killed him too, but he's still alive. Remember, I told you that in order for me to move on with my life, I want closure? Well, this closure is a long time coming and I'm going to get that closure as soon as I'm done here."

I'm confronted by someone who has no qualms about killing. He'll do what he says; kill Marley, then me, and then go for Will. The fact that he won't get anywhere near Will at the hospital is a relief, as is the fact that Jacoby will make damn sure that Will is under protection twenty-four hours a day *after* he leaves the hospital. But the harsh reality of the moment is that Wigand has the means to kill the two of us in this room. The only one who can stop him is me.

I'm debating whether I should rush and disable him with a jolt from the Taser that I have in the pocket of my jeans, when I hear voices.

"See, Hey, see? I *tole* ya she was here." The unmistakable voice is that of Bo, the homeless man who squats in the basement of a nearby building, with his friend Hey. They're coming up the stairs. Bo calls his friend Hey, but he also says hey when he wants to get someone's attention. It used to confuse the hell out of me. I don't want them to get hurt and I know that Wigand will kill them if they come in the office. Innocent people in the wrong place at the wrong time.

"I tole ya I saw the lights before. You know what your problem is, Hey? Huh? Huh? You don't never listen to me. I bet she has doughnuts, yeah, or maybe pizza. Yeah, pizza."

Wigand hears them and he curses under his breath. He wants no witnesses to what he's about to do.

"Pizza. I hope she has pizza, Bo. I like pizza. Cold pizza."

"Yeah, me too, but I like doughnuts too, the ones with the chocolate. Or tacos, yeah, but she never has tacos. I don't think she went to Mexico, no, she didn't, Hey. Not like you did, Hey."

"I never went to Mexico, Bo! I was here on the street. You know that."

They argue back and forth for a few minutes. It's almost a comic relief to hear them talking about food and Mexico while the drama of my and Marley's death is imminent.

There's a hesitant knock on the door, then Bo's voice calling, "Hey, hey Cate, Cate, open up. Me and Hey, we want doughnuts or tacos."

"Pizza!" Hey says in a loud whisper.

"Yeah, yeah, pizza, okay, Cate, okay?"

Wigand goes to stand by where Marley has fallen. He half turns to me and places his finger on his lips as a signal for me to be quiet. Then he holds the gun against Marley's head. His message is clear; if I warn Bo and Hey, he'll kill Marley. His eyes challenge me for a second and I nod okay. I understand. Satisfied that I'll do as he wants, he mouths the words, 'Get rid of them. Now!'

Trying to keep my voice calm, I call out, "Gee guys, I'm sorry. I don't have any food here. Tomorrow—tomorrow Myrtle will go shopping. Come back tomorrow afternoon. I promise we'll have pizza, and doughnuts, and, and even tacos. You have to leave now, okay? I can't let you in. Leave now. I have some work to do and I need quiet. See you tomorrow."

I hear them whispering and then Bo says, "You promise? You promise you'll have tacos too? Promise? I like tacos."

I bite my lip. "Absolutely, Bo. Tacos, yes, I promise we'll have tacos tomorrow. You have to go now."

"Okay. 'Bye." I hear footsteps go down the stairs.

Wigand turns to me. "Didn't lock the door, did you Harlow? You thought you'd get a chance to get away from me? You're as stupid as Weak Wendy here."

He takes a set of handcuffs out of his back pocket and throws them at me. "Cuff her to the desk. Then you and me are going down to make sure that fucking door gets locked. No more visitors tonight."

As he places the gun against Marley's head again, I take one of her wrists and handcuff her to the heavy leg of Myrtle's desk. I have no doubt that he'll shoot her dead if I don't do as he demands.

"You're a real helping hand for weak and needy people aren't you, Harlow? You're so easy to fool, you know that?"

Wigand pushes me forward, jamming the gun between my shoulder blades. If I can only get that Taser out of my back pocket as we walk downstairs. Maybe a quick turn and a jab toward his chest will do it. But I have to be fast, and I have to make sure that I make contact with his body. This Taser is powerful but it's small size makes direct bodily contact necessary to incapacitate someone.

I open the door and we walk out to the stairwell. I'm waiting to make my move.

"Hey. Beef, okay?" It's Bo, standing at the bottom of the stairs. "Beef tacos. I forgot to tell you. Me and Hey like beef ones."

"Bo," I say quickly.

He sees Wigand standing behind me. "Is he going to have tacos too? You have to buy more then, so we have enough, me and Hey."

"I-I'll make sure there's a whole lot of tacos, Bo." The gun is pressed tightly into my back.

"You have to make sure! Please, we love tacos."

"Yes, absolutely, Bo. I will make sure."

"Enough of this shit about fucking tacos," says Wigand. "Shut the hell up!"

But Bo keeps talking. He is like a child when he wants something. He won't stop talking until he makes it clear that you know what he wants.

"Yeah, but, we need a lot. If you're gonna be here, we need more. A whole, big lot of tacos."

Bo starts up the stairs and, before I can stop him, Wigand's arm moves around me. He points the gun dead center at Bo's chest. I shift quickly, knocking him off balance. The bullet goes wild, hitting Bo in the leg instead and he falls backward. I spin, grab the Taser from my pocket and let it go against Wigand's side. He goes down in a spasm of agony. Kicking his gun down the stairwell, I run down the stairs to Bo.

"Ow, ow, ow. My leg! Something stung me, something stung me! It's a big bee! My leg hurts! A bee! A bee!"

"Bo, stay still, just stay still and let me look at your leg."

"Oh no, oh no, oh no...my leg! Oh no, oh no, oh no! Help me, it hurts!"

I bend quickly to look at the wound on his left thigh. My stomach turns at the site. Blood is spurting and is bright red in color. That's bad news. It means the bullet nicked an artery. I need to stop the bleeding fast. I move over to where Wigand's gun landed and hastily grab it. Then I look around for something to make a tourniquet for Bo's wound. There's nothing.

I'm ready to remove my shirt to make a tourniquet when I remember the ace bandage on Marley's wrist. I warn a crying Bo to stay right where he is and race to the stairs. Wigand is still lying on the third step, incapacitated for now. I shove him over roughly and fish the key for the handcuffs out of his pocket. Then I run up the stairs two at a time.

Inside my office, I rush over to my former best friend. "Marley! Listen to me, I have to take your bandage. Bo, that guy who came here before asking for tacos? He's my friend and he has been shot. It's really bad. I need to make a tourniquet to stop the bleeding."

Placing Wigand's gun on Myrtle's desk, I reach for Marley's arm and begin to unravel the bandage. As I do so, I see that, underneath it, Marley's wrist is swollen and misshapen. That bastard Wigand probably broke it at one time and, because she never had medical treatment for it, it never healed properly. I unlock the cuffs and stuff them, and the bandage, into my front pocket, then take the seat cushion from Myrtle's chair to place under Bo's leg to elevate it. I look on Myrtle's desk and grab the heavy metal ruler with "Congratulations on your retirement!" written on it and turn to Marley.

"Get up Marley," I say, tossing her my phone. "Hit the number 8. That'll put you through to Captain Jacoby. Tell him to send the police now and tell him I need an ambulance and EMTs! I have to go stop the bleeding, but I can't leave the tourniquet on too long, so call now!"

"Is he dead?"

"No, Bo's been shot, but it's pretty bad. The artery in his thigh has been hit." I rush out the door of my office.

"Is he dead?"

Without turning around, I say impatiently, "No, I just told you he's—"

"Not him. I mean Eric. Is he dead? Did you kill him?"

"No," I call back as I hurry down the stairwell to help a now moaning Bo. "Eric's alive."

Just as I reach the bottom of the stairs, I hear the slam of the heavy oak door to my office and the sound of the inside deadbolt lock being clicked into place. Marley has locked herself inside before making the call to Jacoby.

But I can't stop. I will lose Bo if I do. I kneel down next to him, ace bandage in hand.

"Bo. Bo! Don't lose consciousness, stay with me, Bo. Come on, look at me, look at me!"

The wound is bad. If I can't control it, he'll bleed out. His eyes are glazing over. I lift his leg as gently as I can, but I see a pained grimace on his face.

"Bo, concentrate on me. Look at me. You're going to be okay. I'll make sure of that. Everything will be fine. Just stay with me, okay? Please stay with me."

Myrtle's cushion acts as a padding under his leg and I wrap the tourniquet several times above the wound. Then, using the ruler as a torsion device, I tie an overhand knot on both ends of it and twist the ruler, tightening the tourniquet, until the bleeding stops. All the while I'm doing this, I'm mentally thanking Myrtle for making me take a first-aid trauma class. I am grateful as hell to have the knowledge.

There is one major problem with using a tourniquet—it can only be used for a short period of time. Blood cannot be kept from its natural flow to the rest of the wounded limb for very long. There's a real danger of tissue damage and paralysis. To prevent that, I have to keep loosening and tightening the tourniquet. Loosen for a count of sixty, then tighten. Enough tight pressure to stop the arterial spurting, then release to save tissue. This has to be repeated every ten minutes or so. Goddamn it, where is that ambulance?

I hear moans coming from Wigand who is still splayed out on the stairs. The cuffs are in my back pocket. I look wildly around the entryway for my Smith and Wesson, the gun Wigand kicked somewhere down here, but I can't find it. Then I remember I took Wigand's Ruger revolver. I reach in the back of my jeans. Where did I put it? Shit! I must have left it on Myrtle's desk. My hand pats my back pocket to make sure the small Taser is still there. Okay, all right. I have to subdue Wigand somehow and the Taser is what I have. It will have to do. I release the bandage on Bo's thigh and count to sixty, then tighten again. Quickly I go back to the stairs, Taser and cuffs in hand.

Wigand looks like a sleeping bear. I don't trust him. I hold the Taser out and nudge him with my foot. No movement. But when I reach over to grab his wrist and cuff him, he grips my ankle and I fall forward on top of him. We struggle and I manage to twist away from him so that I can Taser his arm. The shock is weak; the batteries haven't been charged properly. Still, I manage to stun Wigand enough so that I can cuff him to the old-fashioned sturdy metal spokes in the railing.

"Marley!" I yell up the stairs. "Marley? What did Jacoby say? What the hell is the holdup here? You did call, didn't you? Please tell me you called! Marley!"

I run up the stairs and bang on the locked door. "Open up, Marley! Open it now! Give me my cell phone so I can call for help. My friend will bleed to death if he doesn't get immediate medical help! Please, Marley, open up! I have to call for help!"

I keep banging on the heavy oak door, even though there's no answer. I can't unlock my door with the deadbolt on. Jesus Christ! Without my cell phone, going outside is the only way I can get help. It's late and I will have to go several blocks before I'll find someone. Then I remember Hey. He has to be outside somewhere. He and Bo are never far away from each other.

Bo is moaning and gasping for breath so I go back down to him. Kneeling next to him I release and tighten the tourniquet. "Bo, listen to me. We can't stay here; we have to get help. I have to get you to my car so someone can take care of the, the, uh, bee sting. Okay?"

I don't want to scare him by talking about hospitals and doctors, so I mention the one doctor he knows and trusts. The man who helped his friend Hey after I cracked his ribs when I thought Hey was an attacker trying to get in my car. I tell him we have to go see Dr. Giles Barrett.

"Where's Hey? Is he in the basement room where you two live?" That's the abandoned building a short block away. "Bo, please try to understand me. Is Hey near here? I need him to help me get you out of here."

He doesn't answer me and I shake him, forcing his face close to mine to look at me as I repeat the question. Finally, he seems to focus and says, "By car. Yours. Sitting on ground— wait for me— Hey—wait—Ow! It hurts, it hurts! Hey, it hurts! Watch out for the bee!"

Telling him I'll be right back with Hey, I release, and tighten, the tourniquet once again, then race to the front door and fling it open, calling for Hey to come help me carry Bo to my car.

"Hey! Hey, where are you? Bo is hurt and I need your help!"

CHAPTER 29

J UST AS BO TOLD me, I find Hey sitting on the ground, leaning up against my SUV. I tell him no lies about Bo's condition. Truth is, I am brutally honest in telling Hey that Bo was shot and is bleeding badly. I hate the fact that I'm scaring Hey, but he has a way of wandering off suddenly for no reason, and I need him here.

"We have to get Bo medical help as quickly as possible. This is a real emergency, Hey. You can't leave here, understand me? Bo needs you."

Hey begins to cry, the tears leaving dirty streaks on his face, but, through his sobs, he says he will help me. He runs to the building while I back my vehicle as close to the door as possible and open the tailgate. As we're about to enter the building, I tell him what we have to do.

"We have to carry him to the tailgate, he has to lie flat, with his leg elevated, okay?"

Hey looks confused, so I say it another way. "His leg has to be up. Up higher than the rest of his body. I'll show what I mean once we're inside."

Tears fall freely down his cheeks. "I don't want Bo to die," he says quietly. "Dr. Giles will help him, right? He fixed me. He can fix anybody. He fixed me."

I give him a brief hug. "It'll be all right, everything will be okay as long as we can get him to Dr. Giles. I know you're afraid of hospitals, but we have to take Bo there. You understand?" Hey wipes his nose on the back of his hand and nods yes.

Inside the building, I glance at Wigand who is still lying on the steps handcuffed to the iron railing, then I hurry to Bo who is going in and out of consciousness. Surprisingly the blood doesn't seem to scare Hey. Living on the streets must have made him, if not immune to it, then accepting of bloody injuries. After checking the tourniquet, I show Hey how Bo's leg has to be elevated with the pillow. He nods, follows my lead, and bends to help me carry Bo.

We're about to move Bo, when I hear a noise. There is the soft click of a lock being turned and the door of my office opens slowly, the hinges Myrtle keeps so well-oiled making no sound at all. Marley stands in the shadowy doorway, barely illuminated by the small flameless candle on Myrtle's desk. Her two hands grip Wigand's gun which she holds straight out in front of her. Very softly she says, "Eric," and walks toward the stairs.

"You have my gun," Wigand says stupidly, still woozy from the Taser.

"I thought you were dead. I heard the shot and I thought you were dead."

"But I'm not. I'm still alive." He shakes his cuffed wrist. "I need your help, Wendy. Get the key from your girlfriend over there and un-cuff me."

"No, no I'm *not* Wendy," she says her voice shaking. "My name is—Marley."

"Marley, huh? Who told you that? That bitch?" He points his chin in my direction. "She doesn't know who you are *now*. Doesn't know who you've become. You're not Marley, you're Weak Wendy. I made sure of that. You're scared, dumb, Wendy and if you know what's good for you, you'll un-cuff me and hand that gun over to me before you hurt yourself."

"N-n-no," Marley shakes her head. "I can't, I can't do that." She points the gun right at Eric Wigand's head

"You won't shoot me. You haven't got the guts to use a gun."

"I do. I will."

Her hands shake as she continues to aim the gun at her husband. I remain standing quietly. There's a weapon in play here and anything can happen. Marley can panic, shots can be erratic. So I stand still next to a silently crying Hey, who is kneeling near his friend Bo. My eyes are on Marley.

"Wendy, give me the gun!" His voice thunders in the empty building. I watch my friend trembling as she's shaking her head no. Wigand sees it too and says nothing for a few seconds. When he speaks again, his voice is quiet and soft, almost loving. I turn toward him in surprise.

"Give me the gun, Wendy," he croons. "Come on, do it now, like a good girl. You don't want to hurt anyone, sweetheart. *No one* has to get hurt. I love you, sweetheart. Give me the gun."

"No, I—can't, I—shouldn't."

"Come on, darling girl, come on. Give me the gun so no one will get hurt."

His voice is gentle and caressing, sweet almost. To my amazement, Marley seems torn about whether to give him the gun or not. She comes down a step toward Wigand. I have to stop her from giving him that gun. We're all dead if she does that.

"No," I shout, from where I'm standing, "don't do it Marley, don't. He'll kill you if you give him the gun. You know that. You told me he said he was going to kill you and we both heard him say that same thing right here in this building a couple of hours ago. Give the gun to me and I'll turn him over to the police, but please do this now. The man on the floor needs immediate medical help. It's an emergency. Please, give me the gun."

"Don't listen to her sweetheart. Remember what you told me when we first met? Remember you said that your *friend,*" he sneers the word and nods his head again in my direction, "had everything and you had nothing? You said she was always lucky, remember? Now she wants to take me away from you. She wants to kill me so you have no one, nothing, just like before. She never even looked for you when you left the Public Defender's office, she didn't care what happened to you. Remember? You told me that.

She doesn't give a shit about you. Believe me, sweetheart, she will kill me if you hand that gun to her. Give me the gun, I'll protect you, just like I always have."

My stomach clenches as I see Marley come down two more steps towards Wigand, staring at him, almost as if she has made up her mind to give him the gun. Wigand sees it too and presses on with that gentleness in his voice that is sickening for me to hear.

"We've had some bad times, I know that. But you have to remember that I saved you sweetheart, I saved you. You were drowning in debt, I paid all your bills. Did your friend do that? Did she give you a dime? No. You know why? Because she's selfish, a selfish bitch. Give the gun to me, sweetheart. We'll start over, we'll have a baby. You want a baby. I know you do. We were so good in the beginning, remember? We can be that way again. Come on, sweetheart."

That he has the nerve to call her sweetheart after what he's done to her both physically and mentally disgusts me. The fact that she is even listening to him scares the hell out of me.

"Marley? Marley! Look at *me*, don't look at him." She glances in my direction. "Do you really believe that he will change? You really think that you're going to start over, have a baby, and everything will be wonderful? It won't, Marley. You know what he's done to you. All the physical and mental damage. You told me you miscarried because of all the times he beat you. The one baby you bore prematurely died in your arms. You said he didn't even live an hour. Eric was the cause of that baby dying. People don't change, Marley. They just become more of who they really are as time passes."

I look at Bo. The tourniquet is loose and I see blood seeping from his pants leg. "Marley, listen to me. I have to get this man to an emergency room. He's bleeding, he'll bleed to death if he doesn't get medical care immediately. Please help me and give me the gun."

"Sweetheart."

I turn viciously toward Wigand. "Stop saying that! You don't see her as your 'sweetheart,' you dirty that endearment when you use it. Look at her, you sick son-of-a-bitch. Look at what you did to her!"

"Wendy, sweetheart, don't listen to her. She doesn't want you to be happy, she wants you to be alone again with no money. You were desperate before I came into your life. Give me the gun, sweetheart and I promise you, we'll go away, anywhere you want to go. Please sweetheart."

Marley moves down two more steps towards Wigand. My God, can she really believe what he is saying? Has she been so brainwashed by him that she wants, and needs to believe him?

Bo moans loudly and Hey begins to blubber. "Don't die, please don't die, Bo. I'm sorry I took the last brownie, I'm sorry. I'm sorry! I know you were saving it for yourself but, I wanted it! I'm sorry. Please don't die!"

Marley pauses on the step, her attention diverted by Hey's rambling words. I watch her, then look at Wigand. The look on his face is cold and frightening. He's angry that someone is interfering with his tenuous hold on Marley, diverting her attention from him.

"Shut the fuck up, you retard! Shut up! Who gives a shit if your butt buddy dies?" Wigand's angry voice suddenly booms. "Let him die! He's nothing to me."

"Don't say that, don't say that! Please don't die, Bo, please!" Hey is sobbing and talking hysterically. "Bo, Bo, please—God, don't let him die!"

Marley seems unable to look away from Hey cradling Bo's body in his arms and crying over him as if he were a dying child. She tilts her head and stares. Her eyes seem to glaze over.

That's when it dawns on me. A dying child. She's not seeing Bo and Hey. What she sees is her little baby boy, dying in her arms. Dying because of what Eric Wigand had done to her body. Her baby who lived for such a brief time.

"Help me!" Hey screams at me, "Bo! Oh, God, don't let him die!"

Bo is non-responsive and Hey rocks him back and forth in his arms, crying. Marley stands on the steps, her shoulders heaving with sobs. She's remembering her own anguish at the death of her baby. What she told me upstairs. *Eric buried him in the backyard, as if he were nothing at all to him.'*

Hey's crying shrieks are agonizing to hear, the sound of pain and grief. Marley slowly shifts her gaze from Bo to Eric. She comes down the last few steps until she is standing three steps up from Wigand. With two hands that have miraculously stopped shaking, she holds the gun steady. So quietly that I can barely hear her, she says, "I can't let another innocent baby die because of you. I won't do that." She levels the gun pointing it right at his head.

"Marley, no." I try to talk as calmly as I can even though part of me is hoping she'll pull the trigger and send that evil bastard to hell with a bullet through his brain. But the PI in me wants to see him put in prison for what he did, have his freedom taken away from him, just like he took Marley's freedom.

The situation is volatile, what with Hey screaming, Bo moaning and bleeding, and the look of pure, punishing hatred on Wigand's face.

"Don't do it, Marley!"

"Give me the gun. Now! Give it to me!" Wigand snarls. He struggles to get to a standing position on the steps, the left side of his body bent sideways because of the handcuffs holding his wrist firmly to the railing spoke. He tries but he can't reach her where she is on the stairs. Wigand looks defiantly at Marley, seemingly so sure that she won't shoot him.

I'm not at all sure. "No, no Marley, don't do it. Leave him. Come with me."

Wigand half turns to me and laughs. "Weak Wendy doesn't have the balls to shoot me."

"Please, please don't die, Bo. Please, don't leave me alone. Don't die!" Hey's hysterical voice rises piercingly. Bo moans loudly.

"Jesus Christ, shut the hell up, you little shit!"

The cacophony of screams, moans, and angry shouting is deafening. Marley keeps the gun steady on Wigand. I look at her and see that she hasn't moved one inch. This has to end soon so I can get Bo to a hospital. I have to leave, without Marley if necessary, knowing that she may very well kill Wigand. I don't care about that. But I do care about the possibility that he'll convince her to hand him the gun. If she does that, he will kill her.

"Marley, listen to me. I have to get Bo out of here. He'll die if I don't act quickly."

"Please, God, don't let him die!" Hey screams.

Marley takes a deep, ragged breath and squares her shoulders and nods at me. "You can leave, Ice Cream. Go, now. Leave me here. I'll be okay."

"Marley, come *with* us. I'll send the cops to get Wigand."

"No. Just go now, Ice Cream." Her voice is eerily calm.

Staring menacingly at Marley, Wigand shouts, "This is your last chance, you ugly bitch. Give me the god-damned—"

It all ends with a bang.

The shot echoes through the building. Wigand's words are cut short by a bullet entering his throat. His body lurches back and forth like a floppy wind puppet in front of a car dealership. His free hand grasps at his wound, clawing desperately at it as if he could remove the bullet There is a horrible gurgling sound as he gasps for breath, blood spurting through his windpipe. After an agonizing amount of time, he lies unmoving. Dead.

Marley stands absolutely still on the steps above Eric Wigand, the gun still pointed at him. Hey is screaming as I jump into action and reset the tourniquet tightly on Bo's leg. Then I walk over to Wigand and, kneeling on the bottom step, feel for a pulse. There is none. Marley stares at me uncomprehendingly.

I ask for the gun but she won't give it to me. It will do me no good to try and grab it from her. Someone else might get hurt or killed. I straighten up and look at her.

"He—is he—" she whispers.

"He's dead, Marley. He can't hurt you or anyone else ever again." I draw a deep breath. "I need my phone, Marley. Where is it? I have to call 911 to get an ambulance for Bo."

"He's dead?" Her voice is a whisper as she gestures to Wigand's body.

"Yes. Dead." I pause to let that sink in and then ask her once again for my phone.

The gun still held tightly in one hand, she reaches in a pocket of her jacket with the other and hands me my phone. I immediately call 911 for an ambulance and then call Jacoby.

"Joe? I need you to come to my office building—alone. Alone, do you hear me? You'll find the body of Eric Wigand on the stairs. He's dead. Shot dead. I'll explain it all when I see you. Can you secure the crime scene alone until we can talk? Make sure brass doesn't know about this yet?"

"Wigand's dead?" There's a short pause, then he says very low, "You shoot him?"

"No. I would've liked to, but, no."

"All right. I'm coming now. I'll make sure this stays quiet until after we talk."

"Okay, thanks." I'm so grateful that Jacoby trusts me enough to ask no further questions on the phone. "Oh, and Joe? You might see an ambulance coming here. It's not for Wigand. He shot a neighborhood man named Bo and the man's bleeding badly. The EMTs won't see Wigand's body. I'm moving the man outside for them. They don't need to know about Wigand's dead body yet."

I hear Joe give a low whistle and a short laugh.

"Thought this through, huh? You got a certain, weird, but logical way with you, Cate Harlow, I'll say that."

CHAPTER 30

A FTER GENTLY CARRYING Bo outside the building and placing him on a small patch of soft grass near the street, Hey and I wait for the ambulance. It comes speeding to a stop, the screeching siren fading into a wail as it is turned off. Without mentioning the dead body in my building, I tell one of the EMTs as little as possible about how Bo was shot, and let them know that the police are on their way. Showing them my PI license has a certain amount of clout concerning shooting victims, it seems, and they ask no questions.

Making sure that Bo is stabilized, and that the EMTs are headed to Lenox Medical Center, I send Hey in the ambulance with his friend, promising that I will make sure that 'Dr. Giles' is waiting for him there. Like most people who live on the street, Hey has a terrible fear of anyone in the medical profession. The fact that he even *got* in the ambulance with Bo is a great testimony to their street-friendship.

I put in a call to Giles, who answers on the third ring. After a brief explanation on my part about why Hey needs him, Giles promises to get to the hospital to be there for him. I breathe a sigh of relief.

Joe Jacoby shows up just as the ambulance, sirens blaring

again, speeds off to the hospital. True to his word, he came alone, and we go into the building where the body of Eric Wigand lies on the steps, his throat a bloody mess. Marley stands on the exact same step where she had stood to shoot Wigand, the gun still in her two hands. She doesn't acknowledge us, she's in shock. Her eyes stare, as if hypnotized, at his dead body. My thought is that she wants to make absolutely certain he won't get up and come after her once more.

Jacoby looks at Marley. "She the one who offed Wigand?"

"Yes, she was married to him and, as you can see, she was severely abused, both physically and mentally, by him."

A hardened veteran of the police force, Jacoby winces slightly when he looks at her face, then turns away. Facing me he says quietly, "Can you get the weapon from her?"

"I tried. No dice. I think she's afraid that he's not really dead. She needs it for protection, I guess."

"Jesus!"

"Yeah, well, I'll try again later, but first, let me walk you through what has happened here."

I give him the play-by-play of the night, beginning with how Marley surprised me at the top of the stairs when I came here from the hospital. Then I fill him in on how Eric Wigand played his sick, twisted game by hiring me to find his estranged wife who had been basically rescued, and taken to a safe house, by Will. I tell him how Marley told me Will knocked a drunken Eric Wigand on his ass when he tried to stop Will from taking her.

"Hiring me was Wigand's way of stabbing back at Will. I have no doubt the bastard was going to kill me, as well as Marley, tonight. Then I'm sure he'd find a way to get at Will."

My gut clenches tight as I say this. Life is so precious; no relationship can be taken for granted. I find it hard to breathe for a few seconds and Jacoby touches my shoulder and asks me if I'm okay.

"I'm good, I'm fine. Just, you know, tired."

I tell him about Wigand surprising me at the outer door and how my exhaustion had made me less than vigilant. I describe how he held Marley and me at gunpoint in my office and made me handcuff Marley to a desk, and how Bo and Hey unwittingly saved our lives. I end with Bo being shot by Wigand, my immobilizing Wigand with my Taser, and finally, Marley shooting her husband dead.

"Wigand sure as hell deserved to die, I don't question that. He was a rotten son-of-a-bitch. But, Cate, that woman over there pulled the trigger that killed him. She's still got the gun and she doesn't look too stable right now. We got a potential mess here and we have to be real careful about what we're going to do next. It's my job to disarm her, Cate. That weapon has to be secured before we can begin to do anything."

I nod. Marley did kill her horribly abusive husband, that's a fact. Also a fact, a disturbing one, is that she is still holding that gun and seems unresponsive to anything I say to her. In her mind, she can be envisioning all the past abuse she endured and is certainly not thinking clearly. Jacoby or I can accidentally become a victim if she sees us, in any way, as threatening to her safety.

"Her name's Marley, you said, right?"

I nod yes and add, "Weiner, Marley Weiner. That was her name before she married that piece of garbage." I correct myself. "That *is* her name."

Jacoby slowly walks over to where Marley is standing and gently says her name, "Marley? Hi, Marley. My name is Joe. Can I talk with you for a second?"

There's no response. Jacoby's got a kind face. I know he can be tough, but when he talks to victims, his compassion shows through. He tries again, calmly telling her that he's a police captain, and that he promises her that she's safe. He tells her, ever so gently, that the man she is afraid of, the man lying on the stairs, is dead and can't hurt her anymore.

"So, Marley? Can you hand the gun to me? You don't need it anymore, honey."

Marley keeps staring at Eric Wigand, his Ruger Redhawk Revolver clutched tightly in both hands and pointed dead center at his body. The blood is congealing on his opened throat and I hear the low buzz of flies near the door. Oh, Christ!

Jacoby tries talking to her for a few more minutes then slowly backs away, his hand resting on his own revolver in a holster under his jacket. He's taking no chances and I know that if she spooks and aims at him, she'll be shot down in an instant. I understand the necessity of that cop logic. I don't want to think that Jacoby will shoot Marley in self-defense, but I know he would.

"She's not budging, Cate. We got a problem."

"Joe, let me try, okay? Give me about fifteen minutes, that's all I'm asking."

"That's all you're getting. After that, well, I have to call this in, Cate, you know that. And Cate, you also know that I will have you covered."

"I know." I acknowledge that he will shoot Marley if she turns on me.

I walk over to Marley, take a deep, ragged breath, climb the stairs and sit on the step above where she's standing. She doesn't move or even glance at me. I begin to talk.

"Marley. It's me, Ice Cream. You know what? I remember the first time you called me Ice Cream. It was one of the coldest day of the year and we were working late. You and I, we had had such a crazy day at the Office of the Public Defender. Oh my God! Most of our days were hectic, but that one? We worked until after 8:00 at night because we had so many files, so many names and situations that had to be put into the computer. And those computers were so damn slow. They from the Stone Age. One of the Assistant DAs said they were refurbished junk. And you said, do you remember what you said? You said, 'Refurbished by who? Monkeys without thumbs?' I laughed so hard I fell off my chair."

There's no response from Marley so I keep talking, hoping something I say will get through to her.

"So anyway, we're getting giddy because we're so wiped and we still have a lot to finish. You said that we had to get out of the office for at least an hour. We're hungry, but we don't know where we should go. You want Thai food and I want Italian. So, to compromise we decide to go to a new place that's a couple of blocks away, *Cheeseburger-Cheeseburger*, I think it was called, right?" No answer.

"Okay, so anyway, it's really cold out and when we get there, the place is closed because a pipe was frozen and they had no water! Oh my God, too funny! Now we're kind of at a loss so we walk up the street and turn a corner and there's this little Cuban restaurant. You figure you can order soup and a sandwich. Me too. But when we get inside, I see an old framed picture on the back wall. It's of a man and a woman, sitting on a veranda that overlooks the ocean, and sharing a dish of pistachio ice cream. Pistachio is my favorite. Suddenly a soup and sandwich seem less appealing to me. So, I tell you I'm getting a pistachio ice cream sundae.

"And that server, remember him? He kept saying, '¿Helado? Ice cream? ¿Está seguro? Are you sure? But, miss, it is too cold for ice cream.' I insisted that a pistachio sundae was what I wanted. He brought me hot soup with the ice cream sundae, just in case!"

I glance at Jacoby who holds up his hand, fingers spread, to let me know I have only five minutes left. I rush on, still hoping to reach Marley.

"So I devoured the pistachio ice cream sundae and then asked for another one. I binged on ice cream sundaes while you ate soup! I offered you some but you said you couldn't eat anything cold because you had sensitive teeth. You said I was crazy, but you laughed all the way back to the office. And that's the night you started calling me Ice Cream. Remember, Marl? Remember?"

I sigh deeply and look at Jacoby who shakes his head and pulls out his phone to call for back-up and an ambulance.

"Damn it, Marley," I say under my breath, standing up and walking down the steps. "Did you hear me? Can you just say yes or no?"

"Yes."

Her voice is so low that I barely hear her. I turn slowly to look at her. No sudden movements, but when her eyes meet mine, I know she sees me, really sees me.

"Ice Cream," she says.

"That's right, Marley. It's me, Ice Cream."

Glancing at Jacoby, who has his phone in hand, I take a step toward Marley and make one last effort to take the weapon from her. Once Jacoby makes that phone call, it's out of my hands.

"Marley? Can I have the gun now? You don't need it anymore."

My former best friend Marley Weiner, the spirited, fun-loving red-haired woman with such lousy taste in men, looks at me with the saddest smile I have ever seen.

"No, Ice Cream. I still need it."

I move closer and hear Jacoby say my name, warning me to be careful.

"But Eric Wigand is dead, Marley. He's dead."

She looks at Wigand's body, then back at me, shaking her head no.

"You don't understand."

"What don't I understand, Marley? What?" I feel a chill of fear when I look at her.

"I have to make my final escape from him." With that she raises the Ruger Redhawk toward her temple.

I react instantly, but everything seems to happen in slow motion. My yelling, "No!" and diving forward toward Marley. Grabbing her arm so that the bullet shoots straight upwards into the ceiling, slamming her hand into the side of the railing forcing her to drop the weapon, all of it a slow-motion blur.

Jacoby runs over and picks up the gun while I fall to the stairs gathering a limp Marley into my arms and tell her it's all right, everything is going to be all right. She doesn't cry, she doesn't move, just sits awkwardly with me on the metal stairs and stares at the body of Eric Wigand.

Jacoby makes the necessary calls and within minutes we hear the sound of sirens and vehicles coming to a screeching halt outside the building. Five cops enter the building and Jacoby goes over to talk to them while they view the scene before them. What a sight we must make! Two women, one battered and catatonic, sitting on the steps slightly above a dead and bloody body!

One of the cops, a woman I know who specializes in helping victims of domestic violence, walks over to me. Gently she pulls Marley from me and cradles her head on her shoulder. As she leads her down the stairs, she makes sure to block Wigand's body with her own so Marley doesn't see her dead husband. The cop opens the door and I see my friend being taken outside. She doesn't protest, just lets herself be led by the policewoman.

I stand, my legs shaking from being in a cramped sitting position and Jacoby comes over to grab me as I trip over my own feet. "You okay, Cate? Let's get you outside and get some air."

As we walk towards the open door, I stop. Two EMTs come in carrying a body bag and wheeling a stretcher. They quickly check over Wigand's body, put him in the body bag and onto the stretcher. The son-of-a-bitch is wheeled past us. Through the door I see Marley. The cop has kindly taken her behind one of the patrol vans so she doesn't have a full view of the stretcher being pushed over to the ambulance and Wigand's body loaded into the back of it. The ambulance takes off, no siren, no rush. Just delivery of a dead body to the morgue.

"Are you going to arrest Marley?"

Jacoby nods yes. "She's having her rights read to her right now. I don't know if she understands them, but it's procedure. We're taking her to the hospital to get checked out, then we have to hold her, Cate. She shot and killed Wigand."

"Look Joe, don't cuff her, okay? I'll ride in the back of the patrol van with her."

"You're breaking rules here, Cate. I can't allow that."

"Jesus Christ, Joe! You have no idea of the trauma this woman has suffered for years, *for years,* at the hands of that sadistic bastard, Wigand. Bend a damned rule, can't you? Arrest me too, and then I can sit in the back with her. I'm only asking you to listen to me and don't cuff her."

"Listen to me, Cate, she killed a man, a man I will grant you that completely deserved to be killed. But, you know as well as I do that I would be cuffing her for her own protection, not to mention the protection of those transporting her. It's standard procedure and it's there as a safety measure. I have no idea, and neither do you, of what she might do. She's suicidal and that means she's dangerous."

I look over at Marley standing next to the police van, her head down, her body visibly shaking. Numb. She looks defeated, as if she's just as dead as Wigand. Joe Jacoby sees it too and something, a visceral human emotion for an abused victim, moves him deeply. He slams his open palm down hard on the van. "God-damn it!" With a deep sigh, he pats me on the shoulder.

"Okay, Cate. No cuffs and you can ride with us. But, I want you upfront with me."

I thank him. Jesus, what a night!

As I walk toward Marley, an officer anxiously calls to Jacoby. "Captain? Just got a call from one of our men at the hospital. It's about Benigni. He—"

Will!

Exhaustion and the heightened stress of the last five hours take their toll and my body crumbles. My face hits the pavement before Jacoby can catch me.

CHAPTER 31

F OR THE SECOND TIME in two weeks, I find myself in a police vehicle, sirens wailing, racing to a hospital—and Will. Rather than wait for another ambulance, Jacoby bundled me into the backseat of his police captain's van after I blacked-out, and headed straight to Lenox Hospital. He grabbed one of the officers at the scene and commandeered him to be the driver so he could sit with me in the back.

I can't believe I fainted! I take it as a point of pride that nothing, blood, wounds, week-old bloated corpses, *absolutely nothing* that I have seen in my line of work has ever made me faint. Sick to my stomach, sure, but never unconscious. I am lucky to be able to look at a crime victim critically and objectively.

My mind is fuzzy and my vision blurry, when I slowly come back to consciousness. Marley is seated directly across from me, head down, eyes closed, with her arms tight across her chest in a protective mode. Jacoby, and the cop who took charge of her, sit on either side of her.

I can feel the van zipping around cars and hear the siren blaring as I struggle to a sitting position. Expertly driving the van at breakneck speed is a young, fierce-looking cop who would do just fine on any professional speedway.

"Joe?" I lick my lips nervously.

"Hey, welcome back to the land of the conscious, Cate. Been way too quiet in here without you talking." Jacoby gives me a concerned look and smiles gently.

"How long was I out?"

"Less than fifteen minutes. Your pulse was strong and you were breathing okay, but you scared me there, honey. Never figured a strong, healthy, full-of-hell-fire woman like you would pass the hell out."

I'm afraid to ask but, I swallow hard and say, "Will? You got news about Will back there. Tell me, Joe. Now."

Jacoby reaches across and touches my face. My eyes fill with tears at his tender expression. Bad news is coming, I know it. I brace myself for the worst.

But I'm wrong. Seeing my stricken look, Jacoby hastens to assure me that Will Benigni is just fine.

"Hey, honey," he grabs my face gently, making me look at him. "It's *okay*. Will's waking up, Cate. The call was about *him waking up*. He's finally coming out of that damned drug-induced coma and, God-damn it, it's about time."

The tears fall rapidly down my face. "Oh my God, Joe! I thought, I mean for a moment there, I thought—well, you know. Dr. Charles said it would be about thirty hours until he was conscious. Oh, Joe!"

"I know, I know. I'm a prize jerk for not telling you right away. It's okay, Cate. Will's okay."

I choke back a sob and Jacoby reaches over to the front of the van and takes a box of tissues. Grabbing a handful, I bury my face in them. Without looking up at me, Marley whispers, "Ice Cream." I grab her hand and squeeze it. She's so lost inside herself, I wonder if she will ever again become the gutsy Marley Weiner I once knew. She will need a lot of help and I'm going to make sure that she gets it.

I wipe away my tears and give Marley a sudden hug. "See Marl? Will is okay. He's okay!"

She doesn't answer, but somehow I think she heard me; I hope so anyway.

I face Jacoby. I have to ask another favor. "Hey, Joe? Any way you can find out about Bo, the neighborhood guy who was shot by Wigand? The ambulance took him here. I'd like to know how he's doing."

"Yeah, sure, I can check on him. Don't worry about anything or anyone else. You just go on and see Benigni now. I'll get back to you."

"I will. Listen, Bo has a friend who went in the ambulance with him. His name is Hey and he's afraid of cops but I want to know if he's still here, waiting and all."

Jacoby raises his eyebrows. "Hay? Like hay for horses?"

"No, Hey as in 'hey you.'"

"Really? Hey?"

"That's what he answers to. No idea of his real name. Anyway, much appreciated if you can see if Hey and Bo are okay."

"Only for you, Harlow, only for you." He smiles and then pulls me into a great big bear hug. He muffles what I think is a sob against my shoulder. The captain is a sweet mush under his tough exterior. I hug back.

The driver brings the van to a stop outside the front door of the hospital. Jacoby gets out with me and talks quietly to the police officer in the back seat. She nods and helps Marley to exit the van.

"Officer Corelli will take your friend to get checked out. They may want to keep her for observation, so you won't be able to see her until sometime later today."

Day? I look at my watch. It's 5:06 in the morning. I left the hospital at just before 11:00 last night, and now it's a brand-new day. Unbelievable what has happened in that time frame. I'm anxious to get to Will, but before I do, I walk back to where Officer Corelli is gently taking Marley to the ER.

"Officer Corelli? Her name is Marley Weiner. Call her Marley, okay? She's my friend and she's the bravest person I know. Remember, she is Marley."

The officer nods and smiles at me, then says, "Come on Marley. My name is Liz and I'm going to take good care of you. Let's go inside."

Myrtle, Melissa, and Harry greet me when I enter the waiting area. Melissa envelopes me in a honeysuckle-scented hug while Harry timidly pats my back. Myrtle patiently waits for her turn to hug me and then leads me where she knows I want to go—Will's room.

"He's still a bit out of it all, Catherine. Giles is in there with Dr. Charles." She hugs me tightly. "Go on in there, honey. Will needs to see you."

The cops guarding Will's room talk briefly with me as they get ready to leave. Since Wigand is dead, there's no need for them to guard Will twenty-four hours a day. One officer will still be here, but he'll be in the waiting room. I let them know how safe I felt knowing that New York City's finest were on the job protecting one of their own.

Once inside his room I notice that Will's bed has been raised so that he's in a sitting position while Dr. Charles is monitoring his vitals. Giles is over by the window, leaning against the wall. He sees me and signals me to go over to Will. Dr. Charles finishes his check-up, tells me that the crucial healing process is going well, and says he'll talk to me tomorrow. He and Giles leave the room and it's just Will and me.

"Will." My voice breaks and I start to cry. "Oh, God, Will!"

"Hi, baby," says a scratchy-voiced Will looking at me with sleepy eyes. The endotracheal tube has been removed. "How's my baby-girl? Giles said you were on a case." He takes a deep breath as if the effort of using his voice is tiring. "Worried about you, baby."

He was worried about me! I swallow hard. He looks so exhausted and defenseless lying there. And he's asking *me* how I am.

"I'm fine, I'm okay. How are *you* feeling?"

He reaches his hand out for me and I grab it, then sit on the side of his bed. "Alive and fuzzy-headed." He gives a short laugh then grimaces in pain and places his other hand on his chest. "Damn stitches."

"Will, do you remember what happened to you?"

"Not much. The doctor told me I was hit in the head and then shot. But, the details are a blur."

"So you don't remember who did this to you?"

He sleepily shakes his head no and I decide not to ask any more questions. I'm not going to tell him about anything that has been going on either. There will be time for that. When he's ready, I'll fill him in on everything that has happened.

"Come here. Let me hold you."

I look at the tubes still connected to his body and hesitate. Will pulls me closer to him. "Just come here, baby. I need to feel you in my arms."

I gently settle into the solid, familiar warmth of his body, being extra careful not to lean on his still-bandaged chest. Instead, I snuggle on his shoulder and wrap my arms lightly around his neck. He pulls me closer to him. Under the odors of antiseptic and medicine, I inhale a trace of the real Will. That nice, clean, male smell that I love. His breathing is steady and peaceful and within a short time, we begin to breathe in-synch. Both of us doze on and off, coming awake each time to realize that we're both here, both alive, both grateful as hell to still have each other.

I'm dimly aware of the nurses coming in on their nightly rounds to check on Will, but they don't disturb us. I know it's strictly against policy to allow anyone to sleep in a patient's bed in ICU *with* the patient, but somehow I know that Dr. Charles has broken the rules for me. I also know that Giles more than likely had a hand in the rule-breaking. Seriously, though, if anyone had told me to get up out of Will's bed, and his arms, they would have had a fight on their hands. No way was I leaving the sweet peace and comfort of Will's body next to mine.

Sometime before noon, I am dimly aware of Will's hand softly caressing my breast and sliding down to my hip. He gives my butt a good squeeze before letting his hand rest on my thigh. The hand that squeezes me is a little weak, but stronger than I expected it to be. That, almost more than anything, assures me that the healing process Dr. Charles mentioned, is working just fine. My Will is going to be okay.

CHAPTER 32

THERE'S A GENTLE KNOCK on the door to ICU Room 12. It's Melissa holding a pretty Hermés travel bag. Will is sitting up in bed and sipping orange juice through a straw. I'm looking out the window at a very pretty late afternoon in August. Funny how I never really noticed the blue of the sky or the gentle flutter of leaves on the trees. Or, if I did happen to notice, it was brief and I never gave it much thought. But, today, everything looks beautiful, fresh, and new to me.

Will and I slept until after early afternoon. Neither one of us wanted to get out of bed but Dr. Charles came in and spent considerable time checking Will and talking to him. Will's responses were a bit slow and he took extra time when considering an answer to questions posed by Dr. Charles, but the good doctor seemed satisfied with his examination both physical and verbal.

I take out my phone to see a text from Jacoby telling me that Bo is stable but that Hey is nowhere to be found and that as soon as I can, I need to give my official statement about Wigand's murder to the police. He ends with info about Marley.

'Marley Weiner, aka Wendy Wigand, is detained and being evaluated.'

In other words, she's in the psych unit here, under guard, and will more than likely be transferred to Bellevue if deemed necessary by the doctors. I key in a response that I'll check in with Jacoby later today.

"Hey you two," is Melissa's greeting to us as she hesitates at the door. I signal her to come in. She places the Hermés bag on the only chair in the room.

"Cate, I brought you a change of clothes." She opens the travel bag and hands me soft navy blue pants and a white shimmery top. Both have store tags still on them. Then she pulls out a shoe box, opening it up to reveal a new pair of low-heeled blue sandals.

I take the clothes from her and see that they are from Barney's New York. Then I look at the tags, but the only thing the tags tell me about the clothes is the material content and care instruction of each garment. Of course, Melissa has had the salesperson cut the price cut off each one. I start to protest, but think better of it. Melissa will only make an excuse about some incredible sale or how it's an early birthday present. She gives with her heart.

"And, of course, some lovely new lingerie," she says handing me tissue-wrapped panties and a bra in a soft, delicate shade of light lilac. "I hope you approve," she smiles at Will who gives her a weak thumb's up. He closes his eyes and in a second he is back to sleep.

Melissa comes over to the bed and whispers some spell over him. Then, taking out a small vial from her bag, she gently massages his temples and forehead with scented oil. As she's done before, she moistens her fingers with the oil and runs them through his hair, making his natural sandy color look dark.

Her eyes closed, she murmurs a few words that I've heard her say to Will over and over again.

"*J'en appelle à la volonté des dieux. Votre cœur et votre esprit vont guérir ensemble.*" I call upon the will of the gods. Your heart and your mind will heal together.

I take a shaky breath. Since my own brush with the magic and voodoo of New Orleans and the fiercely powerful saint they call Ursule, I am willing to believe in anything that helps.

Before we leave, she gently spills one drop of the oil onto his chest and then places a soft white scarf with some large red markings on it, loosely around his neck. She tells me the scarf is from her Tante Anjali and has been imbued with tremendous healing spells.

"Let's go, darling. You're eating one of Harry's lovely pastries. Then, you're coming to my brownstone to bathe and change."

Over my protest, Melissa waves her hand. "Cate, darling, Will is fine. You need to get out of those clothes and take a nice, long shower. And the interns' bathroom just won't cut it for that. My, God, Cate, you've been wearing the same clothes for over twenty-four hours! My place is closer than yours, so you are coming there with me."

"I don't know, Melissa. I still feel as if I should stay here, now that Will's awake."

"Darling, please!"

I shake my head no.

"All right. Then, let's do this. Talk with Dr. Charles and, if he feels it's okay for you to leave here for two hours, then you'll say yes and come home with me. Does that work for you? Besides," she adds slyly, "you looking fabulous and smelling of Chanel will do Will a world of good. He needs to see you like that."

I hesitate, but only for a second. The thought of showering in that cat-litter box size interns' bathroom is kind of gross and discouraging. Melissa's large bathroom has two rainfall shower heads at different levels and pale blue marble tile. Those, plus the scented flower petals and lemon verbena she keeps in the room make for a spa-like experience.

"Okay, but only if Dr. Charles thinks it's okay for me to leave. And after I go see Bo."

"Of course, darling." She smiles sweetly and leads me down the hall to where Harry is waiting.

$$\infty$$

Harry's got his pastries piled up on the magazine table in the waiting room and he's handing his goodies out to people who are waiting there while a family member or friend is in surgery. A couple of nurses and doctors on their breaks have come over to partake of Harry's divine concoctions. He's a contented man handing out pastries and napkins to whomever want them. But when he sees Melissa and me, he grabs a box that seems to have been hidden under Myrtle's sweater on a chair, and immediately walks over to us. Myrtle is not here so I'm assuming she's either at the office or at my brownstone.

"Cate! I have your favorite here, I kept it just for you." Harry opens the box to reveal two chocolate cream-filled cannoli. My mouth waters at the sight of them.

I take one and offer the other one to Melissa who politely declines. "I've had two already, plus a divine apple and cheese puff."

After the cannolo and a bottle of water, I feel wide awake. I leave Harry, who is deep in a discussion with a doctor on the best filling for strudel, and go in search of Dr. Charles. I find him in Will's room again. The doctor turns when I walk in.

"Hello Cate. Will is still asleep, but I wanted to check the incision on his chest. It's healing nicely." He nods toward the hallway. "I've finished here. Let's take a walk."

We walk to his office where we sit on chairs facing each other. He looks at me expectantly, ready to answer any questions I may have.

"I'm pleased with his progress, Cate."

"He slept for over nine hours, woke up and fell asleep again. Is this normal?"

"Perfectly normal."

"But I thought that he'd be more awake. I mean he's finally out of that drug-induced coma."

"He is, but you have to remember that the effects of those barbiturates we used are still inside him. He's also on pain meds. All those, plus what his body has been through, the concussion and the surgery, are what's making him doze off and on. But everything seems to be progressing well, so I'm not concerned with him sleeping. In fact, deep sleep is very good for him right now. Don't worry, Cate. His body knows what it needs."

"What about his memory? He hasn't mentioned anything about what happened to him. I asked him last night, but he said it was all a blur. Is that normal too?"

"Yes. He knows where he is and we've told him he was shot and has a concussion. When I asked him what he remembered about the shooting, he was unable to tell me. His memory is cloudy right now, but that's to be expected. In most cases it comes back slowly. Technically he's a healthy man; he's just badly injured and has had a lot of medication. So let's give it a day or so. I'm confident he'll remember."

"Dr. Charles, do you think it's all right if I leave the hospital for a couple of hours? I mean, if you feel it's better for me to stay here, I will. I don't really want to leave. Just that my friend, well, she wants me to go to her place to shower and change and—"

"I think that's a good, positive thing to do," he says putting up his hand in the universal signal meant to politely interrupt. "Will is being carefully monitored and a two-hour break may be just what *your* body is telling you it needs."

I repeat what he just said, "What my body is telling me. You may be right, Dr. Charles."

He touches my hand. "Cate, I do not want to pry into your business, but I have heard what you went through last night. Giles told me some of it and I've heard the officers outside discussing you being held hostage, the shooting of your friend, the murder. You need to get a few hours to clear your mind and take care of yourself. Trust me, Will doesn't need a baby-sitter. He needs to do exactly what he *is* doing, and that's to sleep."

I just nod. What a hell of a night I've had!

"Okay. I'll be back a little later. I have to go check on my friend, the guy who is the shooting victim. He's scared of hospitals."

Dr. Charles stands, gathers an armful of folders, and walks me out into the hall. "By the way, Cate, about your friend who was shot? You not only saved that man's life, you saved his leg from severe and permanent damage. Good going with that tourniquet."

He leaves me to go on his afternoon rounds while I go check to see where Bo has been placed.

CHAPTER 33

MYRTLE IS SEATED NEAR a comfortably sedated Bo who is having his blood pressure taken when I enter his room. He gives me a goofy grin and points to his left leg which is elevated by a medical hoist. There is no sign of Hey. Probably ran away after they got to the hospital. I will have to find him later.

I'm so glad to see Myrtle. Giles must have told her about Bo and this indomitable, kind and gentle woman, who knows of Bo's fears, made it her business to find him.

"No Hey?"

"Um, no, Catherine. Sorry, honey."

"Did you see him at all? Jacoby couldn't find him."

"No. No, um, I haven't. No idea where he is," she coughs discreetly and looks at the technician who's removing the BP cuff from Bo's arm.

"No idea at all?"

"Um, no, um. As I said, I have no idea where he, um, might be."

Something is not quite right with her answers. "Myrtle, are you sure—"

"How is Will doing and how are you feeling?"

Surprised at her interruption, I tell her we're both doing fine, and that I'm going to Melissa's for a couple of hours.

"Good. That will be good for you. Everything is status quo, both at your brownstone and at the office. Only one new case came in, and I took the liberty of taking care of it myself. Just a background check on a potential employee for a restaurant, not anything major. Easy to do."

I raise my eyebrows. "Wow, Myrtle, we'll make an official PI out of you yet."

"No chance of that, Catherine," she says primly. "I am perfectly happy being your secretary and advisor. Checking information online, making a few phone calls, that's all the PI work I care to do."

The technician nods to Myrtle on his way out and she walks over to the bed. Leaning over Bo, she tells him that she has to talk to me privately but that she'll be right back. Then she hands him a large bag with the words 'Paco's Tacos' on the front and admonishes him not to eat them all.

"You have to save some for—um—for later. Do you know what I mean? Save some. And don't let the nurses see you eating them."

"Myrtle!" I laugh once we're outside the room. "Paco's Tacos? You got Bo tacos?"

"Yes, I did, Catherine. The poor man was crying and in pain and kept telling me you had promised him, and his friend Hey, tacos. I had to get them for him. It was the only way I could get him to let anyone change the dressing on his leg."

"I did promise him. I promised him tacos so he would leave the building and be out of harm's way. But it didn't work and it almost got him killed."

I fill Myrtle in on every single detail about Wigand, Marley, and Bo. I tell her about Bo coming back to the office after I had gotten him and Hey to leave, all the way to Wigand shooting him.

"Marley killed Eric Wigand, Myrtle. In my book that's justifiable after all the abuse she received over the years. The miscarriages she suffered, the baby boy dying in her arms. Wigand deserved to die."

"Oh, Catherine. I'm so glad this nightmare is almost over.

First Will being shot and that frightening head trauma, then you being in danger of losing your life! All because of some sick, bullying, violent man. And your poor, poor friend Marley."

She covers her eyes with her hands. For the first time since I've known her, I see Myrtle's seemingly unbreakable façade crack just a little under the cruel pressure called fear. Fear of losing someone you love to unreasonable violence. Just for a brief second she looks old and tired. But her hands come away from her face and when she faces me again I see the ageless, strong, no-nonsense woman I adore, and who has been a second mother to me for so many years.

"Come with me," she whispers, leading me cautiously down the hall to a bathroom that is half-hidden from the view of passersby. She keeps checking to see if anyone is around the area. Curiously, I follow her. Why is she being so secretive?

When we're standing outside the door, she looks around the corner and back up the way we came. When she's sure there's no one coming our way, she taps lightly, three times, on the door of the bathroom. A man dressed in white hospital scrubs comes out and my eyes widen in surprise. It's Hey!

Myrtle quickly walks him down the hall to Bo's room. "Go ahead, Hey, go on in and see Bo. There's a bag filled with tacos for both of you. There's four tacos each and I'm sure Bo has already eaten at least two. Go in now before he eats the rest of them. I'll be out here."

She closes the door and faces me with her no-nonsense look.

"Catherine, Giles called me after he came to the hospital. He called because he knew that Hey was terrified of being here and, since I'm a familiar face to Hey, Giles thought I could help him. Hey hid from Captain Jacoby, I have no idea where, and only came out of hiding when he saw Giles. When I arrived, Hey was outside the hospital with Giles, who was trying to calm him down. He was hysterical. We didn't want him to run off and maybe get lost in the city. He has the mind of a child when he gets upset.

"He's been doing so well since he began living at Bo's place, hasn't wandered off as much. So I told Giles I would handle it, and I did. It may be on the off-side of legal, but I was willing to take a calculated risk. I came up with a plan to keep him here and to let him see Bo. Giles supplied the scrubs and I've been hiding Hey in the men's restroom. I told him that when anyone comes in the bathroom, he is to hide in one of the stalls. He doesn't have to be afraid of doctors or nurses, I can keep an eye on him, and he can see his friend, Bo. So far it's working. Giles is coming by later. Again, this is entirely my idea and I take full responsibility."

I don't say anything. I'm so glad that Myrtle is a take-charge woman who came to Hey's aid. She not only has heart but a practical mind that works to benefit everyone who knows her. I love her.

"Well? Aren't you going to say anything, Catherine?"

"Yes. I'm proud of the way you handled this and grateful from the bottom of my heart." I hug her tightly. "Myrtle, I've said it before and I'll keep on saying it. You are one hell of a gem!" I laugh. "There's only one thing we have to work on concerning your, let's call it, skullduggery."

"May I ask just what that may be, Catherine?"

"You need to develop a liar's poker face and stop saying 'um.' Dead give-away that you're not telling the truth."

We walk back into Bo's room and find both Bo and Hey watching the Disney channel, engrossed in a cartoon show. The Paco's Tacos bag lies empty and crumpled on Bo's bed. I wave in their direction, hug Myrtle, and leave to go to Melissa's lovely brownstone.

I stand under the dual rain shower heads in Melissa's bathroom for over a half hour, willing the water to wash away the filth of my time spent in the company of Eric Wigand. The hot water and the smell of lemon verbena are soothing and reviving. I'll have to remember to get some of this soap for Will when he comes to recuperate at my brownstone. That he will be coming back to my place after he's discharged from the hospital is a welcoming, and positive thought. A positive reality now that he's out of the coma.

I towel off and dry my hair in the massive master suite.

Melissa has left the new clothes she bought for me lying on her bed. It is a pleasure putting on each article of clothing, beginning with the beautiful lingerie. I feel more like myself again. There's nowhere to put my gun. These pants are not like my jeans where I can hook my Smith and Wesson in the waistband. These are too soft to hold a gun. I poke my head out into the hallway and ask Melissa if I can leave my gun in her bedroom until I come back to get it later.

"Yes, I'll put it in the safe in the walk-in closet. No problem."

When I come out into her living room, dressed, and with my hair in its traditional ponytail, I find Melissa on the phone, her appointment book open in front of her.

"Yes, darling, I have been busy. I know, I know. Well, can we change the appointment to next week? Thursday is good. Yes, nine o'clock. That works perfectly. You'll have to excuse me now. I have a call coming in from my beloved aunt, so I will speak with you later. Yes, darling, I'm looking forward to seeing you as well. 'Bye."

She hangs up and clicks on the call waiting button, switching easily to French to talk with her aunt in New Orleans and say that all is well. *"Oui, Tante Anjali. Tout va bien."*

Melissa smiles when she sees me and gestures toward the highboy table near the window where she has set up her Cuisinart coffee maker. Finishing her call, she asks me if I want anything to eat and I shake my head no.

Coffee mug in hand I wander over to the large window facing Central Park. No matter the time of year, the park is always pretty, but late summer is an especially lovely time. While Melissa makes several more phone calls, I sit and watch the joggers and slow-moving foot traffic go by.

All those people down there, living lives that are so secret to strangers. Smiles, laughter, pleasantries pass between us all and nobody, saving close friends and family, really knows us at all. Sometimes, even those closest to us are clueless about our deepest feelings and fears.

"Good morning, how are *you*? Really? That is funny!" I hear her silvery laugh, the one that always reminds me of the delicate sound of wind chimes in a summer breeze. "Yes, seven tonight is an excellent time for me. That new Portuguese restaurant sounds wonderful. I've been eager to try it. Yes, you too. All right, I'll see you later, Giles."

Giles? My Giles? My head turns toward Melissa who is busy writing something into her calendar. Melissa and Giles? It might just be dinner, but I smile at the thought of my best friend and my former lover as a couple. Talk about being clueless concerning those closest to us! Giles never mentioned that he was taking Melissa to dinner. But, then again, why should he?

I daydream about how nice it would be to go out with another couple. Will and I and Melissa and Giles. Dinners, Broadway shows, maybe even a weekend getaway. Fun. We could all get along, I know.

Then a sobering thought hits me. I love both Melissa and Giles, but I also know what Melissa does for a living. So does Giles. I sip my coffee and watch the people passing through the paths in Central Park. Strangers with their own lives.

We all have our secrets.

CHAPTER 34

"**M**S. HARLOW, SHE'S BEHAVING in a manner that is perfectly in line with what she's been through. She will answer to the name Marley, that's a fairly good sign. Out of touch with the real world, though, I would say. She is suffering from PTSD from her years as an abused woman and that's definitely to be expected. She's withdrawing into a shell, not responding and she's also acting out her fears."

I'm on the fifth floor, the Psychiatry and Evaluation area, of the hospital. The psychiatrist sits facing me from across the desk in her office. She's got the psych eval. on Marley on her desktop computer and she is spouting all the medical terms at her disposal.

I fidget. I'm eager to get to see Marley and then go to ICU. Dr. Charles told me that Will might be able to go to a regular private room in a day or two and that I should begin to pack some of his personal items. Several more get-well gifts have come in for Will. One that I know that he'll love is an authentic Yankees baseball bat, signed by the entire team, that Javy was able to get. I re-cross my legs tightly to stop them from jittering.

"Acting out in what way?"

"Well, I can give you one example. When one of our doctors approached her, she began to cringe and then tried to find a place to hide. She was screaming that he was going to kill her. That he had killed her baby. She practically begged us to help her.

"This doctor is a lamb, kind and gentle, yet she became hysterical when she saw him. He had to back off and let a female doctor examine her."

"Is that male doctor on the floor now?" I turn to look through the plate glass walls that separate her office from the patients' solarium.

"I'm not sure, I think he went to the—oh, wait, there he is, see? The man in the dark slacks and white turtleneck shirt? He's talking to that patient over by the window."

I look where she is pointing. The man is short, muscular, and has thick dark hair. The pattern of his shirt makes it look as if he's got white gauze wrapped around his throat. I don't find him threatening but I can understand why Marley might. He reminds me of Eric Wigand and I can just imagine Marley looking at him and seeing the man who tortured and abused her for years.

"Do you know when she might be released? I know that she's being arraigned soon. Any idea when she will be brought before a judge?"

"You'll have to ask that of Captain Jacoby. And, anyway, we're not finished with the entire evaluation. If we think it's necessary, we will have her sent to Bellevue, if that's possible." She closes the laptop with a strong click. "I'm only giving you this information because Captain Jacoby has authorized me to do so. He says that, while technically not her next of kin, you are basically her main contact."

"Any other ways she's acting out?"

I breathe deeply thinking what it may mean if I'm her main contact. I may have to file papers petitioning the court to assign me as her legal representative. Doing that won't be a problem. I still have a lot of strong contacts in the judicial system. It's the responsibility that concerns me. Legal conservatorship. I will be responsible for what happens to Marley until she's deemed mentally fit to deal with life on her own. That's a frightening prospect for someone who, until now, basically cares only for myself and two independent house cats.

The psychiatrist scans her written notes, and then looks up. "Marley seems to think that the man she killed, her husband, is still alive and just waiting to come after her. Every time she hears a phone ring, she jumps in terror. We need to assess her further before completing our evaluation."

I want to talk to Marley myself and make my own my own 'evaluation and assessment.'

"I have to tell you that I spent over three hours with her before she shot and killed Eric Wigand. She told me everything that had happened to her over the past few years. She cried, she was afraid, but she was definitely in touch with reality. She knew what had gone on in her life and, more importantly, what was happening at the moment."

The woman looks at me levelly. This unnerves me, a psych professional looking at me as if she's evaluating me. "That was before she pulled the trigger that killed her husband, Ms. Harlow. Plus, the police captain's report we have says that she somehow believed that Mr. Wigand was still alive, even though you and the captain assured her that the man was indeed dead. She also tried to commit suicide by attempting to shoot herself there in your office building. Her fears are real *in her own mind,* but they are not reality. Trauma, especially the kind your friend has suffered, leads to a person having a so-called split reaction to reality, feeling like she's struggling with two or more people inside her mind. She may have spoken to you coherently then but, now, well, she is in trauma. Marley is extremely fearful and not in current reality. Do you understand?"

"Well, yes, sure, after she shot Eric Wigand she was still afraid that he wasn't really dead, but isn't that to be expected? It's similar to someone being released from prison; hard to believe you're free. I know she was in trauma last night."

"It is our belief that *she* still believes he is alive and coming after her. It is her Wendy persona. That has to be dealt with by professionals."

"She knows she's Marley," I say defensively.

"We note that she answers to the name, yes."

"Marley's not dangerous, right?"

"That depends. If you're asking if there is a danger that she will harm herself, it's entirely possible. If you're asking if she has shown any sign that she wants to harm another person, the answer would be, we don't know yet. You really never can know for certain what she may be capable of doing if her fears overwhelm her."

I'm annoyed at all the medical psycho-babble and words like 'assess and evaluate.' I stand. "I'd like to see her."

"I don't think that's a good idea, Ms. Harlow. Seriously, it is my professional opinion—."

"Seriously, I don't care what you think or what your professional opinion may be. As Captain Jacoby has told you, I am her main contact and, as such, I am *telling* you, not *asking* you, that I want to see her."

"I still don't think it's a wise move."

"I have already filed papers with the court to be a temporary conservator for Marley Weiner," I lie smoothly. It's just a simple lie because I will definitely file as soon as I can call one of my contacts at the courthouse. "Now, are you going to let me to see Marley or do I have to go over your head to get what I want?"

Sighing, she picks up the phone on her desk and keys in a number. I hear her tell the person on the other end that a 'Cate Harlow' has been approved to see one of the patients.

Replacing the receiver, she again gives me an evaluating look and says, "This is not a good idea but, since you insist, her room number is 4. You can't go there alone; someone will have to escort you. Stop by the desk for a staff member to take you to her. I hope all goes well."

She puts out her hand and I shake it. "Oh, one more thing. Before you go to see her, you might want to stop by the cafeteria. Marley keeps asking for ice cream. Good day Ms. Harlow."

∞

The only ice cream Marley wants is me and I know it. Marley never ate ice cream because it hurt her teeth.

I stand in the doorway of the brightly-painted patient's room watching her. She's seated near a barred window, her arms wrapped tightly around her knees which are drawn up to her chest. She looks broken and scared.

Down the hall, a short distance away is one of Jacoby's officers, dressed in civilian clothes. He's been asked to stand there so as not to frighten other patients who are free to walk around. Besides, Marley's door is locked from the outside; there's no need for him to be closer.

"Hi, Marley. It's me. Ice Cream. Here." In my hands is a napkin-covered paper plate of Harry's pastries. I uncover them and bring them to her. "These are really good, Marl."

Tentatively she takes one and holds it in her hand. I make a big show of eating one, hoping that she'll follow my lead.

"Oh, Marley, these are delicious! Take a bite. C'mon, Marley, so good!"

She studies the pastry intently, almost as if there's a message written there in the swirls of powdered sugar on top. Food can be a lifesaver. From traumatized kids to the confused elderly to homeless street people, I've seen how food can help ease fears, if only for a short time. God knows it's always helped me. She stuffs it in her mouth, almost as if she is afraid she won't get a chance to eat again. Quickly I hand her another. She eats it like a ravenous wolf.

"Marley, I want to get you out of here. Okay?"

"Okay," she whispers almost as if she's afraid someone is listening. "I don't want to stay here."

"Of course you don't," I say, sounding to myself like Melissa sounds when she's trying to help me through a problem.

"Listen Marley, in order for me to get you out of here, I have to make some calls. First, I need to contact someone in the court system so that I can file for temporary conservatorship of you. I want to do that today. Do you remember what that is, conservatorship?"

She looks at me blankly. I feel sick inside. Marley was a whiz at legal terminology. Has she blanked out all that she knew?

"Okay, it just means that I'm going to make sure that you're safe and well taken care of. So when we're finished eating, I'll make the call over to the probate clerk downtown and ask to file as your temporary conservator." I stress the word *temporary* hoping that she will somehow know that she will be fully capable of taking care of herself soon. I hope so anyway.

"Then I'm going to call Captain Jacoby. Remember him?"

Another blank look. I get up to throw away my empty plate and napkin. Seeing me walk to the trash can near the door, Marley urgently calls to me.

"Don't leave me. I can't be found. Please!"

I hurry back and sit facing her. "No, Marl, it's okay. This place is safe. You're okay here."

She shakes her head vigorously and grabs my hand tightly. "No, no. I'm not. He'll find me, he always does."

She still thinks Wigand is alive. I sigh. I'll deal with that later. Right now I have to make those calls.

"No, I'm not leaving. I'll stay here for a while. Let me make those calls I told you about. I'll sit right over there, just on that window seat. You'll still see me."

I don't want her to hear me call about being her guardian. The wording *non compos mentis* are sometimes used in a petition for conservatorship and she might remember what that means. The kindest definition for that Latin phrase is unstable. The worst is severely mentally ill.

Reluctantly she lets go of my hand, but keeps her eyes on me as I walk a few feet away. I place a call to an old buddy down at probate. After the usual pleasantries and a few pertinent questions, I set the conservatorship in motion with a promise to make it down to the probate office to sign the legal documents as soon as I can. Second call is to Jacoby and I get his voice mail. Leaving a quick message and the firm, *'Call back as soon as you get this message,'* I go back to where Marley is sitting.

"Marley, everything is going to be okay." She shakes her head. "Seriously, it will. Listen, I can stay for another hour but after that I have to leave. There's Will to think about so, I can't stay too long."

My phone rings and I answer it to hear Myrtle say that she's going to the office for a few hours to catch up on some of my smaller cases. She says she just left Will and that all is good.

"Will was experiencing some pain, so the doctor has increased his pain meds, but he's fine. He's dozing right now and Dr. Charles says that's good."

"He's still in ICU, room 12, right?" I ask. "That's fine. At least I know where to find him."

I don't notice Marley's eyes glaze over in fear when I say, '*He's still in ICU, room 12, right?*'

Or how she is watching me intently when I say, '*At least I know where to find him.*'

Or how her hands clench into tight fists.

I don't notice because I view Marley as a victim and not a threat.

And that is a big mistake.

CHAPTER 35

CAPTAIN JACOBY IS NOT a happy camper. On the other end of the phone, he is giving me a head's up by telling me that Marley Weiner aka Wendy Wigand is going to be arraigned in less than two hours' time. He's telling me that after her arraignment, she will more than likely be brought to Riker's Island, Women's Division. He's not happy about the prospect of Riker's Island for Marley. And he is not happy that I'm fighting him on this.

"Come on, Joe! Riker's Island for God's sake. She'll never survive there."

"There is absolutely nothing I can do about this, Cate. You're lucky that I can even give you these two hours with Marley Weiner and that I'm letting you be the one to tell her that we're coming to take her. Look, Cate, I know how you feel, Riker's Island and all, but this is what I'm hearing about where she'll go. It's not definite but, the Assistant District Attorney on this is a real hard-nosed prick about what she terms is cold-blooded murder with intent."

"Who is this prick?" I'm standing outside the room where Marley is talking with a very nice young psychiatrist. There are no windows on the door, so I can't see how she's doing. "Give me a name. Maybe it's someone I can talk to and see if they can't recommend Bellevue instead."

"Gloria Gedski. Defense lawyers call her Guilty Gedski because, unlike what our laws tell us about people being innocent until proven guilty, Gedski believes everyone is guilty and no one is innocent. Plus, she's got an impressive track record of getting the accused held without bail. You know her? You've been out of the Office of the Public Defender for a long time."

I wince. "Yeah, I know her. My talking to her won't help. She hates me."

"Hates you? Great. Why?"

"I once corrected some legal documents she filed with the Office of the Public Defender. You know we had to proof them for errors."

"Yeah, so?"

"She had a lot of spelling errors in her legal Latin terms. Her English sucked too. Really awful grammatical errors, too. I sent them back to the DA's office circled in red."

"Red?"

"Yeah, red pen. Listen, my parents were teachers, you know. I learned it from them. Anyway she reported me to the DA. The DA laughed at her and told her that maybe I knew more about her job than she did. She's hated me ever since."

"Jesus, Cate. Anyway, I'm coming with two other officers to bring Marley Weiner down to the arraignment. You can show up down there if you want, but you have to go in your own car. I can't let you ride with her this time."

"Right, I understand. I'll follow you down. See you later."

"My suggestion is that you get a seasoned defense attorney for your friend. Don't rely on one provided by the courts. You know what I'm saying, right? Get a damned good lawyer who knows their way around a court room and a murder case."

"Thanks, Joe. I will."

I hang up and my phone rings before I can begin the task of calling a lawyer for Marley. It's my friend from the probate court. He's gotten me a temporary conservatorship and is messengering the documents over to the hospital for me to sign. He tells me to make sure that I show them to anyone in charge so they will know all decisions about Marley Weiner have to be approved by me and that she is in my care.

⸺∞⸺

I show the head nurse the conservatorship papers, allowing me to be Marley's temporary guardian. This allows me free access to see her until Captain Jacoby comes to escort her to her arraignment. I have less than a couple of hours to talk to her.

Before I enter the room where they're keeping Marley, I make several phone calls to defense lawyers that I know and finally am able to secure a woman who is willing to do pro bono work on Marley's behalf. She's dealt with abused women before and is a real mama bear when it comes to saving her clients. I give her all the background on what happened at the office building housing *Catherine Harlow Private Investigations* and tell her about the horror Marley suffered at the hands of Eric Wigand. She agrees that Rikers is the wrong place for Marley and promises to meet us down at the arraignment. Good. Two things accomplished. I'm officially in charge of Marley's welfare and she has an excellent lawyer. Now all I have to do is prepare Marley for the arraignment.

⸺∞⸺

"She's very agitated," whispers the nurse practitioner assigned to Marley. She beckons me to the side of the room, farthest from Marley, so that we can talk privately.

"Has someone told her that Captain Jacoby is coming here soon to escort her to her arraignment? She wasn't supposed to be told yet. Is that why she's upset?"

"No, she knows nothing about it."

"Has she said anything about what has happened, mentioned anyone?"

"Yes. I don't know what it means but she started crying and saying, 'I'm so sorry Will.' Then she told me that he's supposed to be dead."

"She said he's dead?"

"Over and over again, yes."

Will, she thinks Will is—I won't allow myself to even have the word in my mind. I shake my head. Marley is regressing back to Weak Wendy's mindset. I've told her that Will survived and I was certain that she understood it. The psychiatrist to whom I spoke is right; Marley does have her own reality, and goes between what's actually real and what she perceives is real.

"All right, okay. Let me go talk to her and see what I can do to calm her down. It's worked before. She listens to me."

"Good luck. Please buzz the desk if you need help."

My conversation with Marley doesn't go as well as I'd hoped it would. She stares out the window most of the time that I'm talking to her. Twice she asked me, *'Is he dead?'*

When I said no, she asked, "Isn't he supposed to be dead? He was shot!"

"No, Marley, no. He's alive, he's in this hospital. He's here."

"I'm sorry Will, I'm sorry. It's my fault. All my fault."

This goes on for almost thirty minutes. Marley, crying because she believes Wigand killed Will, the way he told her he had. Me, trying to convince her that Will is alive and probably going to leave the hospital soon.

Finally, I have an idea. Not the best one I've ever had, given the situation and all, and the fact that Jacoby is coming soon to get Marley. It is certainly an idea which will involve some illegal moves on my part, but one that I feel is necessary, and in Marley's best interest. Besides, illegal has never bothered me. I justify it as a necessity if it is in any way helpful. Before she's hauled off to prison, she needs to see for herself that Will is alive.

I have to take her to Will's room in ICU.

CHAPTER 36

S NEAKING MARLEY TO THE stairwell by the elevators will not be easy. I need to be able to get her out without too much notice. The cop down the hall is a problem but I think I can arrange to bypass him.

Looking at my watch I see that it's almost six, the time when the staff changes. That's also the time when visiting hours are over for the psych floor. New staff coming in, visitors leaving. A little confusion of people going and coming may be exactly what I need. My mind works quickly, assessing the best way to get Marley to Will's room. If we wait until a few minutes past six, when the hall is full of people, we have a better chance of sneaking out.

Or, maybe, *sneaking out* is the wrong way to go. Why not just walk out with the other visitors leaving the floor! Simply *walking out* is a better plan. Two people who have come to see a patient and are now leaving.

We'll have to be quick to avoid the staff who are also leaving. The stairs are our best way out. My logical bet is that after a full day on their feet, most staffers will take the elevator. Technically, Marley is a prisoner and any staffer seeing her leave will call security.

And then there's Jacoby who's coming to take Marley to her

arraignment. I have to remember that. After we see Will, I'll text Jacoby to pick Marley up in the ICU. He'll be angry as hell that I took Marley out of psych, but he'll just have to deal with it—and so will I.

I turn to Marley and talk to her slowly and deliberately.

"Marley, listen to me very carefully. I'm going to take you out of this room, but the only way I can get you out of here right now is if you promise to do as I say. You understand?"

She doesn't answer so I shake her. "Tell me you'll do what I say."

She flinches from my shake, but nods yes.

"Good. Now we're going to walk out the door when visiting hours are over. We're going to walk out with all the other visitors. We have to appear to be like everyone else. To make sure that no one stops us, you have to be quiet. No crying, no talking. Do nothing that will make anyone look at you. You especially don't want to alert that cop out there. Keep your head down. Got it? Answer me."

"Yes."

"Just walk out the door with me as casually as possible. The new staff won't have time to check rooms yet so, if we time it just right, we can leave without them noticing. Don't look at anybody. Don't say anything to anyone, just walk with me toward the elevators."

She looks at the floor, the same way she did when she was first in my office. I hear her whisper something to herself and watch her shake her head.

"Marley! Do you understand what I'm saying? This is the only way for me to get you out of this room. Please just say yes or no, but give me an answer. Do you understand?"

"Yes."

"Okay, here's what we'll do. We'll be walking toward the elevators, but we're not getting on one. There's a stairwell right before the elevators and that's where we're going to go. We're going to slip away from the group of people and go through the door leading to the stairs."

She nods her head, looks up, and stares at me in a strange

way. Almost as if she is seeing me for the first time. "Is he dead?"

"No, Marley, he isn't dead. I told you and now I'm going to show you," I say gently, thinking that once she sees that Will is indeed alive, actual reality may become permanent. I sure as hell hope so.

The sound of three bells comes over the PA system with the announcement, "Visiting hours are now over. Please exit the patients' rooms. Visiting hours are now over."

I take off my sweatshirt and make Marley put it on. I pull the hoodie over her head and let the sides cover her cheeks. I have to hide her from being noticed by Jacoby's man. We're going to look just like any of the other visitors.

"Ready?"

"Yes."

Opening the door, I wait until I see a group of four people heading toward us down the hall. Grabbing Marley by the hand, I lead her out the door, wait a few seconds, then blend in with the group, and walk with them toward the elevator. I slow down as we come to the door marked STAIRS, and let two men and a woman pass in front of us, hiding us from the police officer's view.

Quickly I push Marley through the door and we run down two flights of stairs to ICU.

It seems strange to see no one standing guard outside Will's room. Even though I know Jacoby has pulled the two cop detail and has only one officer stationed in the waiting room 'just in case', it feels almost as if a needed safety precaution is missing. I know Will isn't in danger any more but still, I liked knowing there were two officers there for his protection.

Will is sleeping on his side, with his back to us, when Marley and I enter. The pain meds seem to have worked because he doesn't wake up when we come inside. Melissa must have put oil on his hair again when she was here today because it looks damp and dark. His throat is loosely covered by the white cotton scarf. The red magical symbols embroidered in the cloth by Melissa's

Tante Anjali are in stark contrast to the white. From the doorway they resemble large drops of blood.

I look at Marley. Her reaction on seeing Will is overwhelming. She's standing there, shaking her head, her whole body trembling with emotion. She slowly backs up until her body is flat against the door.

"No." She is staring at Will. "No!"

"Marley? You needed to see that he's—."

"Dead."

"What? No. He's not dead, he's alive."

"Dead, he's supposed to be dead. He shouldn't be alive. He's supposed to be dead." Her voice is low, but frightening. "He's supposed to be dead! Why did you bring me here?"

"Marley." I touch her arm, but she violently shrugs me off.

"Dead! Dead! Dead! He's supposed to be dead, don't you understand? He was shot dead. Don't you know that?"

I stand back from Marley. She has a crazy look on her face.

"He *was* shot, but he's not dead. I don't know what you mean. He's okay, he's alive. He's just sleeping."

"Why isn't he *dead*?"

"Look, Marley, you have to listen to me. Calm down and I'll explain it to you."

"You told me he was dead, you said it! You lied to me."

"No, I never said—."

"You did! You said he was dead!"

Her whole body is shaking. But, instead of what I had mistaken for an emotional release, I now realize is rage. She is trembling with rage. A rage so hot, my own body feels as if it is standing next to an inferno. Marley's battered face is engorged with an all-consuming hatred. Hatred for Will? But why? He's the one who tried to save her. Her breaths come in harsh and furious spurts.

I hear Will mumble something in his sleep and I lower my voice. "Marley, let's go outside."

She doesn't answer me or even turn toward me. Her eyes are on the sleeping form of Will. My own breathing quickens and I reach out for her. "Marley."

She pulls away from me, her face contorted with a rage that is horrible to see. Her damaged lips pulled back in hatred, she reminds me of a rabid animal.

"You lied! You lied to me! He's not dead!" She hisses the words.

With a strength I didn't think she possessed, she flings me with vicious force onto the floor. She looks around the room and spots the Yankees baseball bat in the corner opposite Will's bed. Running across the room, she grabs it, holds it above her head, and turns towards Will.

"Stop, Marley, no!" I push myself up and run towards her, reaching up to grab the bat. She is wild and her grip is strong. "He has to be dead. I have to kill him or I have to die! I can't let him hurt me again!"

I try to grasp the bat above Marley's hands to give me more leverage. She swings it at Will, aiming for his head, but I twist the bat so that it lands on the edge of the sheet-covered mattress. I scream for Will to wake up and he groggily opens his eyes. He stares startled and confused as he tries hard to focus.

"Will! Get up! Get out of the bed!" I scream struggling with Marley.

The bat slams down hard on the bed frame making a clanging noise. It falls once again against the bed and the vibration of wooden bat on metal causes me to lose my grip. Marley swings the bat toward Will again, but I fling my arms in front of his head and the bat smashes into my forearm.

"Cate? Cate?"

"Will get out of the bed now! Now!" I grab the handle of the bat.

"Cate, what's, what is—Jesus!" Will scrambles as best as he can away from the bat and tries to stand, but he is unsteady from the effects of the pain killer. His legs give out and he falls to the floor.

Wrestling together, Marley and I fall onto the now empty bed and I place a well-aimed knee to her gut. She still doesn't let go of the bat, turning viciously to where Will is trying to stand leaning on the wall for support. As she tries to get up, I hook my foot under her knee, and she falls. We struggle for the bat.

"Get out, Will! Get out and get help!"

I grab Marley with all the strength I have. I'm in better physical shape than she is, but Marley is fighting like a wild savage. Still, I manage to pull her off the bed and onto the floor.

Will staggers crookedly to the door, his legs refusing to obey him, and falls on one knee. But he's able to grasp the handle and pull the door open to yell for assistance. "We need—." His words are sleep-slurred and he curses loudly. "We need—security—here now!"

Marley is crazed, fighting me as if her life depends on getting control of the bat again. Finally, I'm able to wrest it from her and I stand up, clutching it tightly. Marley gets to a kneeling position and screams, "You lied to me! You both lied! He's not dead! You have no idea what he will do to me now!" Then she collapses onto the floor, curling herself into a fetal position and sobbing hysterically. "He killed Will!"

I lean against the wall looking around the room while I catch my breath. I see Will, still kneeling on one knee by the door, his face covered in sweat, his hair wet and dark from Melissa's oil. The white scarf with it's bloody-looking symbols, lying on the floor, looking like a discarded bandage. Breathing heavily, I look at all of this. All the details.

And then I know.

I *know.*

With crystal clear insight, I now understand why she fought me for that bat as if her life depended on it. I know who Marley *really* saw in that bed. Even though they look nothing alike in height or build, in Marley's mind the person she saw in the bed was Eric Wigand. The wet, dark hair that looked like Wigand's hair slicked with gel, the scarf that looked as if blood was seeping through it. She believed the person lying there was Eric and that the scarf covering his throat was some type of a medical dressing.

When she asked me if *he* was still alive, she didn't mean Will. When she said *'he was shot, he's supposed to be dead,'* she was talking about her shooting Wigand in the throat. Saying that Jacoby and I lied to her means she believed we were lying when we both assured her that Wigand was dead. Jesus Christ, Marley, poor Marley! What horror you lived through! You were so brainwashed by Eric Wigand. Why else would you believe that he could be shot as viciously as he was, and still live to torment you!

Two security guards and the officer from the waiting room rush in, guns drawn. With his free hand, and with his eyes on Marley, the police officer helps Will to his feet. "Sir? Detective Benigni? Are you okay, sir?"

Will leans against him and nods, "Yeah, yes, I'm okay." Then looking at the guns held by the officer and the security team he says, "Holster your weapons. She's not a threat now. Call it in and take care of her, officer." The adrenaline from all the activity is waking him up fast and he speaks with some authority.

I hand the bat to Will who leans on it heavily. The officer calls for back-up and then walks over to where Marley is curled up on the floor. I look away as he pulls her hands behind her back and handcuffs her. She makes no sound.

Turning to one of the security people I say, "Go to the nurses' station. Have them page Dr. Charles now. Detective Benigni needs to be checked over for any injuries. While you're there, ask them to call the psych desk on the fifth floor. Tell them they need to have someone come and take Marley Weiner back upstairs to her room on psych. I'm her conservator, I'll sign the papers that will keep her here overnight. In the morning, I'll deal with whatever has to be done to get her the help she needs."

I put my arm around Will as the guard leaves and we stand like that, just holding each other.

Within minutes, the hall is a bustling hive of activity. Dr. Charles comes hurrying through the doorway, obviously puzzled by what has happened here, but all business. Through the door I see Harry watching anxiously and being kept back by hospital security. Will slowly makes his way back to the bed, refusing any help from me or the doctor. Once he's lying down again, Dr. Charles immediately begins to check him for injuries and ripped stitches.

Police back-up arrives almost immediately, along with Captain Joe Jacoby, who surveys the scene but says nothing. Two attendants from the psych floor come in and gently lift Marley off the floor and into a wheelchair.

"Wait a minute. Bring her near the bed."

"We're not allowed to do that," says one of the attendants.

"Do it," I say firmly. "This is Detective Will Benigni. Ms. Weiner and he know each other. The detective helped this woman escape from an abusive relationship, and her husband is the reason the detective is here in the hospital recovering from a gunshot wound and head trauma. She was told by her husband that the detective was killed. Her irrational behavior is due partly to that false fact. She needs to see for herself that Detective Benigni is alive. It's crucial to her recovery."

"I don't understand."

"Just do it."

They turn the wheelchair toward Will and push it closer to the bed. Will leans forward, looking at Marley with a deep sadness. Gently, he says her name. "Marley."

"Will's here, Marley. Look at him."

Marley raises her head timidly and her eyes look straight ahead. She stares at Will. For one brief second, there's something in her stare that makes me think she recognizes him. But just as quickly as it came, the spark of recognition is gone. Her eyes go blank and dull.

"One more thing." I turn to the officer who had cuffed Marley and ask him to remove the cuffs. He glances at Jacoby who hesitates, then nods his okay. When her wrists are released, Marley wraps her arms around her chest in a protective gesture.

The officers follow the attendants out of the room. Jacoby stops at the door and taps me on the shoulder.

"You know that we'll be talking about this incident, you and me, tomorrow, Cate. I'll call you in the morning." Then, he too, leaves.

I sit down heavily in the chair. A nurse who has followed Dr. Charles into the room comes over to me to check me for bumps, bruises, and scratches. I close my eyes and let her do her job.

CHAPTER 37

MORNINGS ARE EITHER a blessing or a curse; it all depends on what's waiting for you once you open your eyes. When I open my own eyes the next day I count the morning as a blessing. Will's alive, I'm alive, and for the first time in weeks I feel in charge of my life. I am determined to keep it that way.

I stretch my arms up over my head and feel every ache and pain of my wrestling match with Marley. Adding to my aches is the fact that two in a hospital bed is not comfortable at all. I fell asleep next to Will, still dressed in the clothes Melissa bought me. I need to go home, shower, and change before I can begin my day.

Kissing Will good morning, I tell him I'll be back in about three hours. It's early, not even seven yet but I have things to do and people to meet. Jacoby first, second, the police trauma expert, Dr. Lara Evers, who can help me navigate the bureaucratic red tape I know I will encounter in trying to get Marley placed where she will receive the best care, and third, speaking with the attorney I retained for Marley. Last on my agenda, and the one I dread the most, I need to see Marley at her arraignment which I'm assuming will be sometime today.

Will interrupts my mental list making.

"I'm starting to remember the day I was shot and I want to talk to you about it. Talking it out with you will help me to remember it better. Talking to some doctor about it just won't cut it for me. I need the connection you and I have."

I hug him tightly, savoring every new minute of our connection. "When I return, I promise to talk with you about the day you were shot." I surprise myself that I am able to say the word 'shot' without a catch in my throat.

"All right baby. I guess I can wait. Just hurry back. I am done with this," he says hoisting himself over the edge of the bed. "God, it feels good to move, weird, but good."

"Will? Marley's being arraigned today. Do you remember what happened yesterday?"

"I do. I was a little out of it at the beginning, but I eventually damn well knew what was happening."

He takes me in his arms. "I'm not pressing charges. No way would I do that to Marley."

"I know you wouldn't."

"And I'm not coming to the arraignment, Cate. I don't think it's a good idea for her to see me until I'm out of here. I'll write up a report for the courts concerning how bad it was for Marley, what Wigand did to her, and how I helped her find a safe house. All of it. I'll make sure it gets to the judge."

On his way to the bathroom, he half turns and asks me to bring him the travel shaving kit he left at my brownstone.

"Not that I don't appreciate having you and Melissa, two very beautiful women, do the shaving honors, but I need, *I want*, to shave my face myself starting today. Got it, babe?"

I smile. We've had the conversation about 'need and want' before. Need is a basic necessity. Want is a gift you can give yourself, what you're determined to have. Whatever makes him feel good and in control, and gets him well enough to get out of the hospital as quickly as he can, is okay with me.

I pass the waiting room. No one is there because I told Harry to go home and take care of himself. Will and I are fine. Harry was reluctant to leave, but after a talk with Dr. Charles and Giles, he left, promising me he'll be back later today with Myrtle and

Melissa. Giles told us there's a good possibility that Will may be moved out of ICU today and Harry views that info as cause for celebration. It is.

Outside the late summer sun is shining and there's a warm breeze blowing. I breathe deeply as I walk to my car. A glance at the fifth floor windows gives me a moment of sadness. Marley's up there somewhere, afraid, among strangers. I know they'll treat her well, but she didn't deserve the horrible reason that led to her being a patient on a psych floor. I will make sure to do all that I can to help her. She's got a long road of her.

And so do I.

My meeting with Jacoby is as bad as I anticipated. He chews me out non-stop while I stoically sit there and listen. I know when I'm wrong and, even though I took Marley down to see Will for the most compassionate of reasons, it was still wrong. Not only legally, but ethically as well. I look at him as he walks up and down in front of me, detailing my, as he puts it, "Not only downright illegal, but completely, *completely*, unprofessional maneuver. What in the goddamned hell were you thinking, Cate?"

Even though the door to his office is closed, his voice carries to all the police personnel in the common area outside. I am desperately grateful that they're trying to look as if they don't hear a thing he's shouting. For that I could kiss each and every one of them.

I don't answer Jacoby when he asks why I did what I did because I know he doesn't want an answer. I'm just deliriously happy that he hasn't once mentioned getting my PI license revoked. At least not yet. So I sit and I take it, making sure to look appropriately apologetic for my misdeed.

"And another thing, you seem to think that you're above the law. That attitude is going to catch up with you one day soon, and I hope I'm there to see it."

Out of the corner of my eye I see Javy pretending to be looking for some papers on a desk. That the desk is not Javy's, but is the one closest to Jacoby's office, isn't lost on me. Good move, Javy. Eavesdropping at its most blatantly subtle form. A short laugh escapes my lips quickly covered by a cough in case Jacoby thinks I'm laughing at him.

After almost an hour and a half of being lectured and harangued, Jacoby has worn himself out. He sits down heavily on his desk chair and fixes me with a stern look.

"Cate, I can only hope that you understand what you did. The illegality of it is only part of it, a big part, mind you, but only part. The real danger was the possibility that someone could have been killed. Do you get this, Cate? Do you know what could have happened here?"

"I was able to subdue her, Joe," I say quietly.

"And if you couldn't have subdued her? If she was able to do what she wanted to do to Will because, in her sense of reality, she thought he was Wigand? What then?"

I look down at my hands.

"You're damn lucky you weren't carrying your weapon, damn lucky. If she had gotten your gun—Jesus Christ, Cate!"

"I know, I know. I'm so sorry, Joe. I really did think that I was doing the right thing." He looks at me sternly. "I mean I *know* what I did was illegal. She was being held on the psych floor and I snuck her out of there."

"Let's be clear about what you really did, Cate. Let's use the legal terms you know so well from your time working for the Public Defender. You broke the law. I know a little Latin myself from being in court. Marley Weiner was *alieni juris*. Remember that term?"

"Under the legal authority of another. I know what it means."

"Correct. She was under *my* legal authority. You removed a woman who had committed murder, who was being temporarily held, by police consent, in a room undergoing a psych evaluation prior to being arraigned. It was your *animus* to go against the law. Got that one, too?"

"Yes. Intention, my intention."

"Correct. It was your intention to take her out of that room where she was being confined. You took her to public access areas of a busy hospital where she could have escaped or caused physical harm to an innocent person. You took her from that room without permission and without the presence of a police officer. You can lose your license for this." He shakes his finger at me. "Don't think that I haven't thought about it."

I don't say a word. Really nothing I can say will change Joe's mind if he's already made it up to start the process of revoking my license. I look up at the ceiling and then back at Jacoby, holding my breath and waiting for the other shoe to drop. Jacoby makes me wait a little longer than I like. He's reinforcing his message by making me sweat. A real cop tactic there, Joe. Then he gets up and walks around his desk, standing directly in front of me.

"But, I'm not going to do that. You're a damn good PI and I should know because I helped train you when you needed guidance. We all, myself included here, make stupid mistakes. And you know that this was a stupid mistake, right Cate?"

I exhale slowly, nod, and keep my eyes on him.

"But when we make the stupid mistakes, we make them from emotion, from the heart, We're human, too. We just have to remember that in law enforcement and the private investigation business as well, we have to keep a tight rein on emotional responses and do what's practical. No emotions. Understand?"

His phone beeps a text message and, as he reads it, I hear him curse under his breath. Looking at the clock on the wall, he asks me one question. "You got a good lawyer for Marley?"

"Yes. She's one of the best and she's doing this pro bono. Marley has no money."

"Good. Now, you need to tell this lawyer that the presiding judge has made the decision to have Marley arraigned in her room on the psych floor. That's in one hour. I just got a text from one of my guys at the DA's office. One hour."

"An hour?" I stand quickly. "Do you know where I can find Dr. Lara Evers? I'm going to need her help when I try to place Marley in a mental health facility."

Jacoby looks uncomfortable, but tells me what he has to say very bluntly. "The text says that where Marley is going has been pretty well decided. After the arraignment, we're taking her to the

Elmhurst Hospital Prison Ward in Queens."

I stare at him in shock. "But that's for female inmates requiring acute psychiatric care. That's part of the Riker's system. My God, Joe. We've all read the horror stories in the New York Times about that place. You've heard stories, from your own officers, I may add, about the vicious treatment patients received there."

"Look Cate, listen to me. There is nothing I can do, nothing *you* can do. That's why I'm telling you to get this lawyer you retained over to the hospital in an hour. If she's as good as you say she is, then maybe she can get your friend transferred to a better facility. Now get going. I'll call Lara Evers and tell her to meet you there as soon as possible."

As I'm leaving, Jacoby places his hand on my shoulder and stops me.

"You have got to promise me one thing here, Cate. No bullshit emotional crap, no playing the savior of someone who has been arrested for murder. You *do not* interfere. Understand me?

"Yes, I understand. I promise; no interference on my part."

"Good. Now go."

On my way out of the precinct, Javy gives me a much needed hug which almost brings me to tears.

CHAPTER 38

Jacoby is as good as his word. Dr. Lara Evers shows up well before the arraignment. I thank her for coming and then introduce her to the doctor who's been evaluating Marley.

Showing him my temporary conservatorship papers, I tell him, "You have my permission to show all of Marley Weiner's files to Dr. Evers and to discuss any and all possible treatments with her. We don't have much time and I need to have her updated on Marley's case quickly."

The two of them, along with Marley's assigned nurse practitioner, go into an office. When I walk by a few minutes later on my way to a conference room, I see them sitting around a table talking and looking at files.

Marley's lawyer, a woman named Brooke Ainsley, sits with me in the spacious room reserved for doctors, patients' guardians, and soon-to-be-discharged patients and family. With her is her paralegal, Jackie. We discuss Marley's case and the options that may be available.

"Can you help keep her out of that prison mental ward?"

"I'll do my best. In her favor are two things First is her physical appearance. That alone speaks volumes about what she has endured. Second is going to be your written statement.

Everything she told you about the physical and mental abuse she has suffered, you're going to tell Jackie here, and she'll write it up. I'll present it to the judge. I have a paper for you to sign which allows me to have Marley placed in a still-unnamed facility. After the judge decides where she's going, I'll just fill in the name of the hospital."

She pauses and smiles. "We're in luck today. We've gotten Judge William Bannister. Long story short. His mother was a victim of spousal abuse. He never forgot what she went through."

Maybe there is a glimmer of hope after all. I can only wish for that.

Marley is dressed in a loose-fitting tunic kindly supplied by Melissa. I have never had a best friend as kind-hearted as Melissa. She sees suffering and she tries to ease it in her own way. Clothes, food, and sympathy are her ways of easing someone's pain. I wish she was allowed to be here at this arraignment.

Jacoby and two other officers walk into the private room where Marley is held. They look tough and businesslike. We don't say hello. Brooke Ainsley hands the judge my statement, speedily typed by Jackie, and the arraignment begins.

Guilty Gedski is a bitch-on-wheels and starts out by spouting words like 'cold-blooded,' 'more than likely premeditated,' and 'malice aforethought,' a unique term for first-degree or aggravated murder. She ends by requesting that Marley be held at the dreaded Elmhurst Hospital Prison Ward in Queens to await trial. Even the judge seems taken aback by that request.

"Ms. Weiner, do you understand the seriousness of the charges against you?" asks the judge.

I'm so glad I told Marley's lawyer to please have her charged as Marley Weiner and not Wendy Wigand. Her first name was never officially changed so, legally she can still use her birth name of Marley Weiner and drop the name Wigand. It hurts me to see her handcuffed, but it is part of the legal process in her case. She has committed murder and she did attack Will. I want to protest, but I don't. As I promised Jacoby, I will not interfere.

"Ms. Weiner?" There's no response from Marley. "Counselor, please direct your client to answer."

Though his directive is firm, his eyes are kind. Marley still doesn't answer, just keeps looking down at the floor. Nothing that Brooke Ainsley says to her does any good. All she can do is make a case for Marley, citing the years of physical and mental abuse she endured at the hands of her husband, Eric Wigand.

"In her mind, Your Honor, she had no choice but to save herself. She could not fathom going back to a life of unbelievable suffering. This was not premeditated murder, certainly not malice aforethought. It was simply visceral, animal fear."

The judge looks at Marley with compassion and shakes his head. Gedski protests vigorously. "Fear? Hardly. The savagely murdered man, Eric Wigand, her husband, was handcuffed to a stair railing and posed no threat to Ms. Weiner at all. She could have called the police to protect her but she didn't. This was calculated, cold-blooded murder."

Marley's lawyer doesn't flinch. "If anyone was savaged, it was Ms. Weiner. She saw Mr. Wigand as someone who could, and would, abuse her again once he got free. If she called the police, and they arrested Wigand, what would happen to her once he was released on bail?"

Guilty Gedski jumps in quickly. "She'd have a restraining order against him that would protect her."

Brooke Ainsley gives an angry look to Gedski. "I believe we all know that an order of protection means nothing. Ms. Weiner was terrified and beyond reason. Your Honor, I beg the court to dismiss the Assistant District Attorney's request that Ms. Weiner be sent to Elmhurst Hospital Prison Ward where violence abounds. It is violence she fears. She needs a safe haven mental facility where she can heal and where she can feel protected while awaiting trial."

Ainsley makes her plea both eloquent and passionate at the same time. I can see the judge is moved. I am more than impressed and grateful.

"I agree with you about where Ms. Weiner should be place,

counselor." He holds up his hand as Gedski begins to object. "It is unfortunately true that Elmhurst Hospital Prison Ward has a reputation for violence, and that certainly is not the place for your client. Therefore, I am recommending that she be placed at New York Presbyterian Hospital where they have an excellent section for victims of severe domestic abuse. We're adjourned."

Jacoby takes charge and leads Marley out of the room, the two officers holding her by the arms. As they pass me, I say her name, but there's no response. I thank her lawyer for everything and she promises me she'll keep me updated on the case. The papers she had prepared for me to sign now have the name of the New York Presbyterian Mental Facility as the place where Marley will be placed. For that small gift I am also grateful.

Before I go to see Will, I take a long walk in the park across the street. The sun is shining and that seems to be so incongruous and not in keeping with the dismal happenings of the day. I hear children laughing and see them running around the statue of some long-forgotten WWI hero. It sparks a memory of a time Marley and I ate lunch in a small park near the Office of the Public Defender.

It was hot and we were sitting on a bench with iced lattes in our hands. Several little boys were running around and one bumped into Marley, spilling her drink onto her new pants. The boy, no more than four-years-old, immediately began to cry. Instead of being angry, Marley told him not to worry. It was all right. No harm done. Then she laughed and said, "I love kids. I hope that I have a baby boy someday."

As I walked, I thought of the way she had looked and smiled at that little boy, dried his tears, and how she said she wished she could have a baby boy. Wishes do come true, it seems. But, sometimes, they don't turn out quite the way we want. Other people can get in the way of our wishes and destroy them.

I turned back toward the hospital and Will. Life needs less wishes and more positive action. And my goal is to live my life with as much happiness and positive action as possible and not allow anyone to get in my way.

My phone buzzes. It's a message from Will.

'It's moving day, babe. Going to room 220 on the second floor ambulatory section of the hospital. Meet you there.'

CHAPTER 39

"SO THAT'S EVERYTHING."

I'm sitting with Will in his new room on the second floor of the hospital. Dr. Charles and his team decided that, even with all that happened yesterday, Will was well enough to leave ICU and settle in a private room. There was no small persuasion on Will's part. He bluntly told Dr. Charles he was more than ready to leave ICU and wanted it done as soon as possible, otherwise he just might discharge himself.

We went over what had happened to him the day he was shot, who shot him and why, and the connection to Marley Weiner. His memory was blurry, but some things stood out. He remembered talking with his condo neighbors and being struck on the head by Wigand. After that nothing, until he was being taken into the ER and seeing me there. He was frustrated that he couldn't remember clearly.

I talked with him the same way I talk with my clients while finalizing their cases. Practical, straightforward, detailed. We had to do it this way, otherwise it would have been too difficult for us. We couldn't make it personal. Will had on his detective face and take-charge demeanor, a look so sexy that I had to smile.

"So tell me about how Wigand hired you. Just found you

online or what? I'm betting he knew everything about you and how you're connected to me. When did he hire you?"

"He hired me about three weeks before you were shot."

"That bastard." Will's face hardens in anger. "He retains you for a missing spouse case, all the while planning my murder. He wanted you to find his wife, a woman he knew that I had rescued and hidden in a safe house, so he could kill her, too. He wanted revenge."

I tell him everything about Wigand, the phone conversations, our one meeting, and my trip to Rural Valley.

"You know, everything Wigand told me was a lie from day one. Telling me that his wife took all pictures of herself when she left. He didn't want me to see a picture of her because he was afraid I'd recognize that his wife was Marley. Almost right from the start, I felt that something was off about the case. But, then you were shot and, I put my suspicions on the back-burner. Sorry, Will. I wasn't up on the case."

"You have nothing to be sorry about, baby. If it were the other way around, and you were shot, I'd be the same way. When someone you love is in danger of dying, you lose all sense of anything else that's happening in your life."

I tell him about Marley and that horrible night. About Bo and my fear that he would bleed out and die. About Marley deliberately killing Wigand, and how I called Jacoby to come alone to my office.

"How did you suspect the woman in your building was Marley?"

"She called me by an old nickname. Then, when we talked, she told me a secret only she and I could know about her mother. That's what made me know it was her."

Will's eyes are closed. "Will? Are you awake?"

Will opens his eyes, stretches, stands up, and looks out the window, concentrating on something. "Yeah, I'm awake. Just trying to remember something. Talking about Marley—there's something else I wanted to tell you, but I lost it. It's fuzzy."

"Don't worry about it. Dr. Charles told you that your memory will come back in spurts, so just relax."

"Yeah, okay. Hey, how about ordering a pizza. Two toppings, pepperoni and mushroom. I am so sick of hospital food."

"Sure I think I can sneak it in. But no wine or beer. You're on meds.

"Not for much longer if I can help it. But, okay, we'll save that for when I'm out and we're celebrating. And," he grabs me by my hips, "we need to celebrate in other ways too. God, you have no idea how much I miss your body, baby!" He pulls me closer. "This hospital bed is big enough for two."

I pull back a little. I don't know if he's healed enough to do this. "Uh, Will, maybe we shouldn't."

"Shhh, baby. Don't worry. I promise I'll be gentle."

On my way to my brownstone the next night, a text message lights up my phone. It's from Will. *'I remembered. Nickname. Ice Cream, right?'*

I turn my SUV around and head back to Lenox Hospital.

Will *was* trying to communicate with me. I knew it! It seems that I was right when I told the nurse that Will was trying to say something. He wasn't just mumbling sounds. When he struggled to say, "I- shh kuh...kree...," he was actually trying to say, "Ice Cream." It was his way of trying to warn me.

In the recesses of his mind, even when he was struggling for his life, he knew that if I heard the nickname I would guess that he meant Marley. And he also knew that if I thought she was involved in the shooting in any way, I would try to track her down and in doing so, find the man who had shot him.

But there was more than that. Will was trying not only to save Marley, but to save me as well. He rightly guessed that Wigand would want revenge because he, Will, had protected Marley. After he shot Will, and killed Marley, I was his next target.

"I was trying so hard to tell you, Cate. All I could think of was protecting you and I wasn't able to do that. I didn't know if I'd be alive for you. I had to let you know somehow. I tried."

He grabs me and holds me in a tight embrace. Tears slide down my cheeks as I realize the strength and love he has for me. Worried about me while he was in that terrible dance with life and death.

What possible good did the universe see in me that it allowed this man to become mine? At some point in time, I must've done something perfectly right.

CHAPTER 40

THE LITTLE WELCOME HOME party I had planned for Will has turned into a much bigger one than I expected. It was supposed to be just the Faithful Five, as Myrtle has dubbed us. Melissa, Harry, Myrtle, Giles and me—the five who faithfully made sure that at least one of us was in the hospital checking on Will day and night.

But it makes me feel good inside to know how well-liked and respected Will is as a detective and as a person. Cops from his precinct have been coming by all day. Joe Jacoby and Will's partner Javy have been here since early afternoon. Even Dr. Charles and Dr. Felicia Hayden stopped by for a short while to see Will.

Melissa quietly goes into another room and when she comes out I find that she has ordered a ton of food from Pasquale's Ristorante, a place that Will and I love. As is typical with Melissa, she refuses to take any money for this. I hug her and pour another glass of wine for both of us.

Dr. Charles comes over to say good-bye to me and I am surprised when he embraces me. "I told you Will was a fighter, and so he. As a doctor I am very pleased with his healing progress. He has to take it easy for a few months and come for periodic checkups at my office but, other than that, I can definitely see him making a complete recovery. You take good care of him, Cate."

I had a talk with Dr. Lara Evers when she stopped by. I asked her why Marley was so lucid when she was talking to me in my office, telling me about her life with Wigand, and how she has now lost touch with reality.

"She is suffering from a severe form of Post-Traumatic Stress Disorder. She was lucid when she sought you out because, for some reason, she had a great need to protect you. But the truth is, Cate, that she is in the full throes of a debilitating mental disorder that sometimes occurs when a person has experienced an extremely traumatic, terrifying event. She has persistent, frightening thoughts and memories of her ordeal. She feels emotionally numb, especially with you, because you were once very close."

"Will she ever recover and live a normal life?"

Lara Evers smiles gently at me. "I don't know. I hope so. She will need a great deal of therapy. Let her get the help she needs, Cate. I'll keep in touch and give you updates. You have to let her go for now."

The day goes on with people coming and going and it is almost sunset when the crowd of people has dwindled down to Jacoby and Javy. It's good to see Will laughing and joking with his captain and his partner. The three of them share a bond that they share with no other. I hear Javy mention Wigand's name.

"He was a dirty cop, Javy. Before your time. Count yourself lucky that you never met him." Will leans back against my couch and sips the one beer he's allowed because of the meds he's taking. "Wigand's name is synonymous with crooked cop. Remember Bluto, Joe?"

Jacoby nods and takes a pull from his beer. I see his eyes flick toward me, concerned. I smile at him to let him know I'm fine and he turns the cop talk to recent happenings in the precinct; who is getting married, who's about to retire, and who's getting a divorce. Everyday chitchat. Jacoby and Javy are busting each other about who knows more gossip. Everyone is laughing. I walk over and sit on the arm of the couch.

"Hey, Javy. Who is that saint your girlfriend always prays to for you?"

"Saint Jude. She swears by him. You know, once when I was a patrol cop, I got shot in the shoulder. Never even entered the flesh. It just was embedded in my leather jacket. Believe it? Man, she swears by Saint Jude."

Giles joins us. "Saint Jude?"

"Yeah," says Javy. He pulls the gold chain and medal he wears around his neck out of his sweatshirt. "Saint Jude Thaddeus, Patron Saint of Miracles and Hopeless Causes. Yeah, man. My girl Wanda, really believes in him. I do too. I prayed to him for my man here." He clinks bottle necks with Will.

"Now that's an interesting coincidence," muses Giles settling himself comfortably on my recliner.

"Coincidence?" Myrtle asks as she, Harry, and Melissa join us, all with glasses of wine in their hands. It's such a pleasure to just sit together and celebrate Will being alive.

I wish Bo and Hey were here too. Harry wrapped up some food to take to them later. They're back in their basement, warm and snug. Bo refuses to be anywhere else. He said that he wants to stay where he feels safe. I definitely understand that.

"What do you mean by coincidence, Giles?" I look curiously at him.

"Dr. J.T. Charles," says Giles smiling. "His full name is Jude Thaddeus Charles. I'd say that was a coincidence, wouldn't you?"

"Man, I can't wait to tell Wanda," says Javy kissing the medal before putting it back inside his shirt.

Melissa winks at me. "See, Cate? The power of believing. All beliefs are magical."

We're all silent, letting that sink in.

The sound of my phone buzzing interrupts our reverie and I get up to answer it. I look at the screen and say, "It's Francesca."

"Put it on loudspeaker," says Will, sitting up straighter.

"Francesca, hi. How're you and how's South America?"

"Hello Cate. I'm well. How are *you*?"

"Me? I'm fine. I—"

"Well, I'm glad to hear that. There must be over twenty

messages from you and Myrtle. I'm sorry I wasn't able to get back to you before now, but we were in so many remote areas. No service. But all those calls! My goodness! You'd think it was a life-and-death situation!"

Suddenly I start to laugh and I can't stop. I keep laughing and laughing. Oh, Francesca!

"Give me the phone," Will stage-whispers. Melissa takes the phone from me and gives it to Will who takes it off loudspeaker. "Hi Francesca. Yes, fine. Uh-huh."

He gets up and walks toward the bedroom and privacy. "Got a few minutes to talk? Good. You, uh, might want to sit down. No, my darling mother, Cate and I are not getting married. No, Francesca, just be my sweet, loving mother and listen to what I have to tell you." He closes the bedroom door.

While I'm on my laptop, Will is doing acrostic puzzles, those interesting mind games where the first letter of each sentence in a paragraph spells out a message. He says it helps him improve his memory. The shooting is still a little blurry and he wants to remember it all in detail. As he tells me, "No cop worth his or her badge should forget the circumstances of how, or why they were shot, or who shot them. It makes me a better detective to be able to remember. It'll help me to help victims of crime."

To serve and protect. He is serious.

"I don't want to be CRS, babe."

"CRS? What does that mean?" Acronyms can drive me crazy.

"It means *can't remember shit*. That's not going to be me. I want to remember everything."

It's been three weeks since Will left the hospital. He's doing really well, but has been ordered to take a three-month medical leave. Jacoby insisted.

"Listen Will, I can order you to do desk duty, but both of us know that we'll drive each other crazy if you're here all day. You like being out there on the streets and not stuck at a damned desk. Make it three months with pay and we'll be fine. I already cleared it with the police commissioner."

I'm surprised that Will seems fine with that order. He tells me that he has plans to do some work on his condo anyway. "Just a little, light physical labor-type stuff," he said. "I can use the time off." He needs to test his body is my guess.

We went to his condo and I saw him hesitate when we walked toward the building. But then the analytic cop in him took over and I saw steely determination in his eyes as he surveyed the shooting scene. He's been back several times without me. That's a positive move.

He went to see Marley at the hospital alone. I couldn't bring myself to see her just yet; I'm not ready. I asked Will how she was and he said she didn't know who he was, just looked at him and started to cry. Her doctor said Marley still believes Wigand will find her and kill her. She hasn't processed that he is indeed dead, or that his death was at her hands. Who knows if she ever will?

We both went to her hearing, and Brooke Ainsley, that superb champion of victims of domestic abuse, cited Battered Wife Syndrome and Diminished Capacity as a mitigating factor in the murder of Eric Wigand. All this means is that Marley, at the time she shot and killed her husband, wasn't able to think clearly, and couldn't control herself. The judge believes Marley's evaluation shows enough mental abuse, and psychological disorder, for any further legal action to be postponed. She ordered Marley, who did not come to the hearing, to undergo further testing at the mental health facility for treatment. Sentencing will continue if, and when, she recovers.

Back at my brownstone, Will asks me if I can get away for two weeks. Before he begins work on his condo, he wants to go on vacation. I'm all for that, I say, as I look at vacation spots online.

"How about O'ahu in Hawai'i?" I ask. "I've never been to Hawai'i. This resort sounds really nice. Let's see, Deluxe Ocean View sound good?"

Will laughs, "Deluxe only means you'll get bacon on your cheeseburger. Try *Premier* Ocean View. And we're flying first-class. We deserve the best, Cate."

And so it is that I book a non-stop first-class flight to the

Kahala Resort on the island of O'ahu where we'll stay in a Premier Ocean View room for two weeks. Life needs to be lived well.

"Okay, Hawai'i, here we come!" I close my laptop with a satisfying click.

Will begins kissing me with an urgency that makes a definite statement about being alive. Clothes are quickly shed and we cling to each other in passion and the joy of living. As he leads me into the bedroom, I make an unbreakable promise to myself that our life together *will* be lived well—and not just for two weeks.

A Kristen Houghton Quick-Read Book

Author's Notes

Domestic violence is on the rise. Many women, like the fictional character of Marley Weiner, live lives of mental and emotional terror and horrific physical abuse. 5% of all royalties from my books go to the URIPALS (People and Animals Living Safely) program in New York City. URIPALS is the first program in New York and, one of the few nationwide, that allows domestic violence survivors to co-shelter with their pets. Nearly 50 percent of female domestic violence victims delay entering a women's shelter because of concerns about leaving a pet behind. Not only does this prevent people from getting help, it also means animals remain in danger as well.

When you buy a Kristen Houghton book, you are helping a victim of domestic abuse and her pet, to become survivors in a safe, secure haven.

My thanks to the wonderful brothers and sisters in blue, New York City's Finest, for all that they do to help the victims of domestic violence. God bless these brave men and women who put their own lives on the line every day to serve and protect. I hope I do you justice with my portrayal of the character of NYC Detective Will Benigni.

On a lighter note, Cate Harlow and company enjoy good food and wine and so, it seems, do the loyal fans of this series. Due to the overwhelming requests from readers who have asked me to do so, I have promised to include any recipes concocted by Harry or Giles in future books. Below you will find the recipe for Dr. Giles Barrett's Cherry Cheesecake Pancakes. As Melissa would say, "Bon appétit!"

I hope you've enjoyed this new format, *A Kristen Houghton Quick-Read Book*. These quick reads are perfect for readers with busy lives who still want to enjoy a good, solid read. Cate Harlow's adventures will continue in 2018.

Dr. Giles Barrett's Cherry Cheesecake Pancakes

INGREDIENTS
Pancakes

- 1 1/4 cups all-purpose flour
- 1 1/4 cups buttermilk
- 1 large egg
- 1/4 cup vegetable oil
- 1/4 cup granulated sugar
- 1 teaspoon baking powder
- 1 teaspoon baking soda
- pinch of salt
- 2 cups chopped frozen cheesecake (I used a 17 oz Sara Lee Original Cream Cheesecake)

Topping:

- 1-8oz pkg of cream cheese, softened
- 1/4 butter, softened
- 1/2 cup powdered sugar
- 1/2 tsp vanilla
- 1 can of cherry pie filling, warmed
- cooking spray

INSTRUCTIONS

- Preheat the oven to 200 degrees F
- In a mixing bowl, combine cream cheese, butter, powdered sugar and vanilla
- Whip until smooth and refrigerate until all of pancakes are cooked
- Warm the cherry pie filling in a saucepan over low heat until all pancakes are cooked

- Pulse the flour, buttermilk, egg, vegetable oil, granulated sugar, baking powder, baking soda and salt in a blender until smooth
- Transfer to a bowl and stir in the cheesecake pieces, keeping them whole
- Coat a large nonstick skillet or griddle with cooking spray and heat over medium heat
- Working in batches, pour about 1/4 cup batter into the skillet for each pancake
- Cook until bubbly on top, about 4 minutes, then flip and cook until the other side is golden brown, about 2 more minutes
- Transfer the finished pancakes to a baking sheet and keep warm in the oven
- Remove the topping from the fridge and microwave until warm and soft
- Serve the pancakes topped with cheesecake filling/topping and warm cherry pie filling/topping
- Enjoy!

www.ingramcontent.com/pod-product-compliance
Lightning Source LLC
Chambersburg PA
CBHW022156170626
46807CB00005B/2226